HALFSKIN

BOOK ONE

TONY BERTAUSKI

BERTAUSKI STARTER LIBRARY_

Get the
BERTAUSKI STARTER LIBRARY
FREE!

---

bertauski.com

God deals everyone tragedy.
Some more than others.

CHAPTER ONE

"Look what I got."

Alex pulled a utility knife out of his pants like an eight-year-old magician. He slid the lever. Parker reached for it.

"No, you don't," Alex said.

"Where'd you get that?"

"Your dad's garage."

Nix stepped back. He wasn't scared of the blade—it was just a knife—it was the look on Alex's face, the way he bit his tongue, like there were ideas bouncing in his head. Eight-year-olds shouldn't look like that.

Parker's dad was on the far side of the pool with the rest of the adults, drinking out of fancy glasses and laughing super loud. Fifteen minutes ago they were sitting around singing "Happy Birthday" to Parker. The kids ate cake. The adults did, too. Then the clown showed up and the adults went to the far side with tall bottles. There was a hot tub over there. The kids followed the clown.

The guy told corny jokes and tied balloons, said he could make any animal on the North American continent as long as it looked like a wiener dog. He smelled like exhaust fumes. Parker, Alex and Nix ditched the clown when the adults popped the tall bottles.

"Don't worry." Alex slid the blade back and shoved it in his pants. "It's just a stupid knife. No one will know."

"What if my dad finds out? He'll know you were in his tools."

"You want your present or not?"

Parker held a box at his side. It was a paintball gun. Aunt Maggy bought it for him. It was cheap and crappy. But it was a gun. And it was strapped into the box with plastic ties a rat couldn't chew through. Parker's mom and dad smiled when he opened it, made sure he said thank you to Aunt Maggy and let him show it off to everyone, but he knew that paintball gun was going back to the store. They told Aunt Maggy not to buy him one. They warned her. Aunt Maggy never listened.

"Let's just get scissors," Parker said.

"Dude, it's not a freaking laser beam. Go get a little wiener balloon with Freaky the Clown if you're scared. Nix and me will cut this loose and have our own little war. Right, Nix?"

Nix had never shot a gun. He'd carved a bar of soap with a Swiss Army knife and shot an arrow at a bale of straw, but he'd never pulled a trigger. Unless squirt guns count. *They don't.*

Parker looked across the pool. Not one adult was looking. Once those bottles got popped, they could do anything they wanted.

"What're you doing?" Jennifer stepped up.

"Nothing," Parker said. "This is a boys' meeting. Go away."

Parker walked quickly around a hedge of azaleas and ducked behind a sweet-smelling gardenia. He laid the box on a bed of leaves. The gun was ready to be cut loose. Ready to lock and load. Alex unveiled the knife. As the razor grew, so did the grin.

New and sharp and pointy.

"Here." Parker held up his hand. "Give it."

"I'll do it."

"It's my present. I'll do it."

"Yeah, I went and got it, so I'll do it."

Nix looked through a gap in the bushes. He shook the blond hair from his eyes. He was the only boy at the party with hair that long.

His sister didn't have time to cut it. That's what she told people. No one argued. When your family had gone through all the things Nix and Cali Richards had been through, you cut some slack. Long hair on a boy, no big deal.

One of the adults in the hot tub said something really, really funny. They were goofing on the clown. Nix's sister wasn't near the hot tub; she was with some of the moms, holding her baby like she was made of glass.

Cali cut her hair super short after she had Avery, said she wanted to remember the day this little angel came into the world. Cutting her hair seemed stupid to Nix, but then everyone said motherhood made her skin glow and the short hair showed it off, like having a baby somehow lit her up all Christmassy. People said she was beautiful—his friends said she was hot.

He couldn't see it. She was his sister.

"Nix, get down here," Alex sort of whispered. "We need you to hold this."

Nix dropped on his knees. Alex was sawing at the plastic bands and Parker was complaining that he was scratching the barrel. Alex pushed his red hair back. If Parker had some muscles, the box wouldn't move around so much and he wouldn't scratch the gun, now would he?

Parker was on one end of the box, Nix on the other. Alex gripped the knife like he was going to stab the gun. A drop of sweat rolled off the end of his nose. He'd gone through at least half of the bands when the gun began to wiggle. Just a few more and it would come loose. Parker's eyes were wide. He let go with one hand, ready to pounce. He'd been friends with Alex long enough to know you had to be ready.

"Don't let go, dummy," Alex whined.

"It's my gun, I'll do what I want."

Nix pressed down on Parker's corner to help out. He didn't want Alex to get the gun, either. It wasn't fair. Besides, Alex was a jerkoff.

A glass broke near the hot tub.

The adults began laughing.

Alex hunched over and sawed another band. *Plink!* It shot into the grass. Parker's right hand hovered over the gun. Alex told him to get back, he couldn't see. Parker told him to shut up and let him have the knife, but Alex told him to shove it up his ass.

An adult shouted about cleaning up the glass and to keep the kids away. Everyone needed to be wearing shoes. Nix wasn't wearing shoes. His sister would come looking for him. He was the only one that had to wear a helmet when he was skateboarding, the only one that still wore a helmet on a bike. She wouldn't give on that. Safety. Safety.

SAFETY.

He tried to sit up straight, just to make sure Cali was still showing off Avery and he wouldn't have to—

SHHHPT.

Nix felt a pinch.

Alex dropped the knife.

He held his hand to his chest. Fear froze on Parker's face. What would happen when his dad found out he was cutting open the paint-ball gun with a stolen utility knife they used to LOP OFF NIX'S FINGER!

Nix was afraid to move.

"Is it bleeding?" Alex asked.

It hurt at first, when the knife sliced through his finger, but now it was numb. He was afraid if he moved it, the pain would come back.

"Come on, let me see it. I don't even think I got you or there'd be blood all over the place."

Something warm seeped between his fingers. It wasn't red and sticky.

It was gray.

"What is that?" Parker asked.

"Looks like snot." Alex reached out.

Nix turned away. He cradled his hand like he was holding his niece. He knew what the gray stuff was; he just wasn't supposed to tell anyone. But then no one ever told him what to say if he cut himself and his friends saw the stuff coming out. He had to say something. You don't bleed snot and just put a Band-Aid on it without explaining.

Jennifer was standing just out of sight. "I'm going to get my mom."

Parker caught her by the ankle. She could've broken free if she wanted. All she had to do was scream and a mom would come running. But Parker had tears in his eyes. Even Alex was sitting still, his lips forming a perfect O.

"Please, please, please... don't tell. Don't tell. I'll promise you anything. Anything, just don't tell."

"Nix cut himself," Jennifer said too loudly. "How is no one going to find out?"

"Please, but... don't... not yet." His lips fluttered. "I'll give you my old iPod, I promise. I don't need it anymore. You can have it, I swear. Just don't tell."

Jennifer put her hands on her hips. "But he's hurt."

"No, I'm not."

They all looked.

Parker crawled back over, hope smeared on his face. Eyes wide, mouth open. If he could wish for anything in the world, it would be for this whole thing to go away. He'd give up the stupid gun if that's what it took.

"Let me see," he said.

Nix pulled his hand away and peeked down like he was looking at a secret. Gray stuff was all over his shirt. It shimmered like metal shavings beneath a rotating magnet. He'd seen that before, at the doctor's office. Once a month, his sister took him to some special doctor, where they'd poke his finger and look at the stuff under some special magnifier before drawing a sample from his arm. No matter how many times they poked him, it only hurt for a second.

This was the first time he'd been cut open outside the doctor's office.

And it wasn't too bad.

He held his hand out like a plate. Alex and Parker leaned over like he was unveiling a dead bunny. The blade had sliced over his knuckle. It was down to the bone. But there was no white tissue gleaming through the gap. It was just a shimmery mass of gray that gyrated between flaps of skin.

"What the hell is that?" Alex asked.

Nix stood up. His sister was sitting in the shade with a blanket over Avery's head. She was probably breast-feeding. She wasn't going anywhere for a few minutes.

"You promise not to tell?" Nix asked.

They nodded, just like eight-year-olds.

"You swear? Because this is a big-time secret. I'm not supposed to tell anyone about this, ever."

"Swear, dude. Swear." Alex held up the Scout's Honor. Parker imitated him. Neither one of them were scouts.

Nix took one more look at his sister. She was far away, not even looking.

He looked at Alex. Looked at Parker.

"Robots."

There was a long pause. "Uhhh, what?" Alex muttered.

"These are robots." Nix dipped his finger in the wound and held up the gray spot.

"I don't know what that means," Parker said.

"I know," Alex said. "It means he's a dope. I oughta punch you in the face, Nix."

Parker didn't take his eyes off the finger. "Why isn't your blood red?"

"Because that's probably a fake finger." Alex reached for it and Nix yanked back. "See, told you. I seen one of those fake fingers at some store next to fake dog crap and fake puke. Come on, Parker. Let's get the gun and shoot him—"

"He means biomites," Jennifer said.

"Dude." Alex's face began to glow. "You got biomites?"

Nix didn't know if this was such a good idea.

"You're not supposed to get biomites until you're twelve."

"Actually, it's fifteen," Jennifer said. "And it's illegal to seed a minor, you know." She crossed her arms and smirked.

"Unless you're in an accident," Nix said. "Unless it's an emergency."

"Nope." She seemed less confident.

"What, you going to tell on him?" Alex said. "Go and tell the biomite police, you tattletale. Go on, see if they care. Nix got mangled in a car accident and they put the mites in him." Alex nodded at him. "Right?"

Nix nodded. That was the truth. Everyone in town knew that.

Jennifer stomped off.

"What's it like, dude?" Alex leaned forward. "Is it like superpowers or something? Can you grab hot coals or punch holes in walls?"

"No." Nix stroked the wound that had nearly sealed. "It feels normal, I guess."

"Oh, man. I can't wait to get biomites." Alex flopped on his butt, staring. "My old man got them to boost the cartilage in his knee and it made him, like, twice as strong."

"My mom," Parker added, "got them to fix her eyes. They changed colors."

"And made her tits bigger," Alex added.

"Shut up."

"You shut up."

Nix was tempted to put his finger in his mouth. He'd done it before; it tasted like aluminum. Actually, he just wanted to hide it. He wasn't supposed to tell. He didn't like the attention. It wasn't like he wanted to be seeded. It didn't make him special. He didn't feel any different than before, so he didn't see the big deal. He was just like everyone else. He just had more artificiality, his sister said. Besides, when they turned fifteen, everyone gets seeded to immunize or correct vision or fix learning disabilities or whatever. And when they were adults, they could fix wrinkles and stuff.

"What's going on over here?" One of the moms came around the bushes. "You boys teasing Jennifer?"

Parker sat on the gun. Alex stared. Nix stared.

Guilty.

"He's got biomites." Jennifer pointed. "And he's a minor."

The mom chuckled. "Well, there's always exceptions. Are you all right, honey?"

Nix turned away with his hand tightly against his chest.

"Let me see. If you cut yourself, we need to get some help. Let me see what you did." She knelt down. The veins snaked blue over the tendons on the back of her hands. Her palms smelled clean. He remembered his mom's were that way. "It's all right."

Nix looked through the bushes, across the pool. The adults were up and walking. The broken glass was picked up. The dads were mostly there. The moms weren't. Neither was Cali.

"Daisy?" The moms were coming around the corner. "Is everything all right?"

"I think Nix hurt himself."

Parker was scooting back into the bushes, using the gun like a disc, hoping to disappear. Nix thought about pointing to the half-loose paintball gun and the utility knife in Alex's pants.

"Nix?" Cali was the last to show. Avery was cradled on her shoulder. "You all right?"

Nix wanted to run to her. To hide behind her.

"Jennifer says he's been seeded."

And then the attention went from Nix to Cali. Parker bolted through the greenery, ditching the gun in the groundcover.

"Is that right?" one of the moms said. "How'd you get him seeded that young?"

"You have connections at the lab?" someone else said. "Eric's having trouble with attention deficit disorder and I can't get the doctors to give him a release. Is there anything you can do?"

"Sally's suffering from constant ear infections and they want to do surgery."

"Benjamin's got acne."

"Nix." Cali stuck her hand out. "It's time to go. Come on."

Nix leapt up and snatched her hand on the fly. They walked briskly alongside the house with a cadre of moms in tow, all of them making their best offers. They were all wealthy, all connected, but none of them could skirt the laws.

Listen, if you want your kid seeded, all it takes is a near fatal car accident and two dead parents and you can have all the damn biomites your heart desires. Hey, it's a blast.

Cali didn't talk as she buckled Avery into the car seat, squealing.

"Sorry."

"Not your fault," she said.

"I didn't mean to tell them."

"Not your fault," she said again.

The moms watched them drive off. A few were waving.

They drove home with the radio turned up, the way Avery liked it. Cali turned off her phone. When they got home, she told Thomas, her husband, they weren't going to any parties for a while.

Nix went to his room. He was different.

He would always be different.

10 YEARS LATER_

THE REAL AVENGER'S BLOG

Shooting Truth-Bullets Since Birth
Subscribers: 3,233

It's the end of time, peeps.

Mark this date, put a black X on your calendar because it's all over, starting today. It used to be that if you didn't like the laws where you lived, you just moved to another state or another country. Freedom existed somewhere in the world. We had a choice. I mean, hell, if you were desperate enough, you could live on the South Pole with penguins and shit.

Not anymore.

Today, it's all over.

Today, Mother was born.

Who's Mother? Our Mother. Already got a mother? Now you got two, only this one will know everything about you. You can't hide from her. She'll know when you're full of crap, know where you stash your porn, know when you pick your nose and when you eat it.

You'll hate her, and she'll know that, too.

Case you've been asleep for the last ten years, the Mitochondria Terraforming Hierarchy of Record is what I'm talking about.

Let's just call her Mother.

A mother that doesn't bake cookies or wash your underwear. She's not getting up to make you French toast or wipe your nose. Nope. This bitch is going to spy on you until you're dead. Which may be sooner than you think.

Mother is somewhere in the frozen plains of Wyoming. No pictures of her exist because no one's allowed to even fly over. But rumors say she's this massive dome, a computer the size of a football stadium, like some artificial brain heaved out of the frozen soil that's wirelessly connected with every biomite in existence.

Did you catch that? EVERY BIOMITE IN EXISTENCE!

Hear that buzzing on your phone? She's listening.

Feel that tickle on your laptop? She knows you're tapping.

All that *Do Not Covet Your Neighbor's Wife* crap? Yeah, that's the real deal now. Mother might tell your wife what you're thinking about doing to Joe-Bob's wife mowing the lawn in a tube top.

George Orwell wasn't even close, man. I mean, Big Brother was just a peashooter compared to Mother. Big Brother was pissing on a forest fire; Mother's bringing the goddamn ocean.

Here's the official statement from Marcus Anderson, chief of the Biomite Oversight Committee.

(BTW, he looks like a gargoyle. Right?)

It is with great pleasure that, after ten years of global effort, I present to you the greatest feat of humankind. I present to you a regulatory system that will keep all people safer and healthier for centuries to come. Bionanotechnology has put us on the brink of greatness, but with that comes uncertainty and danger. The human species has the potential to live forever. Or end tomorrow.

I prefer the former.

Mitochondria Terraforming Hierarchy of Record is linked to every booted cellular-sized biomite living inside our bodies. Its primary function will be to monitor individual levels of biomites and take appropriate action if, or when, they cross a previously determined threshold. This will keep us human.

This will keep us safe.

Forever.

I don't know about you, but this is not a gross infringement on our freedom: it's raping it. I don't want anything or anyone peeking into my biomites; that's none of your business, none of my neighbor's, and it sure as hell ain't the government's.

Biomites aren't evil, dude. They're artificial stem cells, that's all. What's the big deal? If you want to be 100% artificial, be my guest, that's your business, bro. I don't give a rat's pink sphincter what you do with your body. You want to boost your brain with biomites to get smarter? Hey, as long as you got the cash, good for you.

What the chief didn't say in his official statement was what exactly the *previously determined threshold* is.

Want to know?

You should, before you rebuild your kidney or tone those wrinkles, you should know that when your body is 40% biomites, you're a redline. And redlines go to jail.

JAIL.

Think I'm joking?

They call it a Detainment and Observation Center. You can't leave, you don't order takeout, you shower with other redlines. That's jail. You get a federally funded cot and three hots while they watch your biomite levels. On a side note, you'd think the scientists could figure out how to keep biomites from reproducing and slowly taking over our bodies once we get seeded. They are the geniuses, for Christ's sake. Doesn't seem like it should be all that hard.

But all right, whatever. So they continue dividing once they're in our bodies. It's worth the trade-off: they are the answer to every disease, every shortcoming, every desire known to man. They'll figure it out; give them some time.

But here's the kicker. Guess what happens when you hit 50%. Guess, no seriously. Take a stab. When your body becomes halfskin, when it's 50% God-given, good ole-fashioned organic cells and 50% artificial biomite cells, guess what Mother's going to do?

Bitch is going to shut you off.

That's right.

And when she does, when she turns off all your biomites like a light switch, what do you think happens to the other half? The living half?

Yeah. That's right.

It's real, peeps. Real as it gets.

The death of human liberty happened today and you probably didn't even feel it.

Well, I did.

CHAPTER TWO_

Cali knelt down to reboot a server. Her knee hit the concrete, driving spikes up her thigh. She cursed and didn't hold back. She stood a little too fast and steadied herself against the stainless steel rack. A head rush stormed her entire body, weakening her knees. She remained still until it passed and made a mental note to drink some water.

She walked two more rows. Computer after computer blinked green lights at her. No one would suspect she was in a suburban brick house with a pink flamingo in the front yard. The basement looked more like an industrial IT department. It took two air conditioners to keep the house cool.

She couldn't afford to shut her lab down. *Not now.*

No one could afford a setup like that—hell, there were companies that couldn't afford it. But she had money. *Blood money.* When she married Thomas, he joked he'd need another life insurance policy. Luck was not something Cali's family possessed. She thought he was joking, but he took out a ridiculous life insurance policy on himself so that Cali, Avery and Nix would never worry about money again if something ever happened.

And it did.

Cali sat at a desk cluttered with gadgets and monitors, microscopes and assemblers. She sipped at a water bottle while waiting for an espresso-like machine to drip a gun-metal droplet into a flask. No coffee from that machine. It was uniquely constructed to produce congealed biomites: the raw synthetic stem cells with designer DNA coding. At one drop per day, it was a slow process.

She took a heavy flask of mercury-like liquid off the shelf and swirled it under a circular magnifying glass attached to a hinged arm.

Good.

It would take a complete analysis to see if they worked, but she'd seen enough raw biomites to know the subtle colors, just like an Eskimo knew snow. These were brighter than usual, less viscous. Exactly what she expected.

There were six monitors arranged on the wall in two rows of three. The one in the middle, bottom row, was the largest. Numbers scrolled down a column that she occasionally stopped with a mouse-click. Several submenus expanded with another series of clicks. She sat back and let the numbers continue to run. The analysis was taking too long, but the program needed time.

Time was the only thing she couldn't afford.

Biomites were humanity's greatest invention. Forget telecommunications, forget transportation... bionanotechnology changed everything. Once humanity controlled the human body, they could cure disease, heal bones, alter brain chemistry. Biomites were the answer, the one big answer to every question.

Only one side effect. It was a big one. *They were malignant.*

They were exact duplicates of the body's cells but, for some unknown reason, wouldn't accept enzymatic cues to stop dividing. No matter what coding bionanoengineers inserted into the DNA, they always reverted back to runaway division, replacing the body's natural organic cells.

Cali had a theory.

She believed the biomites intuited the weakness of organic cells—their susceptibility to random DNA variability, cancer, disease—and logically replaced them. Biomites were doing what we wanted; they were making the body sound and impervious.

Perfect.

The monitor to the left, bottom row, chimed. Another email arrived and filed at the top of a long column of unread messages. The office manager confirmed Cali's paid leave of absence was nearly depleted. She'd spent her sick days and vacation long ago. Pretty soon, her leave of absence would convert to unpaid. Her employers had been very sympathetic. They gave her more time than they should have. She was a valuable asset, a deserving individual, but a Fortune 500 company can only bend the sympathy branch so far. Pretty soon, they'd prune it.

Cali finished the water and rubbed her eyes. She saw her reflection in the dark monitors. The shadows across her cheeks were long and dark, disguising the red rims of her eyelids and cracked lips. Oily blond hair hung over her eyes. She retied the ponytail.

She rolled the chair to the right and touched the electron microscope. Images lit up a dark monitor, obliterating her deathly reflection. The previous batch of biomites that percolated from the espresso machine was still active. Under magnification, they looked like grains of sand jittering on meth. Excellent stability, that was good. She wouldn't know if they possessed runaway division until further testing, but she didn't care about that. Not anymore.

Priorities change.

She was looking for biomites that would disappear. Not physically, but virtually. Every biomite emitted a frequency that could be monitored. That's what Mother watched, the frequency with which biomites *spoke* to each other. Mother was an eavesdropper, downloading everything they did. There weren't enough zeros to count how many biomites were in existence, but everyone had them.

So Mother knew what everyone was doing.

Cali wanted to change that.

So far, nothing worked. There was still hope. There was still time. But not much of either.

Someone squealed upstairs, followed by a fit of laughter. Avery was about to pee herself. Only Nix could make her laugh like that. She loved that sound, her favorite sound in the entire world. Without Nix, she might not hear it ever again.

This is all my fault. All mine. I knew this day was coming, knew his redline potential, but I waited. I waited because I'm selfish. Nix is going to pay for that. We're all going to pay.

The numbers continued to scroll in a fuzzy line.

She rubbed her eyes and tried to focus, but it only smudged the images further. She didn't have time for this, not now. She could sleep when this was all over; she just needed to focus, to see the data come together so that she could hide her little brother.

Get him off Mother's map.

Mother didn't care what he meant to her, what he meant to Avery. They would come, they would take him, they would take him from her life, from Avery's life, and he was all she had, all she had, he was all she had—

She closed her eyes.

Breathing slowly, breathing deeply.

She relaxed before opening her eyes. The images around her weren't sharp, but she could make them out. She could read them. The analysis was almost over. Once that was done, she could get the next batch started and then lie down for a nap. She'd done it earlier that day (or was it night, there were no windows in the basement), fallen directly into REM. Twenty minutes later, she was brand new.

She took the water bottle to the bathroom and filled it. She heard a bell ring and leaned out the door to see if the analysis finished early. The numbers were still scrolling. She sat back down and took another deep drink—

BING.

That was upstairs.

The doorbell.

Cali stayed completely still, ears pricked with attention. There were muddled voices. A long silence. She remained as still as a stowaway.

The basement door opened and snapped closed.

Little feet danced down the steps. "Mommy," Avery said, "there's some guy at the door talking to Uncle Nix."

Cali stood too quickly and braced herself on the desk. "Who?"

Avery shrugged. "They want him to go."

Cali stumbled to the steps, barely seeing the door at the top rush towards her. She punched it open, slamming it against the wall.

Time is out.

CHAPTER THREE_

Nix just finished draining the dishwasher when the doorbell rang.

He stopped to turn the television off, where cartoons blared loud enough that his sister would hear them in the basement. He was going to take her something to eat and considered mashing up a sleeping pill in some cottage cheese. She swore she was taking naps, but her face was caving in. He'd laced her food once before, when she pulled a week's worth of all-nighters to finish the coding on a new batch of biomites in time for a presentation at a global convention.

He dried his hands and slung the towel over his shoulder. There was a car in the driveway, a black four-door sedan with an unassuming man in the driver's seat. No sunglasses, no badge. Just an ordinary guy sitting like a waxy replication of a normal everyday somebody.

BING.

Nix slowed. He thought-commanded a self-analysis of the biomite population in his body.

39.8%.

He was composed of less than 40% biomites; that meant over 60% of his body was good, old-fashioned organic cells. That meant he wasn't redline. That meant it couldn't be them. But biomite patrol didn't make house calls to see how you were doing. They showed up for one reason.

There's some mistake.

He gripped the door handle.

They'll understand. Gear sometimes needs calibrated.

The door opened.

The man standing there, unlike his partner in the driver's seat, was wearing sunglasses, the reflective kind.

They stood there, facing each other. There were no words. No greeting or informal nods. Just a silent recognition. They'd never seen each other, but they knew what the other was about.

"I'm not redline," Nix stated.

The agent didn't flinch. He unclipped a cell-phone-sized gearbox from his belt. He held it up like a badge and waited. Nix took a half a step forward. The agent lowered the box, pressing it against Nix's flesh between the breastbone and bobbing Adam's apple.

Nix felt the thing whir hotly. Its effect scattered over his skin like electric spider webs, wrapping over his shoulders and across his back, penetrating his body like feeder roots to estimate the biomite population. The agent pulled the gearbox away, leaving Nix feeling weak. He looked at it and turned it so Nix could see the number.

"It's wrong."

"We'll confirm at the office."

"It'll say the same thing, and it's wrong."

"You need to come with us."

Nix took a step back. He considered running. The agent shook his head one time. There would be no running. Any attempt to resist would be met swiftly. Mother was in Wyoming and Nix in southern Illinois, but she could see him like he was standing right next to her. She knew what his biomites were doing, what he was thinking. If he ran, if he disobeyed a biomite agent, Mother would flip a switch. He'd hit the floor.

Obey. Or else.

It's the law.

"It is my duty to bring you into a Detainment and Observation Center to be fully analyzed. You are not under arrest, simply detained for further observation. If our readings are wrong, you will be brought back to your home and compensated for your time. Do you understand these rights?"

Nod.

He brandished a stiff metal ring, the color of a cold weapon. "For your safety and ours, I'm going to place this suppression ring around—"

A door cracked inside the house.

"NO!" Cali bounded across the room and wrapped her arms around Nix. "He's not redline. You can't take him."

"Ma'am, this will be your only warning. Do not interfere."

A car door shut. The driver approached the house.

"Look, look." Cali fumbled her own reader, slimmer and colder, against Nix's neck and shoved the reading in the agent's face. "38.8%. He's under; we still have time."

"He'll be verified at the satellite office. If there is a mistake, he will be back before dinner."

The driver stopped behind the first agent.

"No," she whispered.

"Ma'am."

Her hand clamped on Nix's arm.

There was a long moment of staring. Nix could sense all the thoughts floating around them like transparent bubbles. He couldn't hear them, but he sensed them. Thoughts of escape. Thoughts of apprehension.

Violence.

Nix reached up and gently squeezed her hand. It would be bad enough to be taken away. He wouldn't be able to handle watching his sister punished for it. She was still shaking her head, mouthing the same word over and over.

The agent reached up and lowered the suppression ring over

Nix's head to rest around his neck. It was cold against his skin, warming quickly.

Heaviness fell on him as the biomites in his body slowed down, diminishing their activity. They were not deactivated, just reduced to keeping him alive, to keeping him subdued for his safety and others. Thoughts became dull; memories began to pale.

But worst of all... *Cali is alone.*

Nix was guided to the car. A few of the neighbors watched. One leaned on a rake, relief on his face that it wasn't one of his kids.

Cali wasn't in the doorway when Nix sat in the backseat of the new-smelling sedan. The front door was closed. She was already in the basement.

The suppression ring wasn't fully powered. There was still time to say goodbye.

Nix laid his head back and closed his eyes. The car rocked as it backed over the curb. Traffic sounds faded. He no longer heard the cars passing or felt the pavement grind under the tires. The world around him disappeared. Nix went to his safe haven, went to a place he discovered many years ago, a place that protected him from the world. Where he wasn't different.

He went to a lagoon deep inside his mind.

CHAPTER FOUR

THE LAGOON WAS DEEP AND CLEAR WITH STRIPED MUSSELS AND bright starfish on the sandy bottom. Sometimes sharks would find their way through a small channel that funneled water from the ocean. They would skim near the beach, their dorsal fins cutting the surface. They'd come so close that Nix could run his hand over their slick skin.

A fire smoldered from inside a pile of sticks, a thick column of smoke withering in the still air. There was no scent, no sting in his eyes. He smelled very little in this dreamland, good or bad.

The smoke obscured the view across the lagoon where, above the palms on the far shore, blue cliffs rose up. Halfway up was an opening that spewed water like a giant faucet, its roar heard a mile away. The water poured forth and sprayed misty droplets, leaving an ever-present rainbow stretching into the palms.

[*Away.*]

The smoke twisted away like a vacuum simply pulled it in the other direction. The waterfall hadn't changed much over the ten years he'd been coming to the lagoon. In fact, it was exactly like the day he first saw it. He was only eight. In fact, it was the day after he showed his best friends, Alex and Parker, the biomites in his finger.

Even though he was just a kid, he knew the dreamland wasn't normal.

But, then again, Nix was anything but normal.

He knew his body was in the back of a biomite agent's car. Time between the dreamland and fleshland wasn't synced. Dreamland time went so much slower. Still, the ring would suppress the biomites that powered dreamland.

Maybe he'd never visit again.

He looked around for Raine. The fire was there; she must be getting ready for something. Nix pulled a stick hard against his shin, heard it crackle until the dry fibers gave way and split open. The pain on his shin was dull and slight.

He dropped the branch on the smoldering fire. Sparks spit out from the bottom. He gathered the bark that flaked off and piled it onto the embers, waving and blowing it back into flames. Smoke billowed up. He squatted, rubbing his hands, as if he could feel the heat. Perhaps he could, but it was tepid. Like day-old dishwater.

The foliage rustled behind him. Something dragged through the weeds and then across the sand.

"Is the fire ready?"

Nix smiled.

"Such a slacker." Raine pulled a cord with a wild boar tied to the end, the tusks curled out of its mouth. Raine's skin was brown. Her black hair, cropped and choppy. Her eyes green, like the green of verdant forests when the sun rises.

She was about Nix's age, he guessed, eighteen years old or so. Her body was taut with muscle roiling around the bikini top. She showed up at the lagoon about five years ago. Before that, he would explore on his own, but now they did everything together.

She slid a knife from a holster tied on her leg and cut the hog loose. Nix piled more sticks on the pathetic fire and watched her dress dinner. Grit and sweat smudged the perfect skin on her shoulders. She wiped the back of her neck with the knife wedged between her fingers.

He swore he could smell her, that her fragrance—that essence that was Raine—permeated everything inside him. He knelt behind her, kneading the cords of muscle that flexed over her shoulder blades. She agreed with a guttural *mmmm*.

"You know, I'd rather have a fire than a massage."

Nix pushed his thumbs into her back and worked the knots loose. He kissed her neck, a distant taste of salt.

"Stop, now. I want to catch some waves and that fire looks like an ape built it." She clapped. "Chop-chop!"

She finished dressing dinner while he set up the spit. Reluctantly, he shaved more bark and gathered kindling. A fire was roaring before she was ready. He watched her wash tubers in the clear water of the lagoon and slice them into the beast's splayed belly.

They rested against a fallen palm trunk while dinner slow-roasted. If it all ended, he wouldn't be disappointed. This was a good way to say goodbye. She nestled into the crook of his arm and lightly snored. He never got tired of that sound: the sound of her sleeping against him. The way her lips fluttered. The way her fingers twitched as dreams came.

Did she dream? Did she snore when he wasn't there to hear it?

Nix always thought that question exposed the self-centered nature of humanity. If a tree fell with no one around to hear it, did it exist? The snoring question was different, though. The lagoon was his dream and Raine was part of it. Sometimes, he wasn't so sure, but perhaps that was wishful thinking. The only thing that existed at the lagoon was what he wished to exist.

The sun was close to setting when Raine pulled the meat from the roasted carcass. He wondered where the car was in fleshland—how close it was to the satellite office—as Raine dished the meal onto primitive coconut bowls and piled cooked tubers onto it. They ate with their fingers. The food didn't do much for Nix's appetite. He didn't have one. And he hardly tasted it. Raine moaned with each bite. Grease glistened on her lips. She licked her fingers. Her joy pulsed through him.

"You crying?"

Nix wiped the corner of his eye. No, he wasn't crying, but she caught him wishing this moment would never end. This might be the last time he watched her eat like an animal, listened to her snore, watched her swim...

So, no, he wasn't crying. "The fire... smoke... making my eyes itch."

They left the fire burning, left the meat for scavengers if they got to it in time. Raine grabbed a well-worn surfboard that she carved from the trunk of an ancient tree years ago. "Come on," she said, shoving his on the ground. "Let's catch a wave."

He lay there in the sand. The sun was low. Her skin, darker.

"Something wrong?"

He shook his head, smiling. "Go on. I'll catch up."

She hesitated, sensing the secret inside him. Or did she already know it, preferring to enjoy their last moments instead of soaking in them. He watched her push into the glassy surface, plowing the water with sun-kissed arms, powerful strokes driving her towards the narrow channel that led to the ocean, where she'd catch perfect waves.

Always perfect waves.

The water shimmered. Turned white.

Then black.

Nix stared at the black sedan's roof. The biomite agent stood next to the car with the door open. He helped him out and led him toward a small brick building where they'd test his biomite population again. Where they'd officially call him a redline.

Where they'd power up the suppression ring.

Where he could say goodbye to dreamland.

CHAPTER FIVE_

Albert Gladstone turned fifty years old.

That was a few days ago. He ate birthday cake. It was vanilla with chocolate frosting. His wife and two teenage kids were there. They sang "Happy Birthday" and watched him blow out the candles. Someone cut the cake and took pieces to his family. His son ate. His wife and daughter didn't.

Albert ate his piece. Even licked the icing from the paper plate. It wasn't particularly good.

But that was a couple days ago.

He didn't have an appetite now. He couldn't feel much of anything.

Albert wore loose-fitting pants and a shirt that looked more like hospital scrubs. Felt like pajamas. He sat in a comfortable chair in a small room. A small empty room. The chair was cushioned but could've been made out of stainless steel and he wouldn't have known the difference. His biomites began dumping synthetic morphine into his bloodstream an hour earlier.

Life was bad, but didn't feel as such.

49.8%.

"Jenny from across the street was walking her dog this morning,"

Albert's wife was saying on the other side of a thick square of glass, "and sends her best. She's got four cats and three dogs now. I think it's too much, if you ask me. But she says what else is going to happen to these animals? I mean, she goes to the shelter and finds these poor pets that were abandoned by their owners and they're going to be..."

Her words trailed off.

She covered her face. Words had always been a buffer. They usually didn't fail.

An elderly woman put her arm around her shoulder. That was Albert's mom. And behind her stood his dad and two kids. His daughter was leaking stained tears. His son wore a mask without emotions. Unlike his mother, he dealt with loss by killing his emotions.

Albert could hear his wife's sobs through a speaker. They sounded like tiny hiccups strung together with squeaky thread. His daughter stepped forward and smudged the glass with her hand.

"Do you feel all right, Dad? Does it hurt?"

Albert smiled as brightly and widely as possible, but it only translated into a slight upturn of his lips. He nodded once. The cushioned back of the chair crunched on the back of his head.

49.9%.

"I'm proud of you, kids." His words were amplified into the other room. "If I was God and had to build a daughter and son, they would be just like you. I wouldn't change a thing."

He took a moment to draw in a breath. His lungs felt smaller.

His daughter's face was streaked with charcoal tears. She pressed both hands on the glass.

"This is inhumane!" The old man shook his fist. "How can you murder a good man and refuse to let his family be with him? How can you force us to watch him die from another room? This is... this is... it's diabolical! I am a lawyer and I will see to an end of these sinister laws! I will make sure this will never happen to another human being!"

The old man hammered the glass with both fists.

"THIS IS MURDER! YOU ARE A COLD-BLOODED MURDERER!"

He was speaking to the odd-looking man that was in the room with Albert. Marcus Anderson stood off to the side like an observer, wearing a finely tailored suit and silk tie. He occasionally looked at a device in the palm of his hand. He represented the government in these halfskin matters. Anyone with a loved one near halfskin status knew his face well, a face one would not call handsome. He was the same age as Albert but looked more like Albert's father. His thinning hair was prematurely gray, his head slightly misshapen much like the slight hunch on his back from an outward curvature of his spine.

He was as emotionless as the son.

A guard politely and gently guided the old man away from the glass, but words of protest still trickled through the speakers.

"It's all right," Albert could be heard whispering. "We all have to end. This isn't so bad."

They didn't believe what he said. Later, they told the press that the gargoyle (they refused to call Marcus Anderson by his name, he was a monster, leave it at that) had drugged him so he would say stuff like that. They probably shouldn't have called him a gargoyle.

"Shhhhh." Albert was too tired to say anything else, so he just made that sound so they would feel comforted.

He didn't want them to feel sad. He knew the rules. He knew he was pushing his luck with his biomite population. He'd exceeded the biomite seeding recommendation to his brain stem, but it had paid off. His memory and analytical abilities were computerlike. He won a record number of federal grants for his lab. He thought the seeding would boost his intelligence to find a cure for the runaway biomite replication before he went redline. It was a gamble.

But Albert wasn't much of a gambler.

If he was honest, he didn't like the way it felt. The more the biomites replaced the organic cells in his body, the less present he felt. He was smarter, more successful, more secure... but he was just less... *real.* The agents took him from his lab the moment he went redline. And as he neared the halfskin threshold, he wrote to his wife that everything felt the same, he just felt less real.

He couldn't explain it any better than that.

Shutting his biomites down wasn't such a bad idea. Not the way he felt.

50%.

Marcus put the device he was obsessively watching into his pocket and respectfully folded his hands. A doctor entered the room.

The sandman began pouring his magical dust into Albert's body. It started at the top of his head and filtered down to his toes. He was becoming heavy. Gravity pulled him into the chair. His head lolled back and forth like he was refusing. He barely heard the sobs get louder.

His eyelids were too heavy.

He wanted to see his kids one last time, but that wasn't to be. He wouldn't hear them again. All he heard, as the biomites slowly shut down, pulling his life with them, was the sound of a leaking tire. A sound that slid through his lips.

"Shhhhhh."

The doctor knelt next to Albert and pressed his fingers to his neck. He checked an instrument that he briefly pulled from his pocket. He stood and nodded.

"MONSTER!" The old man had to be restrained. "My son... was good—"

The speaker clicked off. The glass dimmed.

THE FAMILY WOULD REMAIN in the room to grieve. Once Albert was fully examined, they would get to see him one more time but would not be allowed to take possession of his body for burial. Albert would be cremated and his ashes sent to them.

Marcus Anderson let his people attend to Albert's body. The man known as Albert Gladstone was gone from this world. If anyone asked Marcus, the man began dying the moment he chose to be seeded.

Marcus stopped outside the room to rub antibacterial gel on his hands. He went directly to a room on the bottom floor of Cleveland's Detainment and Observation Center, where a cadre of reporters would want a statement from the chief of Biomite Oversight and Regulation regarding the shutdown of another halfskin.

He would be happy to report one less halfskin in the world.

CHAPTER SIX_

MARCUS ANDERSON SANK INTO THE SOFT LEATHER OF THE heated backseat, taking comfort in the laptop's blue glow. His flight from Ohio was uneventful. He stayed long enough to answer questions and went directly to the airport to fly home.

The driver turned into the Washington, D.C., neighborhood of Spring Valley. The streetlights illuminated the wet pavement.

He adjusted the Bluetooth in his ear. The press secretary wanted to be briefed on the halfskin shutdown. When laws regulating biomites went into action, there was revolt throughout the world. But the evidence was overwhelming: if something wasn't done to curtail biomite integration, the human species was in danger.

The models predicted that biomites would essentially consume the human population within twenty years without regulation. The Halfskin Laws declared that—until biomite replication was cured at the cellular level—no citizen would be allowed to contain more than 50% biomites. Once over that threshold, you were more machine than human.

Marcus couldn't agree more.

The result of shutting down a person's biomites was always death of the body. The president was concerned about the family and the halfskin's comfort level. The president had signed the Mother Over-sight Agreement with the United Nations; America would abide by its laws. But still, the president needed to show compassion for the victim and his family.

He is not a victim. He simply failed to exist.

That was how Marcus framed the definition. If a healthy human could not exist without the assistance of biomites, then it was a failure to exist. There was a flaw in the definition (people were kept alive by artificial assistance all the time), but Marcus simply drew the line with biomites. These weren't plastic arms or legs, they were artificial living cells. Replacing your God-given bodily cells with man-made ones was Marcus's beef. A plastic arm was one thing, trading God's temple for a slimmer, stronger, faster body with killer blue eyes was quite another.

The car eased to the curb. The brick house was set back from the street; a sidewalk meandered toward the front door. Marcus packed his leather briefcase and checked the mailbox on his way inside. Crickets sang and the night smelled wet. He didn't get outside much.

One of the kids was crying upstairs while Marcus hung his coat in the closet. His shiny shoes clapped on the bamboo floor, making a harder click as he turned onto the kitchen tiles.

"Good evening," he said.

Janine was sitting at the breakfast table with a phone pressed against her ear, surrounded by eternal stacks of documents. He'd had a discussion with her about that—orderliness of body brings orderliness of mind, especially for lawyers—but there were many things they disagreed upon. Their marriage was not a good one by conventional definition, but it was fruitful. It was powerful. Their children would be very successful, given the gene pool from which they were spawned. (Marcus knew this because he had their genomes mapped.) So, they called a truce on the paper stacking. *Pick battles, not wars.*

"Dinner is just about ready," Ariel, the head nanny/cook, said. She stirred a pot of red sauce. Marcus stopped to smell.

"Then you can get the children."

"Yes, sir."

MARCUS CLOSED HIS OFFICE DOORS. The wall along the back was curved, with a mahogany desk centered in front of a bay window. The heavy curtains, drawn. Shelves lined the walls with classically bound books that were authentic, but never read.

He checked his emails while sipping a freshly pulped glass of carrot juice. He didn't answer any of them, but glanced through the headings before stripping off his clothes and changing into a pair of shorts and T-shirt folded neatly in the bottom desk drawer. He mounted a recumbent bike tucked into the corner to the right of the desk and eased into an exercise routine. He didn't like exercising on a full stomach, but there wasn't much choice. If he didn't, he wouldn't exercise at all.

The television flickered to life. There was only one channel he watched: news. All-day news. As he dug into the next level of exercise bike's resistance—his empty glass flecked with orange spots—he watched protesters march around the Capitol with signs that condemned the Halfskin Laws. They were always out there.

Change is difficult.

To lead a nation, one accepted protest. People did not like change. They wanted things to stay the same, forever. Whether they were suffering or not, whether change was logical or absurd, they wanted things to stay the same. They would hate you for it. Sometimes kill you for it.

The television went to commercial and came back to Marcus's press conference following Albert Gladstone's shutdown. He touched a button on the exercise bike and brought the resistance up another level while he watched himself climb to the podium. He hated seeing himself on television. The lights made his skin ashen and always seemed to catch his left eye, the slightly misshapen one. If it weren't that, it was from an angle that made him look like a hunchback.

Damn liberals. Always showing my bad side.

"It is with regret that I hold this meeting…"

Empathy. Sorrow. He'd nailed every emotion, dead-center perfect. He wasn't lying; he did feel for the family of Albert Gladstone. They had to watch their beloved father-husband-son destroy himself. Marcus was not to blame. He was innocent of such malevolence, just a man helping humanity—infantile in their desires and bottomless in their greed—save themselves from themselves.

"How do you respond to critics that this is government-sanctioned murder?" he was asked.

And he answered with a stern expression. "We're simply shutting down biomites that have reached a threshold of willful domination in Albert Gladstone's body. The human body is an organic being, not a computer. If it cannot survive without assistance of bionanotechnology, then it has reached its end."

His empathy waned.

If the reporters all dropped dead simultaneously, he wouldn't show sorrow. He doubted he could even suppress a smile. That would be sinful, but nonetheless. Some of those rats with a pen were direct descendants of Satan. And that, he felt certain, was a fact.

He watched the rest of the conference, suppressing the urge to vomit.

God didn't make machines. Man did.

His office doors opened. Janine slung her briefcase over her shoulder. "Office called; I have to go."

"It's almost ten o'clock."

"Deadline is tomorrow and the world is ending."

Marcus climbed off the bike and mopped his forehead with a

towel. He wished for another freshly squeezed juice. Ariel was most likely gone.

Janine pursed hairpins in her lips while she fixed her hair back. Her face was blotchy and oily. She rarely wore makeup, especially when she went in late.

"Did you see the press conference?" he asked.

She nodded. "I did."

Janine squeezed his shoulder. He hated when she touched him like that. It was a pat on the shoulder and proud expression, and she never really looked at him when she did it. It was so... *scripted.*

A melodious tone muffled somewhere. Janine finished clipping her hair and dug through her briefcase as she headed for the doors. "This is Anderson."

Marcus followed her down the hall, hearing the lawyer-speak that he loved so much—a language of order and righteousness—before turning into the kitchen as she exited the front door. He watched the car back out of the driveway, the headlights swinging across the lawn before fading down the street.

He returned to the office with another juice and prepared for his nightcap. The kids were asleep. The wife, gone. Still, he drew the curtains closed and locked the doors.

This moment was forever secret.

CHAPTER SEVEN_

Cali pulled off to the side of the road. The Center was across the field.

The Detention and Observation Center.

She sat twenty minutes north of Carbondale, Illinois, just off Highway 51. Once a fertile field that farmers tilled for corn and soybeans, the ground that separated the road from the Detention and Observation Center lay fallow now, giving rise to yellow-flowering weeds and cocklebur. There used to be a community center over there for farmers, a place they could play bingo or drink coffee and talk about the weather. They wrecked it to build a secure building, one for detaining and observing. The farmers' sons put down their plows and took up badges for a steady sip from the government, to protect this land from the 40% biomite-infested redlines.

This Center was just one of many across the nation. And unless the laws changed or biomite replication was solved, they would become modern-day death cubicles. When that day came, overpopulation would not be a problem as Mother shut off halfskins by the thousands... *daily.*

The new-age holocaust.

That was how Cali saw it. Of course, critics were confident that something would change, surely the human race would evolve, they would solve the replication problem. They wouldn't allow the mass extermination.

But those same critics didn't have a loved one detained and observed. So Cali was a little... jaded.

She'd been to visit her brother once a week, every week, since they took him. That was six months ago. If she wasn't visiting, she was in the basement.

Working.

She'd taken an unpaid leave of absence from the lab. They understood. They didn't terminate her. She could always come back when she was ready, they told her. When Cali told people she wasn't well, that she needed some time to sort things out, they didn't ask why. Those that knew her gave her all the space she needed.

Poor thing.

The Center would see her car parked across the field. Someone would eventually come out. Cali just needed a moment. She came to visit every week, but it wasn't getting easier. The closer she got to this sick and twisted place, the more her hands shook. No one seemed to care that her brother would be dead without biomites.

Now he's imprisoned for it.

There was no justice in this universe. And if there was a God, she'd smack him for meting out such imbalance. The Christians were right; God had to be a man. Who else could make a woman's life hell?

She fumbled with her purse and tapped out a cigarette. It took a couple clicks of the lighter to get it puffing. She blew a cloud out the window. The mentholated smoke settled her nerves.

She was used to southern Illinois humidity. Nix was born in Illinois, but Cali grew up in South Carolina and this was mild compared to that. However, she still wasn't accustomed to the flatness. When she drove the country roads, she could see for miles in every direction, like God had scraped the edge of his hand over this part of the world. She craved the trees and hills where she grew up, the wetlands and smell of pluff mud and the rank odor of the paper mill on wet days. She missed home, a place where she belonged.

If she went back there, she still wouldn't find it. Home was gone. *Gone, gone, gone.*

"Better get *go-ing...*" Avery sang from the backseat.

Cali looked in the rearview. Her eyes—ringed as if with soot, capillaries showing where the whites were supposed to be—looked back. She pushed the hair out of her face and took a drag before adjusting the mirror. Avery was strapped into the backseat, watching her iPod. Her backpack was next to her, holding all the essentials: water bottle, change of clothes and Pogo, the stuffed rhinoceros.

"You'll get in trouble if they come out here, Mama. They won't let you see Nix."

"I know, honey. I just need a moment."

The little girl hummed like she'd heard that excuse before. She dragged her finger across the screen and sang, "Better get *go-ing...*"

Cali smiled. What would she have in this world if that little girl wasn't with her? God had taken everything else but Nix.

There was nothing left to take.

She sucked on the filtered end and hung her hand out the door. Cali put the car in gear. A white dust cloud followed her to the stop sign, where she turned right and passed a tan truck. The truck turned around at the intersection and followed her to the gate.

Avery was still humming.

Jennifer Adams wore a pair of khaki slacks and a white blouse. A small metal American flag was pinned above her left breast. She wasn't sure what to wear to a press conference, one where she'd meet her half-dead husband. This seemed appropriate.

Her daughter rode on her hip, resting her head. The pacifier squeaked compulsively. Jonathan held her left hand. He wanted to wear his Cub Scout uniform. He tugged at the yellow kerchief snug against his neck. It seemed appropriate.

Along the wall to their left were reporters and photographers from major outlets across the nation. Cameras clicked and phones buzzed. A man in uniform patted her shoulder and whispered something comforting in her ear (she didn't understand it; she couldn't understand anything at that moment) before rustling the boy's hair and tapping the little girl on the nose.

Jennifer was going to stain her blouse with vomit.

In front of her was a brown podium with several mics. The American flag was behind it. The curtain on the wall was pulled aside. Her breath caught in her throat. It was hard to let out. A man stepped out. He was dressed in hospital scrubs for the announcement. Walter Reed Hospital wanted the world to see what they had done with Jennifer's husband.

That had to be good. Right?

Still hard to breathe.

"General McGee and other members of the army," the doctor said, "ladies and gentlemen of the press, thank you for coming."

He took a moment to look at the podium and adjusted his cap.

"Jennifer." He smiled. "Thank you for your patience. I know this has been very difficult for you and your family. Your husband, Lieutenant Adams, was gravely injured during an assignment on foreign soil. He returned to the United States on life support. He lost his arm above the elbow."

The doctor signaled with the edge of his hand somewhere in the middle of his left bicep. Jennifer looked down for a moment, unable to push away the memory of her husband. When she saw him in that bed with the ventilator and the bruises and the swelling... he looked so small. So fragile.

It wasn't him.

Cameras clicked to capture her raw moment.

"I know this is quite a spectacle we've created, but it is an event the world needs to see. Lieutenant Adams' injuries were fatal. The best we could hope for was to prolong his life with prosthetics and life support. But with the advent of bionanotechnology, his injuries were treated with artificial cell regeneration. We hope to show that this new approach to medicine will change the way not just our service men and women heal, but all Americans. Lieutenant Adams has a new spleen and lung, his vision has been restored, his arm..."

The doctor adjusted his cap again. He looked around slowly.

"Let's not let words get in the way."

Jennifer couldn't feel her knees. She lowered her daughter to the floor before she dropped her.

She knelt next to her son.

Her hand quivered over her mouth. She couldn't breathe. She stopped trying.

Because when the curtain pulled aside—

When a man stepped out—

She recognized him. At last, her husband had returned from the war. All of him.

And the cameras snapped and snapped and snapped.

CHAPTER EIGHT_

"Your turn."

George sat on the other side of a transparent door. The collar on his uniform was open, his neck unshaven. He tipped back on the chair and dropped his boot on the corner of a small table. The chess pieces rattled slightly. A smile was hidden beneath a mustache bush.

Nix stood in the center of his cell. *His room.* It wasn't a cell, he was reminded often, it was a room. He wasn't a prisoner, he was a ward of the United States under the Halfskin Laws. Nix was under watch, twenty-four hours a day and had been for the past six months and would be as long as he registered above 40%. In the history of biomites, no one's population had ever decreased. It was likely he'd have a room for a while.

At least until he hit halfskin.

The walls were white and barren. There was a bed and a toilet and a sink and a desk and a chair. All white. The desk wasn't for writing since pens and pencils weren't allowed. Recent studies proved certain biomites could spread through liquids, even ink. Seeding usually required specialized equipment, but some of the new breeds of biomites could simply be inhaled as vapor or liquid. No one wanted to be seeded against their will, so Observation and Detainment Centers banned them, and desks became more for stacking things than writing. They'd bring him a laptop, if he asked, but it was quarantined and couldn't remain in the room. It was too dangerous. They hadn't explained why.

Currently, there was just the stack of papers that was in the middle of the desk—the only thing on the surface—crisp and colorful drawings from a ten-year-old girl. Cali brought him one every week from Avery. If he were allowed tape or anything sticky, he'd put them on the wall. Sometimes he spaced them out on the floor and walked through a labyrinth of blue skies and green grass and yellow, smiling suns and brown ponies; he always picked them up and stacked them neatly when he was done.

Time went so slow in the room.

At least it was comfortable. At least it was safe.

Nix stared at the monitor over the sink. It was not his reflection that looked back—mirrors weren't allowed—but a monitor. He was dressed in (what else) white. He had no hair. None. Not on his head or brows, under his arms or anywhere south of that. All of that fell out after wearing the suppression ring for six months.

Everyone reacted differently to the ring. It was only supposed to suppress the biomites to slow their replication and activity. *There's some dangerous redlines out there,* George the Guard used to say. *Got the strength of a chimpanzee. Got to slow the mites down, Nixy,* George would say.

Nix's biomites slowed down. And they dumped his hair like a chemo patient. But that wasn't the worst of it. The no-hair thing wasn't a big deal. It was convenient, if you asked him. His skin, perfectly smooth. No, the worst of it was the vibration.

He heard it and felt it in the middle of his head like an itch he could never reach, like someone struck a tuning fork deep inside his brain. It was always there, day and night. It took away his dreams. Scrambled his thoughts.

Took away Raine.

He sometimes remembered the last time he saw her. The color of her skin. The way she paddled through the water. Other days, she was just a hazy figure in his memory. Someone he used to know.

He tried to sketch her when he had the laptop and his memories were good, spent hours with a doodle program to recreate the lagoon and the blue cliffs and the waterfall. Each time, there were fewer details. Fewer memories.

Without the lagoon and Raine, he felt empty. Alone.

And he couldn't remember the last time he felt that way.

Nix craned his neck. From where he stood, he could already see his next move. He anticipated what George was going to do, even though George was cheating. He was using his phone to log the moves into a chess program, telling him what to do.

"Got you now, halfskin." George chuckled, hands laced behind his head. His eyes were nearly hidden in folds of fat and untamed eyebrows. Nix had a feeling it'd take a hundred suppression rings to make George hairless.

Nix pulled his chair to the door. He studied the board through the embedded crisscrossed wires. He pretended to be thinking. He liked George. Anything was better than nothing. Most of the guards were good at their job, but not George. He talked with the redlines, got to know them.

Where'd you get the name Nixon? George asked the day he arrived.

My dad was a fan of dead presidents.

George thought about that. It was the next day he came back, tapped on Nix's door and then tapped his head. *I got that,* he said. *Richard Nixon, I got that.*

He saw Nix playing chess one day on his monitor and, the very next day, set up a little table. Said he was going to teach this eighteen-year-old halfskin what a real man could do. Didn't matter Nix wasn't halfskin, he was redline. But that was a technicality. Really, he was a halfskin, just hadn't fulfilled his destiny, George would say. George would show him what a whole man could do. How a pure man could think.

Not a halfskin man.

George was still convinced the biomites were giving Nix superpowers, making him smarter. Maybe he was right. Nix wanted the game to last. If it ended too soon, George would take his game and go home. Might not come back. And then Nix would be alone.

Keep the game close; give him hope.

"Six months," George said, "but I'm finally going to beat you."

Nix planted his chin on his knuckles. Pulling off the con had become more fun than beating him. Watching him walk into the trap was a hell of a good time, too.

"Good run, kid. I've beat every mite-infested halfskin in this place but you. It just goes to show you, God-given talent always beats the machine." He tapped his temple. "Creativity, son. It's the power to adapt and create; that's what God gave us, not you with the power to program your little computer-cells."

He leaned back some more.

"You had a great brain, but you had to ruin it, had to eat the mites to get better than the rest of us and now look at you."

His eyes twinkled between thick lids. "You're paying for it now."

George thought Nix chose biomites. Most people did. You don't have a choice when a drunk driver caves in the side of the car. But why spoil the fun, just lump all the redlines together: a bunch of greedy turds.

"You're going to owe me, William!" George shouted down the hall. "Got the kid stuck."

Nix cringed. He may have strung this one out too long. He didn't want to draw George too far into the trap of disappointment. Once, when he trounced George with a seven-move checkmate, the ring got turned up and Nix's head rattled all night. The biomites damn near shut down. No one knew how the ring got turned up, but George winked at him the next morning. Nix couldn't get out of bed for a week.

"There's a cure out there," George said. "A way to get rid of all the mites in your body."

Nix remained pensive. "Why would I want that?"

"You like what you are?"

Nix shrugged slightly. *Sure, why not.*

The front legs of George's chair hit the ground. "As long as you got mites, we know where you are, son. You got mites, Mother's going to always know what you're thinking, where you're going, whether you're picking your nose or sniffing someone's underwear. You get purged, you can be just like me—a whole man, free to do whatever you want. Why wouldn't you want that?"

Nix studied the pieces. George had been reading too many gossip mags. There was no such thing as a biomite purge.

"If you go to a plastic surgeon," Nix said slowly, "and cure your ugly, will you still be you?"

Someone laughed down the hall. They were listening.

"I may be ugly, but I'm real."

"So are chimpanzees."

"I'd rather be a monkey than a machine."

Nix sat back and crossed his arms, stroking his baby-smooth chin. He looked up from the board for the first time. George stared back, eyes glittering and mustache quivering.

"What were you doing seven years ago?"

George's eyes disappeared. "Hell, I don't know."

"You weren't doing anything, that's why. Because you didn't exist."

"The hell that supposed to mean?"

Nix leaned forward, pretending to look at the board. "Did you know it takes seven years for all the cells in your body to be recycled? That means all the cells that composed your body seven years ago have all died and been replaced by new ones. So, for a pure skin like you, the answer is simple, George. By your definition, you didn't exist because that wasn't your body. That is, if who you are is your body."

"Don't twist facts, kid. I ain't changed, I'm still me. I'm still flesh and blood and you ain't, no matter how you slice it."

Nix hummed, rubbing his chin. "You ever get cavities?"

"Do you ever shut up?"

"What do you do, let them rot?"

"Course not. Go to the dentist, don't *seed* a bunch of mites in my mouth to fix it."

"You get fillings, then?"

"That's right, kid. I go to the dentist and let her fix my cavities. Chimps don't do that and neither do machines. Real people do."

Nix nodded. "Is your mouth fake?"

"It's fixed."

"Does it make it less real?"

"Does this look like a mirage?" He snapped his coffee-stained choppers with a hollow bite.

They stared.

"You got me there, George. You got me there."

George smiled for a while, thinking about it. Nix got up and crossed the room. He folded his arms and tapped his elbows.

"Queen to G-6," he called over his shoulder.

A piece slid across the board. George's chin stubble rasped in his palm. He checked his phone a couple times, acting like there was a text.

Nix turned on the water and splashed his face. The chess game was over.

George just didn't realize it, yet.

CHAPTER NINE_

CALI FLASHED HER ID AT THE GATE. THE GUARD HARDLY
looked at it. He glanced in the backseat but didn't bother talking to
the ten-year-old picking her nose. He stepped back into his little
station and the flimsy chain-link gates opened.

He didn't bother telling her where to go.

Cali parked her car in the middle of the visitors' lot with half a
dozen other cars. The Center was only two stories tall but sprawled over
seven acres with a courtyard for exercising. But there weren't tattooed
gangsters pumping iron in the yard, just everyday people that redlined
too many biomites. Doctors, lawyers, farmers... no one was spared.

Walking, talking machines, she remembered a politician once
said when federal money was available to build these Centers and
create jobs in his district. *Biomites will turn us all into walking,
talking machines. Unless we do something, this is the first step in the
extinction of the human race.*

Cali checked her face in the rearview. Her face had a strange
color, something closer to bruise-yellow than blush. She didn't care,
just didn't want Nix to worry. She took a few minutes to doctor her
complexion and ran a brush once or twice through her hair.

She took a deep breath and closed her eyes. Her heart rate was up. She counted her breaths to ten and felt her blood pressure settle down. She couldn't look out of the ordinary. She always made herself look a little nervous when she arrived, so that when this day arrived, her emotional state wouldn't look out of place.

But not too nervous.

Cali looked through her bag, flipped through files and made sure a bottle of water and an ink pen were at the bottom. *Distractions.* She reached into the backseat and pulled a drawing from Avery's bag, a scene of the ocean with a dolphin leaping out of the water and a yellow sunset. It was quite good for a ten-year-old. Almost too good. She might have an artistic future.

"You going to be all right out here?"

"Yep." Avery didn't look up from her movie.

"I'll be in there for about an hour."

"I know."

"Of course you do." She rustled her daughter's hair. "You're a big girl."

"Can you kiss Uncle Nix for me?" Her eyes were wide.

"Not yet."

Avery stuck out her bottom lip.

"Maybe soon, though."

"Okay."

Cali stretched over the seat and kissed her daughter's forehead and whispered, "I love you."

"Love you, too, Mama."

CALI STOOD at the door until it buzzed.

The floor was hard and shiny. The walls empty. At the end of the short hallway was a counter with a door to the left of it. Cali walked the thirty or so steps while the man behind the counter—wearing a blue uniform, hands folded on the countertop—watched her the whole way. He smiled in neutral.

"Where's Greg?" Cali dropped her bag on the counter.

"Called in sick."

The man's ID badge was clipped to his collar. One Mr. Franklin Moses, here to protect and serve. Franklin gestured to the right. Cali swiped her ID through the scanner.

"Dr. Cali Richards." Franklin looked to his left and pecked a keyboard behind the counter.

"I'm not a doctor."

"It says here you have a Ph.D. in Nanobiometrics."

"Don't call me doctor."

Franklin raised his eyebrows. He'd touched a nerve and, wisely, stepped off.

Cali slid her bag to the right side of the counter onto a black scanning plate. Franklin watched the monitor to his left. The plate vibrated, then stopped.

"Please empty your bag."

Cali let out an exasperated breath. She pushed her hand through her hair and began pulling out the items. She stacked the folders and placed Avery's drawing on top. She put the bottle of water next to it. Franklin picked up the water and turned it around. He looked at her.

"You have a doctorate in nanobiometrics and you don't know that liquid is not allowed in a Detainment and Observation Center?"

"This is a prison. And if I wanted to contaminate you or anyone else with a new strain of biomites—a super strain of biomites that I could control—I wouldn't have to bring it in a bottle of water, I'd just seed my salivary glands and spit in your eye, Franklin. All it would take is the most inconspicuous fleck of spittle to go airborne, one you'd never notice, and you'd be mine, just like that." Cali grabbed the ink pens from the bottom of her bag. "Taking liquid from people isn't going to make them safe. It's too damn EASY!"

Franklin's eyebrows went higher. He slowly put the water down and began to turn around.

"I'm sorry." Cali reached for him. "I get a little... stressed out coming here. You know biomites can't go airborne, I was just making that up. I'm sorry, I'm just... a little tight."

"You can't joke about that, Dr. Richards. Not someone of your caliber. And biomites can go airborne, that's why we confiscate any form of liquid. If it's atomized, there's a brief period that a person could be seeded with an unknown strain."

"Yes, yes, I know. I just... my brother... he's just... I don't agree with all this, you know. He doesn't deserve to be locked up. He didn't do anything wrong."

"He's not a criminal, Dr. Richards."

"He's being treated like one."

"No, he's quarantined. It's not illegal to be seeded, but it is illegal to contain too many. I don't make the laws, Dr. Richards. That's just how it is."

Cali locked her lips. She'd said enough. Anymore and he'd throw her out and she'd never come back. She needed to look concerned and worried, not unstable. Not a threat.

"I'm sorry." Cali took the drawing off the folders and pushed it across the countertop. "Look, this is all I want to bring to visitation. Could you send it up to Nix? It's from his niece. She'd come, too, but she's scared of this building."

Franklin paused. He put one finger on the piece of paper and slid it closer.

"She used colored pencils," Cali added. "It's all solid medium, the paper and everything. There's nothing there that can vector a viable biomite. It's like all the other drawings in his room."

He picked it up while staring at her. He lifted it toward the overhead lights and looked through it.

"You can run it through the sterilizer, if you like. Greg knows how much these drawings mean to Nix. And, look, I'm sorry about snapping. I just want to make sure my brother gets a little something every week. Imagine what it must be like in here."

Franklin looked at the dolphin and ocean and sun for a full minute. He placed it on the counter and nodded curtly. "Very well."

The door to the left clicked.

———

ANOTHER GUARD.

He motioned for her to come closer and put a cell-phone-sized box near her throat. She tasted metal.

The humming died. "You're 39.9%, Cali."

Cali nodded.

"You're one-tenth of a percent from redline."

"I'm aware of that."

The guard looked at it while he snapped the reader back on his belt. There was a long silence.

"Can I go?" Cali asked.

"Sure," the big guard said. "Get comfortable. You're probably going to see this place from the inside, *reeeal* soon."

Cali tightened her lips. She wanted to explain that exponential growth of biomite cells was not an absolute and that her research in the last couple months was showing signs that it could be suppressed by injecting growth regulator code that limited biomite division. Even though she slowed it down, she doubted it could be reversed. Either way, she wasn't about to tell anyone, not until Nix was out. And they weren't going to just open the doors and set him free.

She planned on doing that.

CHAPTER TEN_

NIX USED THE WHITE WASHCLOTH TO WIPE HIS FACE, HIS HEAD, rubbed the film off his teeth, and changed into a new white jumper. He did these things every time Cali came to visit. Ritual was key to remaining sane in solitary.

And he didn't want his sister to worry.

Nix folded the old jumper and placed it at the foot of the door, where a guard could switch it out when he dropped off food. The small table was on its side in the hallway, the chess pieces scattered on the floor. Nix imagined George's computer program suggested he offer a draw after a few more moves.

Or kick over the table and leave.

Nix returned to his desk and straightened the only stack of papers on it. Every week, Avery sent a drawing. Sometimes it was animals, sometimes people. Most of the time, it was scenery, like the mountains or a lake. Regardless, it always had the sun. The sun was bright yellow and shiny, just like he remembered. He could see the sun rise from his window, but it wasn't the same from inside the Center. The sun didn't rise the same when freedom was gone.

He rubbed the waxy, yellow circle peeking over the lush hills. No liquid there. Just a sterilized piece of paper. Nix smelled it. It reminded him of home. Reminded him of when Cali and Thomas would be working at the lab late at night and Nix would put Avery to bed. He'd take a book from her nightstand and open it and the smell of the pages would fill his nose with memories. That's what those old pages smelled like: memories. They were old books, books that Cali read to him when he was little.

Remember the wild rumpus?

He smelled the paper again. He knew they were watching him. There were cameras that captured his every move, little eyes in the corners. Nothing went without record.

He was counting on it.

Nix pulled the chair in front of the monitor. He placed the pictures on his lap and waited.

Hours later, the monitor flickered.

HIS IMAGE DISAPPEARED, replaced by another sitting in a similar chair in a white room, hands on her lap.

"Little brother."

Nix smiled. He was always surprised how much the sight of his sister could warm him. Even if she was a faint shadow of what she used to be. A waif. A troubled soul. Her shoulders were pointy, her cheeks drawn. The room was well lit but, still, shadows darkened her eyes.

"How are you?" he asked.

She looked at her lap, picking at her fingers. "I'm well."

"You're eating?"

Nod.

She's too demure. She's thinking about it too much.

"How's the little angel?"

The shadows lightened. Her teeth showed pearly and white. She told him about making cookies. Avery came up with her own recipe: chocolate chip and potato chip cookies. Sounded gross because it was. They made jelly bean and peanut cookies, gummy worm cookies, and, finally, a batch of sugar and syrup cookies. They decided to take them to the volunteers at the animal shelter. They were going to form a group called Baking a Difference and would get the neighborhood kids involved.

Cali loosened up. She always felt relaxed when she talked about Avery. They went on to talk about other things, like the new playground down the street and the neighbor's new baby.

Something slid under the door.

Nix saw the drawing. The corners of the paper were folded up. He looked at Cali. She was speechless.

He retrieved it and sat down. This one was an ocean with a dolphin. It was jumping out of the water with a big smile, free at last.

Free at last.

Nix touched the sun.

"She misses you." Cali sniffed. She didn't have to pretend. "She wants to know when you're coming home."

"What do you tell her?"

"I tell her soon."

"Maybe you should tell her the truth."

"I've petitioned the government to open a new branch in our lab. Our research was showing strong signs of biomite remission when exposed to RNA injections before they cut funding. If we can just have a year or two, Nix, I know I can bring your biomite levels below 40%."

"A year or two."

She looked back at her fingers. She was making all this up. There was no remission evidence in laboratories, public or private. Maybe in the basement, but not at the lab.

"You'll get me out of the redline?" Nix muttered.

"And out of here, if they just listen."

"That's a lot of ifs."

"That's all I got." Cali wiped both eyes. "You're all I got."

There was a lot of truth to that. Only Nix was aware of just how true it was. He stared at the picture, remembered going on vacation to Folly Beach outside Charleston, South Carolina, and seeing dolphins for the first time with Avery. Remembered sleeping on the beach towel in the afternoon while she built castles and Cali and Thomas went for a long walk. That was vacation. That was a long time ago.

"She worked hard on that," Cali said. "I got her a new set of pencils with special colors just for you. She must've spent months drawing that one."

"I like it." He held it up. "Tell her thank you."

"Maybe one day you can tell her."

They talked about neighbors. Talked about his old friends. They filled the gaps with words, making it all seem normal. Finally, Cali stood up.

The screen went blank.

Nix sat for several minutes, looking at the colors. It was just like the other ones, pictures from a lovely girl to a loving uncle. He lifted it to his nose and breathed in the waxy aroma.

His sinuses tingled. A tickling sensation penetrated the porous bone plate that separated his olfactory senses and entered his brain like a virus. Like living cocaine. He held the back of the chair and kept his eyes open even though the room was spinning.

Special colors just for you.

Nix made it to his bed and lay down without looking suspicious. Cali told him on the last visit that Avery was working on a special drawing. He knew something was coming. Intuition told him to smell it.

Something embedded in the colors.

His sister was a genius. She spiked the drawing with something—probably a new breed of biomites, ones that eluded the ring's effect. Nix could feel them spread out in his head like cold webbing. If the guards suspected something, they would already be in his cell.

She'd discovered something new.

Something undetectable.

Nix lay back and closed his eyes. For the first time in a long time, since the day that ring went around his neck, he smelled the ocean.

CHAPTER ELEVEN_

CALI WIPED HER EYES WITH A TISSUE. IT WAS THE FIRST TIME she'd teared up during a visitation. She'd cried when they took her little brother from the house, but not since. Not ever. She'd never allowed herself to feel those emotions, but the thought of her little brother coming home was just too real.

It got to her.

It probably didn't hurt her performance. It would be completely expected, probably bored all the people watching.

She walked out without a word from any of them. She stopped outside the final door. The sun was overhead. Nix didn't see that very much, at least not on his own terms. That's what he always requested of his niece to draw for him: suns. *Draw me something yellow,* he would say.

Cali peeked through the back of the car. Avery was laid out on the seat, eyes closed. Cali closed the door behind her quietly so she wouldn't wake the angel. She stopped herself from giving her daughter a hug, giving her the good news.

Uncle Nix will be home soon.

CHAPTER TWELVE_

The head of the table was empty. Marcus entered.

The other chairs were filled with children. His wife, Janine, was seated at the other end. Her head was bowed. He could tell when she was thinking. Always thinking. Never here. Always somewhere in her head, combing through facts, through paperwork and scenarios. A lawyer's work never rested. *Not for good ones*, she would say.

The children had their hands on their laps, heads slightly bowed. They weren't thinking of clients and affidavits. Only dinner.

Marcus sat down. "Let us pray."

Their heads bowed deeper.

"Bless us, O' Lord, and these Thy gifts which we are about to receive from Thy bounty. Through Christ, our Lord. Amen."

The clinking of china was preceded by signs of the Cross— Father, Son, Holy Ghost. Ariel moved into action and helped the children spoon sauce over their noodles. Marcus smoothed a cloth napkin over his lap and watched that no one put their elbows on the table. All the napkins were in place. His wife was on her second glass of wine.

Pick battles.

He began eating. The dinner proceeded as it had every night, in relative quiet. Nothing but the *tink-tink* and the occasional slurp. Not too many. They were kids, after all.

Marcus twirled noodles on his fork and, before filling his mouth, pointed at the empty seat he hadn't noticed. "Where's Andrew?"

"Fever and a sore throat, sir." Ariel filled Janine's water glass.

Marcus chewed carefully and spoke again once he swallowed. "Is he getting clear liquids?"

"Yes, sir."

Another bite. Swallow. "Have you given him herbal tea for the sore throat?"

"Yes, sir," Ariel said.

"It helped a lot, sir," Margaret, the new part-time nanny, said. "He fell right to sleep when he was finished."

Marcus nodded thoughtfully. He wasn't thrilled with another nanny, even part time. But his job had him away from home more often and Janine was too busy playing lawyer.

Janine asked the children how their day at school was and how they were feeling. No one felt the least bit sick, although someone puked in William's class after recess. He started to describe the smell when he was cut off. He managed to say *chunks of meat* before his name was called. Sternly.

"You know, my sister's son, he's seven," Margaret said, helping Clifford cut his noodles, "and he come down with a fever and they took him to the pharmacy, where they got these little temporary biomite injections. Have you seen those?"

She held up her fingers a half inch apart, indicating they were real small.

"They fight infection and then get washed out through the kidneys. They're not like regular biomites that reproduce. He was better that evening."

Marcus chewed slowly with his lips closed. He flipped a glance at Ariel, who did not return the look. The meal finished without much conversation.

Marcus unzipped the suitcase and threw it on the bedspread. He began the weekly ritual of packing for a trip. He started with his underwear—pressed and folded. All of them white with tiny red stripes on the elastic band. Next were socks, followed by gym shorts for working out in the hotel exercise room, bathing suit for the hot tub, and T-shirts for lounging. His suits and ties would be packed in a hanging case.

He went to the bathroom—open to the bedroom—to pack toothpaste and the rest. Janine came out of the shower room, rapidly working the water from her ear with her finger. She was wearing a white robe, not the one he'd gotten her for Christmas but one she'd bought a year before that. She always said she liked the way the old one felt, she'd get to the new robe one of these days. Just not until she was finished with the old one.

Janine fished through the drawer to the right of the sink, found a pair of tweezers and went into the walk-in closet. She sat on the bench in the middle of her closet and hiked her foot up on the stool and began to work on her toenails, digging out the ingrown portions.

Click.

She liked to pick.

Click.

She'd been to the doctor but preferred to work out the problems on her own.

Marcus found his razor, his cologne, shaving cream and the rest, shoving it into a toiletry bag, and went back to the bed. It was one thing to listen to the *click, click,* but quite another to see the cottage-cheese-laden legs beneath the frayed edges of that worn-out robe. He used to rub those legs, when she was in law school, when she'd be up seventy-two hours at a time, sleepless from leg aches.

She didn't look like that then.

More like a linebacker, now. And not one from Harvard. More

like NFL All-Pro. Marcus gave her a P90X for Christmas. Never got opened.

Click.

"I've arranged for Ariel to bring the kids home after William's play," Janine said. "Will you at least see some of it?"

"Afraid not. I'll be on the West Coast, starting in Seattle tomorrow morning and finishing in San Francisco on Thursday."

"His performance is on Wednesday."

"I'm not flying back for that, Janine."

Long pause. Not an empty one.

Marcus finished packing his carry-on. He pulled three suits from the closet and laid them on the bed. They were pressed and clean and spotless. They went into the hanging garment bag.

"How many halfskin shutdowns are you going to attend?" Janine leaned against the closet door frame.

"As many as there are, dear."

"They'll only increase." Her tone was final. "This... biomite war you're waging... you can't win it, Marcus. People are going to keep seeding unless they become illegal."

"Then we'll keep turning them off."

"Until what? Until you've wiped out the human race?"

"Just the seeded ones."

"This is an infringement on their liberty—"

"Spare me the lawyer speak." He dropped the suitcase on the floor and snapped out the telescoping handle. "People will destroy themselves if we let them."

"That's their choice."

"Then why not just legalize everything, Janine? Why not just set up heroin shops and cocaine dens outside the kids' school? Let's not have a drinking limit; it's their life, after all. It's their choice to destroy it."

He hung the garment bag on the top of the bedroom door and paused. Janine dropped the tweezers in the drawer. Her robe crumpled on the floor. Her granny panties snapped around her waist. Marcus didn't turn around.

"Technology will catch up," she said. "They'll be able to control runaway replication at some point."

"I hope it does. I don't like shutting down halfskins."

"I think you do."

Immortality is meant for the soul. Not the flesh.

Marcus slid his feet into moccasin slippers and pulled his suitcase with the garment bag over his shoulder.

"In case you're wondering," Janine mumbled, "I'm going to a fundraiser tonight with Helen. Make sure the children have brushed their teeth. Alexander has not been flossing."

She was standing in front of the mirror with bobby pins in her mouth, pulling her black hair back. Her nipples pointed at the faucet.

"Tell her I said hi." He started and stopped. "And I want the new nanny fired."

"Mmm-mm."

Marcus went to his office. He texted Ariel to make sure Alexander flossed.

CHAPTER THIRTEEN_

Nix stared at the ceiling.

He was cautious not to daydream. He kept his attention on his breath, emptied his mind. It had been weeks since Cali delivered the special drawing. She continued her weekly visits, as usual, and asked how he was doing.

Good. Real good.

Then they talked about Avery needing braces, how the Holloways' dog got hit by a car, how crappy the weather was. She didn't bring any more pictures, just said that Avery was probably going to make him another one in two weeks. She was pretty clear about it. *In TWO weeks.*

But Cali wasn't bringing another picture.

She was telling him how long to wait.

She had embedded biomites into the waxy yellow sun. They were undetected by the ring that registered him at 48.8%. But Nix felt the effects. They weren't suppressed at all.

They were fully active.

The ring had no effect on these new-breed biomites, had no recognition of their proliferation. His senses slowly enhanced as they integrated into his body. He smelled the subtle odors down the hall, knew when the guards were eating, when they last showered. He saw more colors, felt more textures.

The new-breed biomites heightened it all. He had become... *more*. If he had to guess, they put him over 50%. He was probably halfskin and no one knew it.

Cali told him to wait. Wait until there were enough of them, until the levels of these new-breed biomites were more active. Then he'd know what to do.

Waiting was the hard part.

At night, he closed his eyes and fell into rhythmic breathing. If anyone was watching, he was sleeping. But these were opportunities to smell the lagoon. Occasionally, he could hear Raine's laughter. Maybe he imagined it.

Maybe not.

Each night, he hoped to know more, perhaps to see the blue cliffs and the trees framing the crystal water. Each night, he only sensed a glimmer of that world. He'd wake in the morning, still a prisoner.

On the week that Avery's next drawing was to be delivered—four weeks since he snorted the yellow sun—Cali didn't come to visit.

GEORGE WAS WAITING outside his door.

It had been a month since he last saw George, but there he was with the table and the box under his arm. George began setting up the board. He didn't say much, just pushed the pieces around.

Nix smelled something new about him, something metallic, the ting of aluminum on the edges of his tongue. He looked at George sorting out the blacks and whites. That's when the new-breed biomites whispered Cali's plan. Her ghostly voice was inside his head. It was a recording that was triggered by the sight of George and told him what to do.

Told him it was going to hurt.

Such a hypocrite. Such a liar.

George was 10% biomite. Maybe more. Nix realized he could read George's thoughts. Somehow, Cali's new-breed biomites were seamlessly scanning and connecting with other biomites within a short range, like wireless computers. And the biomites he was sensing were in George's brain.

Like a book.

"A game?" George tapped the small table outside the door. "Or you have somewhere to go?"

Nix looked up from his bed. He sat up and rubbed his eyes, sleepy.

"Heh-heh," George added. "I've been thinking about our last game, where I went wrong... I have to be honest, I was cheating."

"I know."

"I know you know." George touched up the pieces, centering them in each of their squares. "But I figured I should come clean. I was using a machine to beat you and that's not fair. I'm here as a man, as a human being—" he thumped his chest "—to redeem the spirit of Man!"

George muttered a little pep talk. He clapped his hands and asked what color Nix wanted. Nix balked, so George took white.

"The good guys," he said, and moved queen's pawn two spaces.

Nix went to the sink and splashed water on his face. He wiped his scalp, the back of his neck. Dabbed himself dry with a hand towel. He just realized that, in his dreams, he had hair. *I had hair before. And now I'm this.*

I've forgotten what I look like.

"Come on, already." George looked at his watch. "I go on shift in an hour and you're over there making yourself pretty. You ain't got a date, halfskin, and I ain't easy to look at, either. So let's go."

George wasn't a bad guy. Maybe not good, but not bad. Nix felt a pang of guilt for what he was about to do to him.

But George was his ticket.

It needed punched.

Joni Neisler's blue placard poked her in the chin. She walked to the slender mic at the front of the stage, far too timidly for someone at the National Championship. But probably just right for a five-year-old.

She tugged at the pleats in her dress.

The judges were conferring.

There was a man behind them. She couldn't see him so well, it was dimly lit beyond the judge's table, but she saw enough. He sat there with his barrel arms latched over his chest, next to his tiny wife. He was scowling. They both were. They'd been doing that ever since the contest started. Always at her.

The judge looked over his laptop, his face bluish. "Spell 'Otorhinolaryngological.'"

Joni was supposed to take a deep breath. She was supposed to ask the judge to use it in a sentence. Ask the origin of the word. Her father told her to make it look like she was thinking it through, but the lumberjack dad and his little wife kept staring at her.

They were so angry.

She just wanted to get off the stage.

"Otorhinolaryngological.

"O-T-O-R-H-I-N-O-L-A-R-Y-N-G-O-L-O-G-I-C-A-L.

"Otorhinolaryngological."

Joni went back to her seat. She didn't wait to hear if she was right. She was right. She spelled everything right. She didn't know what was so hard.

The crowd rumbled. There was shifting around. The judges leaned their heads together as the next contestant went to the mic. None of the other kids looked at Joni. Joni was half their age, but that wasn't why they always looked at her strangely. It was something else. Probably the same reason the lumberjack dad was mad at her.

And he was standing, now.

He pulled his wife up, too. They were scooting down the aisle, not making much of an effort to walk sideways like you're supposed to when you walk down a crowded aisle.

"Quiet, please." One of the judges, the nice one with perfect teeth, said, "Please settle down."

"We're done here," lumberjack dad said.

"Sir, you need to take your seat or your son will be disqualified. Distractions need to be kept to a minimum."

More disruptions.

Someone else stood.

Lumberjack dad stared at the nice judge. Joni thought he was going to slug him one.

"You test her?" He pointed that giant arm right at Joni.

"You have no right!" Now Joni's momma was standing up.

"Did you test her?" Lumberjack dad didn't pay any attention to Momma. "The rules clearly state this is a natural-born spelling bee. There are competitions for biomite-enhanced young ones, but this is not one of them. And even if it was, that girl is five. She's too young to be seeded; it's against the law. So did you test her?"

Arguments broke out in the studio. Judges were standing, crew from off the stage were coming over, and security was already putting hands on the lumberjack dad. People were walking out. One of the contestants' dads came up on stage and dragged him off by the arm. He gave Joni a mean look.

That's when the first tear came out.

"Did you inspect her brain stem?" lumberjack dad was shouting over the chaos. He was pointing at the back of his neck while security ushered him away. "There'll be a knot the size of a BB where the seed point is."

One of the judges left. The others were calming the crowd. Joni's face felt hot. Her papa came out of nowhere and put his arm around her. She hid her face while people stomped off the stage. The lights turned up. There was a call for recess, a call for order.

And Joni cried in her papa's arms. She rubbed her tears, smearing them on her cheek, and reached behind her ear. Her little fingers crawled through the hair braided on the back of her head, the braid her mama did for her before the event, and searched the base of her skull.

Where she found a knot the size of a BB.

CHAPTER FOURTEEN_

Cali unpacked.

Avery's clothes were on top. She placed them in the empty drawers, all the shirts nicely folded and cleaned. All perfectly stacked. Next, she took hers out, placing them in the larger drawers, not so meticulous with them.

She dragged the large bag to the corner and unloaded the toiletries around the sink. The Chicago Marriott welcome kit was neatly arranged against the mirror. Cali took the time to unload the toothpaste and deodorant and brushes and soap and everything else to keep the bathroom area in order. They'd be staying in the suite for the next couple weeks and Cali hated a messy bathroom.

Avery jumped from bed to bed, giggling with each leap, crumpling the floral bedspreads in heaping wrinkles.

Cali wanted a smoke. It was too far to walk down to the street. She brushed her teeth, instead. They'd been in the car long enough to pound out a pack of cigarettes. Her chest wheezed. She hated the city —too big, too cold—but she hated not knowing even more. And she came to Chicago, not knowing if things would work.

They have to. They have to.

Cali dug a clot of clothes from the drawers and went to the bathroom.

"Going to take a shower, Mama?"

Cali mumbled something and closed the door. She missed the light switch and, in the dark, kicked the toilet. Pain seared her big toe, shooting over the top of her foot. She found the light and half a toenail on the floor, still covered with chipped orange polish from the last time Avery painted them.

Blood bubbled on the exposed nail bed.

She quickly ran the shower, undressed and stepped in to wash off the dirt, to wash away the emotions, to clean her mind. The steamy water covered the sobs hiccupping in her throat. Blood washed in diluted rivulets to the drain. Cali wondered how many of those red platelets were biomites just imitating blood. *How much of that is me?*

She reached out and hit the light switch.

Showered in the dark.

"Stop jumping."

"Yes, Mama." Avery climbed off the bed nearest the window. "Do you feel better?"

Cali brushed her teeth again and decided to wear the robe instead of getting dressed. She found a Band-Aid at the bottom of her bag and wrapped her toe. Avery was standing on the window frame, arms out, palms pressed against the glass. Cali cleaned the blood off the bathroom floor and retrieved the brittle toenail—that was the second time she'd cracked a nail in a week—before Avery saw it. Blood creeped her out and made her lose her breath.

"Everything's so *biiig*," Avery announced, smudging the glass with her lips. "The people look like ants."

Cali smiled. That's what she said when she was a little girl and her dad brought them along on a business trip and took her to the top of what was called the Sears Tower. She remembered her stomach lurching and the cars looked like toys.

"I want to spit." Avery had a very big smile. "What do you think would happen if we spit, Mama?"

"You'd get in trouble."

"No one would know it was us. There's like a million windows on this building, Mama. No one would know."

"How are you going to get the window open?"

Avery examined the glass. She ran her fingers along the edges. "How come it won't open?"

"They don't want anyone falling out."

"Oh, my." Avery covered her mouth, her eyes wide but smiling. "What would it feel like to fall?"

Cali wondered the same thing. *What would it feel like?*

Would she feel anything in her empty stomach? Would she feel alive, for once? Or would it bring relief?

"I'M HUNGRY." Avery stumbled into the office area of the suite. "When are we going to eat?"

Cali was still in her robe. There were two tablets and a laptop open and running on the desk. CNN was on the TV. She slouched in the chair, head resting on the back.

"You want to call up room service?"

"Yes!" Avery leaped and clapped. She scuttled into the bedroom and picked up the phone.

Cali kept an eye on her screens. The lights were off. The room shimmered data blue. CNN might pick up the story she was waiting for, but she knew she'd see it on her company's—BioMed—news feed first. She logged on with an encrypted connection and watched story after story of anything biomite related scroll down the laptop screen.

She reached out and tapped Nix's name with one hand. The news feed spit out past stories regarding his initial seedings and development, including confidential data. She punched in a date to limit the stories to current ones.

The information stopped.

So she waited.

She kept her eyes on the empty screen, waiting for a story. Waiting to hear anything on her brother while her stomach turned and her eyes grew heavy and reporters droned on the TV.

She waited.

She waited.

THE ROOM WAS DARK, lit only by the television's flare.

The computers were asleep.

Cali wiped the spittle from her mouth. The other room was silent and dark, as well. She sat up and tapped the space bar.

The screen was full of words.

Full of stories.

All containing Nix's name.

...Nixon Richards is en route to Northwestern Memorial Hospital's biomite wing...

She scrolled the mouse wheel, her eyes racing over the words, looking and looking. She clicked the next story describing more details.

...his condition critical...

Cali flopped in her chair, eyes stuck on those two words. Condition critical. *Critical.*

But he's alive.

He's out.

It worked. He's out of the Center.

And he was at Northwestern Memorial, in the nation's most advanced biomite technology wing only two blocks from where she was sitting. She let out a breath. A long stale one. Perhaps one she'd been holding for several months.

Avery was lying on the bed, the iPod inches from her face. Electric shadows stretched over her cheeks. Cali looked around.

"I thought you ordered room service?"

"I didn't know what you wanted," she said dully. She did not look up. "And you were sleeping."

Cali lay next to her, stroking her daughter's hair. They watched a few minutes of a movie.

"Did you get good news?" Avery asked.

Cali kissed her cheek. "Yes."

CHAPTER FIFTEEN_

George needed a victory. Something. Anything.

All he had was this place, this job.

He had no life outside of it.

It wasn't always like that. He used to be somebody. He was starting left guard for an AA state champion football team. He had an associate's degree in criminal justice. And he was eight years from retiring to Florida, where he'd find a trailer and fish until the sun went down.

Some people had it worse than old George, but, still, he needed a victory. He needed something to remind him he was worth something.

This little... *chess game...* it was nothing to Nix. That kid had nothing else but time to think about it. George had responsibilities, he had alimony and child support, he had a sick mother and an asshole father. He had all sorts of things occupying his mind, but he was damned if he'd use that as an excuse. He was better than that.

He was better than a machine.

And that's just what Nix was. He was damn near 50% biomite, something like 49.9%. One-tenth of a percent didn't make you human. You were half human, half machine. No way around it.

George, on the other hand, was only 10% biomite. That wasn't much. And he didn't choose to get seeded. He was diabetic and alcoholic, and those were treatable diseases with biomite technology. The doctors assured him he was seeded with suppressed varieties that doubled in population once every fifteen years. That meant he would be dead before he redlined. If a little seeding made his life a little less miserable, then praise the Lord.

He rested his elbows on his knees. He decided last time there was too much chitchat. Nix threw him off balance with all the talk. He needed to concentrate. Besides, his act of confession about the last time was just a decoy. He'd downloaded some chess code and had the doctor seed his brain. It was only a 1% biomite boost, but guaranteed to make him remember more and analyze faster.

And it was working, he could tell.

It used to be he only had one or two moves planned, but now he was planning five or six. He felt good, felt right. Felt like today was his day. He could even see a way to checkmate this snotnose in seven moves.

George felt his scalp tingle. He wiped the sweat with his sleeve. The hallway was getting warm, the A/C was down. No matter, he was on a roll.

George lifted the knight with two fingers, placed it on C-6 and studied the board. If he had things figured right, Nix would take the bait and swipe his bishop, which would leave him open to get his queen in position.

He lifted his hand. Move made. He looked up.

On the other side of the glass...

Sitting in a chair on the other side of the glass... door...

He wiped his eyes. They were blurry with sweat. He needed a drink; he was parched. His throat was scratchy and hot. He wiped his forehead again.

"You all right?" Nix asked.

George waved the kid off. "Shut up and move."

The kid watched him. George looked away, irritated. But then he moved exactly where he wanted him. The little dummy took his bishop, just like he planned.

Good God!

George could hardly keep calm. He forced himself to sit still, forced himself to refrain from moving too quickly. He pretended to think for a full minute while sweat ran down his temples and his brain quivered with excitement.

He made his move.

Queen to F-3.

He refused to look up; he couldn't be distracted. Not again. Not like last time. Whatever the hell brought that weird thing up a minute ago was... it was nothing. He focused.

Focus. And never look up from the board.

He executed every move just like he planned. Nix castled his king into safety. Or so he thought. George pushed his pawn up a square. All he needed was one more move and it was a done deal. The rook would slide up to C-2 and he could accept the kid's submission—

"Bishop to G-8."

George shuddered.

His head was vibrating on the inside, like someone jammed a vibrator between his ears. His eyes stung from the heat. *Will somebody turn up the goddamn air-conditioning?*

He reached for the black bishop. His hand moved like a sandbag, dropping on the pointed end and sliding it across the board.

He didn't see that coming.

He didn't...

See...

George looked up. He looked through the glass door. He didn't see the kid... it wasn't the kid... sitting there. He wiped his face, rubbed his eyes, moved his mouth like it was filled with paste and looked again.

It wasn't the kid.

It wasn't Nix.

James?

"Hey, Georgie. How's it going, bud?"

My best friend?

The guy he grew up with was sitting on the other side of the door. His buddy, his friend for life, his best man at his wedding...

James was sitting in there. His blood brother.

The man that slept with my wife.

"Georgie, remember this one?" James kicked the chair across the room and got on his knees next to the bed. "Remember the time you came home from work early and saw this? You remember?"

James's hips gyrated, grinding into the mattress. He closed his eyes, head back. James's fingers caressed the sheets. The frame squeaked with every thrust. It began to sound like a woman moaning. A woman loving it.

Loving every second of it.

"Remember that, Georgie?"

Yeah. He remembered.

He remembered the best man that took his life away... he remembered the best man he'd take a bullet for, the man he'd die for, the man who was doing that with his wife... HIS WIFE... AND THAT MAN WAS RIGHT... IN... THERE!

Click.

George touched the monitor on his belt. The door unbuckled. James backed up. George came in, fists clenched. He'd waited a long time for this day. He waited a long time to tell his best man what he thought, what he felt... all these years.

Chess pieces fell on the floor as he stepped into the cell. The door latched behind him.

His head was vibrating. It was so hot.

Like fire.

CHAPTER SIXTEEN

Nɪx ᴡᴀᴛᴄʜᴇᴅ ᴛʜᴇ ᴍᴀᴅɴᴇss ᴜɴꜰᴏʟᴅ.

He hardly looked at the chessboard. Instead, he watched George's memories like streaming videos. He wasn't sure how he was doing it, just looked up and there they were. At first, Nix misunderstood, thought he was remembering something in his own past. But he was remembering someone else's life, someone middle-aged.

Sitting right in front of him.

The new-breed biomites had something to do with it. Cali's message was clear: Nix would know what to do. He had to get out of the Center. He couldn't just walk out, even if he had George tied with his hands behind his back and a gun to his head. They'd simply shut off Nix's biomites and it was over. Like that. Cali had another plan, a way that would force them to take Nix far away from the Center, to a place with less security. A place easier to dupe.

But it was going to hurt.

So Nix sat there watching George's memories, sorting through the painful ones. There were so many to choose from, but there was one that continued to rise to the surface. And that would be it. That would trigger the escape.

Nix made that memory a reality.

George saw what Nix wanted him to see. None of it was real, but George wouldn't know the difference. Maybe it wouldn't work on someone else, someone smarter, someone who didn't drink or had more refined biomites with security patches. As it was, George wanted to believe his thoughts, he loved to be entertained. His reality was what his brain biomites told him was reality. And they told him that his best friend, his greatest betrayer, was ten feet away, mocking him.

Nix knew all too well that the mind can make people see what they want to see.

When the door popped open, when George entered his room, Nix thought-commanded his new-breed biomites to dull his nervous system. He stood up numbly and backed away. George came through the doorway, the door shutting behind him. This needed to be beyond anything they could handle in the Detainment and Observation Center. They would need to get him out after this.

George looked like a grizzly. His chest expanded, his eyes red and wild. Teeth bared. He backed Nix into a corner, hot air streaming out his nostrils. Before the first blow landed, the new-breed biomites connected with the surveillance cameras and began downloading the video stream, capturing every last second of the mauling that took place in room 204.

It was a beating that lasted three minutes, with guards begging him to stop. A beating of pure hatred, bent vengeance, total destruction.

When it ended, no one would recognize the face that belonged to Nix Richards.

The cameras would never forget.

CHAPTER SEVENTEEN_

Marcus loosened his tie.

Down on Van Ness Avenue, three stories down, was a line of people. A line of gays and lesbians and hippies. The lesbian with the crew cut was bellowing into a bullhorn.

Only in California. Only in San Francisco.

He'd been to almost every state to witness a halfskin shutdown and he'd never seen picketers. There were scathing editorials and dirty looks, but Americans understood this was a problem and the government was looking out for them.

But not in California.

They were saving the world one tree at a time, hiking up their sleeves and making humorous signs that belittled the grave danger biomites presented to humanity. And the liberal media was more than happy to slurp it up, regurgitate it to the general population so that teenagers around the world believed the government was a big bad wolf coming to blow their house down.

They were all going to hell.

God did not look kindly on the free-sinning lifestyles of California. He did not approve of their dream worlds. If these people got a job, if they lived in reality, they wouldn't have time to kick off their shoes and parade in front of the Detention and Observation Center. They'd be home, taking care of their family. Taking care of kids.

California.

It was federal law to establish secure centers for detainment and observation. Somehow, converting a five-story building on a downtown street did not conform to what Marcus considered secure.

These jerkoffs were right there at the entrance.

He watched his car coast down Van Ness Avenue. It slowed near the entrance but continued without much notice. He'd phoned down for the driver to meet him on Polk Street. He'd take the back exit and walk the block over.

He dug a camera from his soft leather handbag and snapped a picture of the bullhorn lesbian. He'd get her identity. He'd make sure he attended her halfskin shutdown. That, he'd enjoy.

He folded his jacket and tie and stuffed them into his bag, snapping it shut. He hoped if any of the hippie protesters saw him, they wouldn't think much.

The door opened. "Sir, the Secretary of State is on the phone."

Tim held the cell phone to his chest. Marcus walked around the shiny conference table, hand out and fingers wiggling.

"Yeah." He spoke into the phone, closing the door on Tim. "Just leaving."

Marcus wandered back to the window.

"It went fine, just a little backlash at the front door."

He listened to the voice on the other end.

"Chicago?" Marcus spouted. "Why'd they move the kid out of the Center?"

The Secretary of State explained the public relations waiting for him at Northwestern Memorial Hospital. The kid had been nearly beaten to death by one of the Center's guards.

"That's not our problem. That's on the Center."

"They suspect a bad biomite seed caused excessive aggression," the Secretary said, "in the guard."

"Look, I don't know why you're calling me. People snap all the time; that's not on us. I suggest you get him back to the Center, let him heal and then we'll shut him down when he's halfskin."

There was discussion.

Marcus pulled the phone from his ear and looked at the photo uploading to his screen. He took a deep breath, putting the phone against his head.

"That gets out," the Secretary said, "we got problems."

The Secretary was right. People like those on the street would send that around the world. By morning, the media would paint the administration as blood-lusting animals sending their redline babies to meat factories where they'd get battered and raped before they got shut down.

"Listen, the president wants that kid nursed back to health; he wants us to care for him, to do everything we can do. He's sitting at 49%. We can't shut him down while he looks like that because one of *our* people snapped."

"All right."

"It's not us against them, Marcus. Get over there and clean this up."

Marcus looked out the window. "No one goes near that kid's hospital room besides doctors and nurses. Post security; I'll fly out tonight."

He dropped the phone on the table.

He went out the back way.

Things would be so much easier if people didn't get in the way.

CHAPTER EIGHTEEN_

Avery was swimming with some kids at the other end of the hotel's pool. Cali watched from a lounger. Big, round sunglasses hid her eyes even though they were indoors.

She was thinking.

There were always problems. She was an engineer and knew to plan for contingency. She thought they'd let her see her brother. She had waited a day to go to the second floor of the hospital so it didn't appear like she was already in the city, waiting for him to arrive. She saw the guy sitting outside her brother's room, reading a paper. She explained who she was, showing her identification.

He simply shook his head.

No one, absolutely no one, is allowed to see this kid. Not his sister, not his mother, not Jesus Christ.

She stood in front of the guy, clenching and unclenching her fists, until he told her that she needed to move on before he escorted her out.

Cali wandered down the hall, turned the corner and leaned against the wall. She didn't know where to go, what to do. There were a dozen options, but none of them had long-term viability.

She needed to think.

She needed to do something, fast.

And that's when the small, freakish-looking creep walked past her. He reeked of government entitlement. His pants were wrinkled, collar undone. His stride was bold, his shoes clapping the floor like it offended him. He oozed power.

She knew who he was. Every nanobiometrics engineer knew what Marcus Anderson looked like. He put that guard there.

He was just the person she needed.

She went back to the hotel room, but it was stuffy.

She came to the pool to change the scenery, to give Avery something to do besides jump on the beds. There was only one couple, the ones with the kids splashing around. The man's name was Paul. His eight-pack abs rolled like hardened sand dunes. His sunglasses were askew, mouth agog. He was 35% biomite, used them to burn fat and build muscle without exercising. He also allocated a significant percentage to increase strength and eye-hand coordination to dominate his golf league. The remaining biomites boosted memory and analytical ability, aiding his successful legal skills. Paul had about five years before he redlined, but he figured something would come out before then.

Shelly—his gorgeous wife—was shopping on her tablet. She was only 10% biomite, something that controlled her metabolism and suppressed her appetite and boosted her memory. She planned on going back to college. She wanted to be a teacher.

Cali's new-breed biomites knew these things, downloaded them from Paul and Shelly like data. They were none the wiser. Cali's new breeds were networking with Paul and Shelly's biomites like cloud memory. She knew everything about them: bank accounts, passwords, social security numbers, memories.

Paul was two years into an affair.

"Mama! Watch!" Avery splashed into the deep end. "I'm going to touch the bottom; count how long I'm under water."

Cali smiled at her daughter. "Okay."

"You ready?"

"Yep."

Avery pinched her nose and somersaulted beneath the surface, her feet splashing her deeper. Cali loved watching her swim. She remembered when she couldn't touch the bottom and clung to her arm like a barnacle.

Avery emerged in a hurry, breathing heavily.

"How many?" she asked.

"One hundred seconds." Cali smiled.

"*Moooom.* You didn't count."

"Let me finish up and then I'll come swim with you, how about that?"

"Yay!" Avery pinched her nose for another dive.

Shelly put on sunglasses, acting like she wasn't staring.

Cali set up her laptop and found some basic information on Marcus Anderson. He was involved with the boot of Mother and a leader of the Halfskin Laws. He was witness to all shutdowns to date.

If he only knew what I invented.

It wasn't hard to find his office phone number and email. That information was available to the public. Cali wasn't interested in those. Anyone who sent a message or called would get an assistant, guaranteed to never reach him.

She needed a more direct line.

Cali analyzed thousands of Marcus Anderson accounts. In seconds, she cracked into his home computers—accessing documents, bank accounts, vacation photos and personal email and cell phone.

She didn't bother calling. He wouldn't answer.

She texted, instead. Uploaded a video.

[*Send.*]

She sat back. Her coffee was cold.

Paul was still asleep and Shelly was filing her nails, still pretending not to sneak peeks at Cali. Avery climbed onto the ledge in front of her, pushing her wet hair back and spitting water.

"You said you were going to swim."

"I am, sweetie. Almost done."

Avery whacked the side of her head, knocking water out of her ears. She complained when she couldn't get them clear. Cali pulled a bottle of alcohol from her bag and waved her daughter over. Avery lay on the lounger while her mother squirted alcohol into her ears, making a funny face because she hated the way it felt.

Shelly was watching again.

Avery dried her hair, looking at the laptop.

"When are we going to visit Uncle Nix?" She touched the picture of her uncle that was frozen on the screen.

"Soon."

"I can't wait to see him."

A cell phone chimed. "Me too. Why don't you jump in and I'll be right there after I take this call."

Avery cannonballed into the deep end. Cali flashed five fingers twice and Avery was pleased with scoring a perfect ten. The caller ID reported a restricted number. Cali touched the screen and held it to her ear.

"How'd you get this number?" a man said.

"There are more important matters to discuss."

Silence hung on the other end of the phone. His voice muffled through his fingers as he said something. The receiver scuffed and he pulled his hand away.

"I'll have you arrested."

"The video is genuine. You may take your time authenticating it, if you like, but I only have so much patience. You don't want that released to the public."

Another long pause.

"What do you want?"

"I just want to see my brother. I will arrive at the hospital at noon today."

Cali turned off the phone.

He'd have his people analyze the video, have them figure out how she got it. The new breeds seeded in Nix's brain pirated the video and uploaded it to an anonymous FTP site that Cali immediately shut down. She forced herself to watch it. Dry-heaved when it was over.

She really didn't expect to use the video; it was only going to be a last resort bargaining chip if things got bad. But getting locked out of the room sank every other plan she had. They would keep him isolated until he healed enough to return to the Center.

Or turned halfskin.

That's what really freaked her out, seeing that man in the hall, knowing he was there to see this to a tidy end. She knew she couldn't play nice. She was all in. If the gamble didn't work, she would start blowing up careers and take as many people down with her as she could.

Starting with Marcus Anderson.

"You coming?" Avery called.

Cali stretched her arms and back. She was ready for a swim. She needed to cool off. Just before diving into the pool, she made a suggestion that the new breeds passed along to Shelly. When she emerged halfway across—throwing her wet, blond hair off her face—she heard Shelly. And Paul trying to explain all the emails he'd received from someone calling him lover.

CHAPTER NINETEEN_

Antiseptic.

Beeps.

Pinpricks on his arm.

Something pumped, in and out. Inflating him like a balloon then allowing him to leak before filling him up again.

Nix knew the sounds and smells of a hospital. His earliest memories started at five years old, when he woke in one of the tilting beds with the side rails and a nurse tending a needle in his arm. He watched her through the slits of his eyelids, fascinated there was a needle in his arm and he couldn't feel it. In fact, he couldn't feel much.

That was the day he realized he was cursed.

His father, a brilliant nanobiometric engineer. *Dead.*

His mother, an outstanding computer programmer. *Dead.*

His sister, a nanobiometric engineer like her father, the only family he had left. She was beside his bed.

She was cursed, too. Just didn't realize it yet.

He couldn't open his eyes. It might have been hours or days. Weeks. He floated in the lonely darkness with his memories. Occasionally, he heard muffled voices or felt the dull prick of a needle sliding into his arm. He was still wearing the suppression ring, his biomites offering very little help healing his broken body. If not for the new breeds, he would be in agony.

They helped control the pain, dulling his nervous system, but did very little to heal. He was mending the old-fashioned way.

Time.

Until then, he lay comatose with his memories.

He didn't control George, didn't make him open the cell door. Didn't make him attack.

He merely baited him.

The first punch was all that Nix actually remembered. He covered up, but George's fist landed on the side of his head like a club. The memories went dark after that, but Nix watched the incident from above, like an out-of-body experience from all corners of the room, like his eyes were surveillance cameras. He lay in the darkness of closed eyes and watched George drop bombs.

His face broke on the third shot.

His ribs caved on the fifth.

George picked him up by the neck. Nix hung like a slab of meat.

The guards stormed through the door. Nix's face was red. It took five of them to peel George's hands off. The video ended just after George fell on his knees, looking at his bloody hands, weeping.

The new breeds knew where to send the video.

Cali saw it. She owned it. She would have it to bargain, if she needed it.

Until then, Nix faded in and out of consciousness, yearning for all his biomites to be fully online. That's when he'd heal. That's when he'd wake up.

And, maybe, he'd get to see Raine.

Jonny Miser took the ball from the catcher halfway between the mound and home plate. He chicken-winged his glove under his right arm and rubbed the new off the ball with both hands. He made one loop around the pitcher's mound, careful not to touch the dirt until he was back around the front.

Bad luck if he did.

Wrigley Field fans were on their feet. Even the fans on the rooftops were up and waving and whistling and shouting. He wiped the sweat off his forehead.

It was hot for October.

He blinked, focused on the scoreboard. A one-run lead. Three balls, two strikes. He looked around the diamond; St. Louis Cardinal base runners looked back from all three bags.

Last game of the season. *Win, you're in.*

The sort of pressure Jonny loved.

He couldn't hear the crowd. The voices blended together in a blur of white noise. The whole world was watching. People were on the edges of their seats at home, on their feet in the bars across the nation, all of them ready to watch Jonny Miser close out the St. Louis Cardinals to win the division.

It was all up to Jonny.

He did hear one of the voices. The one in his head.

Don't blow this.

He toed the rubber, digging his cleats into the divot. He wedged the side of his foot against it and looked at the catcher. His arm dangled at his side, the surgically repaired elbow tingling.

He shook off the first pitch. Took the next one.

The heat.

Jonny would propel his team into the playoffs by blowing a fastball past the batter. Put it all into this pitch, the last one of the season.

It would also be the last one of his career.

Jonny Miser went into his stretch, the crowd frenzied, the batter waving his bat, the umpire crouched behind the catcher.

He kicked his leg.

He threw the historic pitch.

The umpire never called it. He stumbled, eventually falling on his back. He never saw it.

The sound of the ball was described as a wet gunshot that shattered the catcher's hand. If it had missed the glove, it would've ended his life.

It was later explained that the Tommy John surgery performed earlier that year utilized a small amount of biomites to repair tendons in Jonny Miser's arm. The low levels were monitored by the league and remained at less than 1%. However, it was later explained the biomites responded to elevated levels of cortisol and norepinephrine —stress hormones—and induced an immediate proliferation. In minutes, the biomite population had consumed his arm.

Impossible, said nanobiometric engineers.

The pitch was clocked at 204 mph.

Cali sat in the back of Northwestern Memorial Hospital's chapel. The room was small. The wooden pews were padded with long cushions. She propped her feet on a burgundy kneeling block.

Chicago was a foreign land. She'd been there with her husband. He bought two tickets to *Miss Saigon*. Neither one of them had ever been to the city (at least not when they were older), but he insisted they just needed a map. Of course, city streets were a lot different than small towns and they ended up in Cabrini Green below the train. She thought she was going to cry.

Avery fell asleep on the pew.

An elderly woman fumbled prayer beads in her fingers. Pretty soon, she fell asleep, too. Cali sat with her head against the brown paneled wall and listened to soft snoring. It was music to her ears, hearing her daughter sleep. Sometimes she leaned over to feel her warm breath on her ear. When Avery was young, she would crawl into bed and cuddle against her, breath tickling her neck.

Cali preferred the chapel to the waiting room. She'd spent enough time in hospitals to know that—between services—it was quieter. There were fewer people, too. She didn't think she'd be able to sit long in the waiting room, surrounded by people with all their heavy emotions and thoughts of dying.

Especially now.

The chapel was better. It contained hope, a sanctuary for the religious faithful that brought their belief in God with them. Sometimes, in the face of the hopeless, the illusion of a spiritual being carrying her through life's difficulties was helpful.

But she wasn't interested in that now. Cali just needed somewhere to focus, to steel her will and sharpen her wits. Battles were fought with the mind long before muscle joined the fight.

"Honey." Cali gently shook Avery. "Do you want something to drink?"

Avery's head rolled across Cali's lap. She blinked a few times and looked around the strange room. She sat up and yawned.

"You thirsty?" Cali asked.

Avery nodded.

"Here, take this to the cafeteria and get yourself something to drink and eat."

Avery took the money and yawned. "Do you want something?"

The elderly woman woke up and looked around.

"No, thank you, sweetheart. You help yourself. Do you have your phone?"

Nod.

"Okay, good. I'll be right here."

Avery started away.

"If you get lost, just come back here, all right?"

Nod.

Cali returned to a quiet place in her mind and closed her eyes, where thoughts fell away. Where she could just be present. Where she didn't think. The time for thinking was reaching an end.

SHE FELT them before they arrived. The new breeds sensed the arrival of security outside the chapel.

Cali opened her eyes.

There were a few more people in the room. A preacher was at the podium, leafing through pages. He pushed his glasses up his nose. Two men entered the room. Their hair was cut proper and their dark jackets concealed weapons. They didn't bother walking down the narrow space along the pews. One of them signaled Cali with his finger.

She quickly texted Avery. Wait for me in chapel. Going to see Uncle Nix. I'll come back for you.

She would be upset, but Cali didn't want her to see her uncle like that.

The gentlemen patiently waited. Cali handed her bag to them. They didn't bother asking her for identity. The one on the right—brown hair and a tiny soul patch—looked through the bag while the other one, the one with slick black hair, pressed a scanning device on her. Cali tingled as her biomites responded to the device.

The new breeds remained quiet.

"39.9%." He put the scanner away. "You're almost a redline."

"So I'm told."

"We'll be holding onto your bag," Soul Patch said. "Do you have any liquids on you?"

"Didn't the scanner tell you?"

"We have to ask."

"To give me a chance to lie."

He blinked slowly. Waited.

"No," she said. "Just me. Can we go?"

Soul Patch led the way out. Slick followed.

CHAPTER TWENTY-ONE_

The elevator opened.

A hefty nurse intercepted Cali and her escort. She was doughy with a hook-shaped scar at the corner of her mouth. This was her floor. Soul Patch engaged her while Slick guided Cali past them despite the nurse's protests. A man sat at the end of the hall next to a door, his ankles crossed and a newspaper spread open. He folded it beneath his arm and stood up.

"Turn around." He made a twirling motion with his finger.

Cali faced the other direction and felt a scanner pressed against her back, evidently too shy to press it near her throat. "Didn't we already do this?"

She heard the instrument slide back into the sheath on his hip. He tugged her shoulder so that she turned back around, and stepped aside. Slick nodded at the door. They waited as she hesitantly placed her hand on it. It swung open, heavy on the cushioned hinges, and she heard Slick ask the other guy if he saw the baseball game.

The room smelled like the hallway—clean, germ-free, and artificial. It was darker, more points of light—greens and reds and lighted numbers—dotted medical machinery on the wall and rolling carts.

Plastic bags hung from hooks with clear tubes that dangled down to a bed—

Her back hit the door, pushing it closed.

Seeing the video... but this...

There wasn't much to see, actually. His body was covered beneath sheets and wrapped in gauze and casts. His head was fully encased and the nose was covered. Only the eyes were exposed, the skin dark purple, tinges of yellow. A tube exited his mouth, taped in place and attached to a ventilator that whooshed in and out with air.

She knew the extent of the damage; she knew what she was going to see. She saw his body at the end of the video, but seeing it in the flesh was...

I made a mistake.

A man stood at the foot of the bed, hands folded in front. His head was shaved, his face expressionless. The neck larger than the head.

"Four guards," she said. "You act like he's a criminal."

"He is." Marcus sat beside the bed, legs crossed; he eyed her with the larger of his two eyes.

"How many has he murdered?" she asked. "How many has he robbed? Raped?"

"Worse. He's spreading the disease of biomites."

"Then everyone is guilty."

"Your brother is guilty of excess."

"And that's worse than murder?"

He smiled. "They are one and the same."

Cali went to her brother's side. She held the two exposed fingers. The ventilator hissed at her. She wanted to kiss his forehead and whisper in his ear, tell him things were going to be all right like when he was little and things hurt. She wanted to tell him she was sorry.

But didn't.

"Wait outside, James," Marcus said.

There was laughter in the hall. The men peeked inside as the door slowly closed.

Cali rubbed his fingertips. Despite her best efforts, a tear escaped the corner of her eye.

"I KNOW THIS MUST BE HARD," Marcus said. "Tell me why it happened."

"I should be asking you that question," she said.

"You hack my personal information, show me the security footage of your brother getting beat to a pulp and I'm supposed to believe you don't know anything?"

He laughed, looked away and shook his head. Thinking.

"The guard had no history of violence. His wife slept with his best friend and he didn't even slice the guy's tires. Now you want me to believe he flew into a murderous rage because he lost a chess game? Did you stick around and watch what happened after they peeled him off your brother? He blubbered like a little girl. He tried to hug your brother. He wailed apologies all the way to a holding cell and tried to kill himself the next morning."

Marcus paused. He leaned forward, lowering his voice.

"You ruined his life, Cali. He's going to prison for a long time. You should be ashamed. Now, you want to tell me how you did this?"

"My brother's half dead and you want me to feel sorry for the attacker?"

"Your brother should be dead. If the hospital didn't keep his biomites suppressed, he'd be halfskin by now."

He had more thoughts, but was cautious she might somehow gather more evidence. He suspected something more was going on, a gut feeling he was way behind the true nature of this incident. Marcus was an intuitive man. He was usually right, but he didn't know how she got the video and couldn't be sure she wasn't recording this. He didn't want to give away too much.

Screw it. The truth is the truth.

"He should be dead," he continued. "Without his biomites fully activated, there's too much damage. Somehow, he lives. Want to explain?"

"It's medicine. We're not in the Dark Ages."

"The doctors are mystified. They say his internal injuries should have been fatal without fully activated biomites, but activating them would make him halfskin. Either way, he should be dead. I'm confused. Do you know something I don't?"

"I'll tell you what I know. My brother took a beating from a federal employee, a beating the world would love to see. A beating your political career wouldn't. Neither would the president."

"How'd you get it?" His tone deadened.

Cali looked back to her brother. She wanted to take the tube out of his mouth. It had to be uncomfortable.

"I know your tragic past," he said. "Believe it or not, I can make it worse."

"None of that will help you," she said, not looking up. "Not when the video is released to the press and the pro-bionanotechnology protest groups. Not when your personal information is released with it."

Her expression was as lifeless as his.

"Surely you have some secrets," she said. "Something you don't want anyone to see."

He didn't flinch.

"We have our own public relations. Truth can easily be spun into lies and urban legends. The Associated Press won't run it, not from a warped source like you. Unstable, unemployed. Damaged. We'll smear your reputation and your brother's all over the world."

"Politics isn't about truth. It's making people believe the story. They'll love what I have to show them. And it just happens to be the truth."

Long pause. Blink.

Smile.

"I suppose we have a stalemate," he said.

"That would mean we're tied, but I don't care. I've got nothing to lose. You have everything."

She remained placid.

"That's not a stalemate."

He watched her. The smile remained but quickly hollowed. Thinking, thinking...

"What do you want?"

"I want visitation rights to see him whenever I want. I want the right to be in the same room with him at all times and relate to him as a human being."

Marcus didn't move.

"I want the biomites fully activated so that he can heal quickly and painlessly, despite the threat of halfskin. I want him treated like a boy that's not imprisoned for living."

"You forgot to ask for his freedom."

She didn't respond.

"Oh, but why ask? If this is a ploy to help him escape, I promise you that won't happen. We'll have security inside and outside of this room. You won't get outside this hospital. If this is a chess game, Cali, then you're in checkmate. Your brother will heal and return to the Center. I imagine after we fully activate the biomites, though, he won't get that far. I won't even have to fly back to Illinois, I'll just sit in the waiting room until then and watch him shut down. You're welcome to watch."

If she was recording, he was screwed. He'd be seen as the tyrant the public and the press always suspected. But she threw the first swing. Marcus wasn't fond of cowering. You don't get far in politics with that.

"He's family," she whispered. "He's all I've got."

"I sympathize. But that's got nothing to do with my job."

"Perhaps you would better understand if your wife, Janine, took your boys to the store and they were in an accident."

Marcus's complexion turned a shade chalky.

"Maybe your tone would change if Janine died. Only Andrew

and William survive, but Andrew doesn't for long. He's brain-dead that evening. By morning, all you have is William. They have to seed him with biomites to keep him alive. It works. Your son is alive and you watch him grow up. You come home every day and ask him about school and his friends and take pictures before football games.

"And then the authorities show up. Mother has reported he's redline. Despite all your protests, all your explanations, they take him from you. Despite all your connections, they treat him like a criminal when all he wanted to do was live. All you wanted was for him to live. All you wanted was to not be alone. Because the law's the law, Marcus. There's nothing you can do but watch him get turned off."

Cali held his gaze. "Maybe then you'd feel differently."

Marcus was surprised at how that felt. He could separate work from family. Always could.

"Are you threatening me?" he said. "I could have you arrested for suggesting the murder of my wife and child."

"If you do, this goes live."

Cali held up her phone. The video of Nix's beating started with George bursting through the door. He didn't watch it. He didn't fidget, just looked off at something far away.

Thinking, thinking...

Marcus went to the door and stopped. He was about to say something, then left.

CALI WAITED a couple minutes for him to return. When he didn't, she dared to smile while she reached for her phone. She tapped the screen and pressed it against her cheek. It rang four times. Each one pulled her stomach tighter. Colder.

"Hello?"

"Avery." Cali let go of a long-held breath. "Come up, honey."

The tears cut loose.

CHAPTER TWENTY-TWO_

Marcus walked into the hall. Arms folded, eyes cast down.

His security team watched him pace away and lean against the wall. Minutes ticked by. The guards began whispering about strip clubs and a fight. Baseball tickets were mentioned and something about calling an old college buddy...

He knew her past.

He knew everything about her.

He couldn't blame her. That family was cursed. But she was dangerous.

She knew things, things about biomites that he didn't. He didn't like her being in that room, but there was nowhere to go. There was no escape. He needed time to think this one out. The video couldn't get out, not yet. And the kid wouldn't die, not soon enough. Not with the doctors looking. He needed time to clean things up, make arrangements.

"James." He waved his security guard over.

James squared his shoulders. Marcus kept his head down, voice low.

"I'm going to talk with Dr. Erickson about removing the biomite suppression. His sister will be allowed to stay in the room, but I want you to keep her in your sight at all times. You can rotate the watch with those two."

James listened.

"She's not allowed to leave. If she's got a hotel room around here, send someone after her stuff. As far as I'm concerned, she doesn't leave the hospital. Understand?"

James nodded. Marcus stared at him. He turned toward the other two.

"Hey!" They snapped quiet. "This isn't a frat party."

Their expressions shifted, darkly.

Marcus, half their size and not nearly as strong, stayed in place a few seconds. Thinking.

He told James to get in there.

And then he was down the hall. He was going to talk with the chief biomite doctor. After that, he was going to find where she lived and turn her house inside out.

If there was time, he'd text his wife.

CHAPTER TWENTY-THREE_

CALI STARED OUT THE WINDOW, CLUTCHING HER ELBOWS. THEY were pointy. She rubbed the chilly bumps that seemed to always be rising on her skin. The room felt colder.

Avery didn't complain.

She was in the corner, telling a story with two stuffed animals. Security brought all their stuff from Marriott that first night. They went through it, she was sure. They wouldn't find anything. She'd purged her laptop, databombed the hard drive and wiped out all her accounts.

The same was true of the house. Sooner or later, they would find the basement lab. Once this was over, they would haul everything out and pull it apart, piece by piece. But they'd find nothing. Cali knew she wasn't going back. Everything she needed was inside her.

And her brother.

New breeds.

Sometimes Avery would sit on her lap and tell a story, one she made up on the fly. Cali told her to write them down so she could practice becoming a writer. She would do that on scraps of paper and leave them around the room. Eventually she got bored and started telling the stories out loud again.

"What do you think the bad guy's name should be, Mr. James?"

The security guard didn't answer. He never did. He just stood there watching them. Didn't read, didn't watch TV. Just watched with his mouth closed.

Outside, it was raining big gray drops, blurring the city below. Cars were jammed up and pedestrians walked beneath umbrellas of red or black or whatever. Some took cover beneath an awning. It was probably warmer outside than it was in the room, but the loneliness seeped through the glass like a wet kiss, springing a fresh layer of chilly flesh.

"Momma, I'm hungry." Avery pressed Mr. Pillsbury—a fat, brown bear—against the window. "Look how far up we are."

"I'll get something to eat pretty soon."

"Can I get ice cream?"

"The cafeteria probably has something good."

Avery cheered. She walked Mr. Pillsbury across the room, stopped in front of James and did a little dance.

Three days of this.

Three days since they activated Nix's biomites and started an aggressive healing program. Almost fifty trillion cell-sized biomites were mending bones and tissue. Internal bleeding had stopped. His body temperature was slightly elevated from all the activity, but the color around his eyes had turned from black water to jaundice yellow. The respirator sat quietly in the corner. Nix breathed easily on his own.

Still, he lay unconscious.

Come on, Nix.

There wasn't much time. Marcus had given her everything she asked for, but there wasn't much of a window here. She was feeling the pressure. *What was I thinking, we'd just walk out of the hospital?* She doubted herself, wondering if it would've been easier to bust out of the Center than escape the hospital. This wasn't what she planned. Nix had to be healthy to leave. Had to be awake.

Before he became halfskin.

She needed him to wake up.

"Mr. James?" Avery called. "I have a question. Do you have a dog?"

James didn't answer.

Avery continued about what kind of dog she wanted and what she would name him.

Cali leaned her head against the window. The glass felt good. She wanted to stop thinking but didn't want to leave Avery all alone. Her head was filled with a white noise, like static, electric cotton. It fogged her focus. She hoped these weren't side effects from the new breeds. She didn't have time to test, just seeded herself in the basement lab. It was stupid, but there wasn't a choice. If they were failing now, well then, it was game over.

"What's your favorite ice cream?"

Silence.

"I like chocolate chips in mine but not too many. Have you ever put peanut butter in your ice cream?"

Silence.

Silence.

Silence.

"WILL YOU ANSWER HER?" Cali swung around. "She's not asking you to put your gun up your ass, she just wants to know what your favorite ice cream is."

James turned his head, regarding her without expression. Avery pulled her legs onto her chair and wrapped her arms around them. She hid behind Mr. Pillsbury.

"I'm sorry." Cali flopped into the chair next to the bed. She pulled her legs under her and rubbed her tired face, scratching her scalp.

"You need something to eat," James said, his voice deep and demanding.

"I know." Cali laid her head back. "I'll get something soon."

Avery shuffled across the room, leaning against her mother. Cali made some space for her to sit. She squished next to her, nice and warm and cuddly. Cali laid her cheek on top of her daughter's head.

"Tell me a story," she whispered. "A good one."

Avery started with a bright sunny day. She was on the porch with her mother, and Uncle Nix was in the backyard, digging a hole to the middle of the world, where they would make their home. Where no one could hurt them.

Cali closed her eyes. She smiled.

Then she projected a thought, one she hoped would be heard.

[*Wake up, Nix. Wake up.*]

CHAPTER TWENTY-FOUR_

Trapped in a long night.

Pain wrapped around Nix like a coffin. He willfully fled into unconsciousness. The new breeds kept him alive, but they couldn't heal. The longer he stayed in bed, the less they helped.

He got worse.

It got painful.

Not what he expected.

Minutes were days. Hours, months.

There was no rest. The large blank periods were not measured in time. He returned to self-awareness somewhere in the formless space of his mind. He couldn't sense the confines of his body, just the agony. He couldn't move his fingers, his toes. Couldn't open his eyes.

He sensed pressure. Felt disharmony. Experienced floundering organs and broken pieces. If he could disconnect entirely, he would.

Death.

That would be a good deal.

It would only take a thought-command directed at the new breeds working so tirelessly to keep his body alive.

Cease, and it would be over. *Cease,* and peace would be on him.

No more suffering. No more hurt.

No more, period.

He could rest. Finally.

All his life, he'd gone from one disaster to another. He'd seen those around him die, seen them suffer. Watched them break down. And after all of that, here he was imprisoned in his own body. Life was hardly fair. In fact, it was vindictive.

He often wondered what he had done in a previous life, if there were such a thing. He often wondered what the point of continuing to live would be with such suffering. It made no logical sense. Death was a prime option. *Why suffer? Why live a miserable life?*

He couldn't answer that. At least not with anything that made sense, not to his little mind.

But, live, he did.

He continued, and didn't know why.

The night appeared to be endless. He imagined Cali sitting by his side, watching him fade. Perhaps it was best if he stopped this madness. She could let go of him, finally. Stop taking care of him.

Face her demons on her own.

He didn't want to do that. She needed him. But if she could look inside him, if she could see the night, even she would tell him to let go.

Let go.

Let go.

And the ceaseless night brought him to the brink, where he loaded the thought-command to cease. He placed it in his mind. He felt the new breeds hesitate, sensing it. All he had to do was confirm it as a purposeful directive and they would stop. The organs would fail. His brain would fade.

And Nix would rest.

He could find peace.

BrrrrrrrrrTHG.

Something engaged.

A switch was thrown. Followed by—

MmmmmmmmmmmmmmMMMMMMMMMM.

A whine.

A thrum.

Light.

Warmth flooded his consciousness, trickling through streaks of pain, taking away the sparks and bites and stings and pressure...

It went away.

Disappeared.

She did it. She activated all the biomites!

Nix felt as if he was smiling, even though his body lay as still as death. Inside, he smiled. Inside, he basked in the glory of suffuse light penetrating everything. It was blinding and good and flowed with a silky essence.

Pure existence.

And from somewhere in its endless penetration, a form took place. He heard the water rushing, heard it crashing. He felt the foamy fingers slide over smooth sand. Felt the craggy rocks rise up.

The light condensed.

It was white. Then yellow.

Orange.

It solidified into a ball just above a sharp line. He felt its warmth. He was the warmth. The water thrummed a beat on the shore. It crashed inside him.

He pulled away from the sensations.

Felt a body that was separate from the sun and ocean and beach. Feet on the wet sand, toes buried beneath it. A bare chest for the rising sun to kiss. Hair falling over eyes that could see.

Could see.

See.

Far to the right, hundreds of yards, she walked down a steep dune, between the sea oats and the soft sand. She reached the hard-pack, where the water skimmed over the top in bubbly sheets. Her skin dark and unblemished. Her feet flung the water as she ran.

Nix turned.

He ran.

He went to her. To the girl in dreamland.

They embraced. They fell in the water, rolling over and over. His face buried in her thick hair. Inhaled her.

And the sky broke open.

Rain poured from the heavens.

The lagoon wept with joy.

Nix is home. Nix is home.

"Raine," he whispered.

Nikki had seen houses that big; she'd driven by them, just never walked up to one. Now she was standing on the porch made from some sort of dark tropical wood. Ceiling fans turned lazily above them.

"You sure about this?" she asked Carly.

The house was dark except for a single light in the back somewhere. It didn't look like anyone was home. It looked haunted.

"Don't get your panties in a wad," Carly snapped. "This is the address."

But we don't know him. That's what she wanted to say, but Carly and Kim weren't interested in caution. They were sixteen. Their best years were now, baby.

As in, NOW.

Carly thumbed the doorbell. Inside, a melodious series of bells echoed. When the last one trailed off, Kim was giggling too hard to press it again. They dared each other to do it. Nikki had her heels on the top step when Kim's finger hovered over the button—

The door cracked open.

They screamed. They jumped.

An eyeball peeked through the crack. Then a smile. "Hello," it said.

"You scared us!" Carly slapped the door.

"What took you so long?" The boy opened the ornate door. He was illuminated by the streetlight humming at the curb, his complexion bluish, shadows hiding his eyes. Even so, Nikki could see his complexion was smooth as marble. His teeth straight, white and perfectly square. Lips wet and full.

Like an airbrushed centerfold.

"Come in, come in." He stepped aside. "Welcome to my humble abode."

"This isn't your house," Carly said.

"Mi padre's casa es mi casa."

"Ooo... he speaks another language." Carly and Kim hugged each other on the way inside, laughing along the way.

The boy stepped out and took Nikki's hand. "You must be Cinderella."

His eyes peered from shadows, cold as winter rain, blue as a frozen sky. His hand, though, warm as a soft blanket.

A large chandelier greeted her inside the foyer. She could see a grand piano in the shadows of a great room on the right and a spiraling staircase on the left. The back room, the only light in the house, was the kitchen.

Ten teens sat in a circle. A candelabrum burned in the middle. Perfect skin. Perfect teeth. They laughed with perfect pitch and cadence.

Perfect.

The boy leaned into her. He smelled like new leather.

"Watch."

And Nikki watched. One of the girls tucked her knees together and bowed until her forehead touched the floor. One of the guys wrapped something over the back of her neck. They sat back and watched her convulse. Nikki stuttered back, but the boy put his arm around her, drawing her close.

The girl threw her head back.

Eyes bright.

Smile vacant.

She sat back with a dopey grin while the boy and girl on her left and right held her steady. Nikki swore she saw her cheekbones lifting, cheeks draw in and lips plump up.

"Spiking," the boy whispered. "We're overriding our biomites, reprogramming them to do what we want. To look like..." He smiled, beautifully. "This."

"How?" Nikki muttered. "You need to be a doctor—"

"Or have the right connections."

The candles flickered in his eyes.

Each of them took their turn, always bowing, always coming up with a smile.

And always looking more perfect than before.

"You got to try this," Carly said, ten minutes after her turn. "Don't be afraid, girl. It's a rush."

Nikki noticed her blemishes were gone. And her nose seemed... slimmer.

"I don't know."

And around it went. Around it went.

Nikki nearly turned and left. The boy, though. Each time he smiled, she melted. And when he said he'd do it, he'd be the one that put the spiker on her neck and held her hand, she let him. She let him take her down to the floor. Let him guide her head to the cold floor.

And wrap the thing on her neck.

It was heavier than she thought it would be.

And warm.

Then hot.

It poked spots around her vertebrae. Flooded her brain with hot soup. She melted like a puddle of wax thrown on a hot plate. Colors swirled in a psychedelic mind storm. She was tossed into the sky, landed in Oz and skidded down the yellow brick road, tumbling...

And tumbling.

And laughter.

Her head was lead. She pushed with both hands to lift it. Candlelight flickered like stars and the perfect people laughed and smiled and—

Screamed.

They scrambled like rats, hands clawing the slick floor.

Nikki's cheeks rippled like waves. Her teeth were filling her mouth. Her nails slid out of her fingers like utility blades.

Later, it was reported, her biomites had an adverse reaction to the reprogramming module. She was dumped outside the emergency room.

Her head the size of a pumpkin.

CHAPTER TWENTY-FIVE

Marcus swirled the tumbler of tomato juice and ice, looking out the twenty-second floor of the Allerton Hotel. Chicago at night, Michigan Avenue was electric fire. The streets were streaked with taillights. He lifted a small pair of binoculars and spied the janitorial worker in an office building across the street. He scanned the other floors. No one working late or otherwise. He could always find someone up to no good. The month before, while in New York, he watched a couple getting busy on the roof. They both faced the same direction, watching the city lights while he thrust from behind. Their bodies synchronized.

"Yeah." He tapped the Bluetooth in his ear.

The voice on the other end was coming from his office in Washington. No funny business in those rooms.

"I'll be here another two, three days, I imagine," Marcus said.

He'd been on the phone with Janine, explaining the urgency in Chicago. He texted, but she called. He told her the boy's sister had him in a corner; he was taking care of that. He needed to stay. She complained about missing a parent-teacher conference. In fact, he'd missed all of them so far. But what was he going to do? Let the country fall apart so he could make sure William got a seat near the front?

He was staying in Chicago. He was cleaning up.

"Not acceptable." He loosened his tie and unbuttoned. "It needs to be done by tomorrow."

He sipped the bottom of the glass.

"I don't want any excuses, Chad. Tell the boys it needs to be done tomorrow by nine a.m. or they're looking for work, understand? I'll make sure they never find a job that even remotely deals with computers, trust me. Text me when it's uploaded."

Marcus pulled the drawer out and sorted through the neatly folded clothes. A small leather pouch was beneath a layer of T-shirts. He unzipped it, digging through razors and small tubes of toothpaste, finding the small silver cube about the size of a billiards chalk.

Chad was still relaying details about his assignment; Marcus half listened to the excuses. People, he'd learned, needed pushed. They could tolerate much, much, MUCH more discomfort than they believed. People needed a leader, they needed someone to give direction and incentive, to put a boot in their ass when they slowed down; otherwise they'd toil in mediocrity, and where would they be then? Where would the human species be if they sat around fires playing bongos all day long?

"Pull some of the techs off their other assignments; get everyone working on this. It has to be done by morning, Chad. And that's final. Do you have any more questions?"

Silence hung in the Bluetooth. Then, "When will you be back, sir?"

"If all goes well, I'll be back in three days. It could be longer. Peterson will monitor the halfskin program while I'm gone. He'll attend any shutdowns, in the meantime, and he will report to the Secretary."

Marcus pulled the bedspread onto the floor. He rolled the cube into the middle of the linen sheets.

"Nine a.m."

"Yes, sir."

Marcus pulled the phone from his ear and tossed it on the dresser along with his wallet and watch.

He gazed at the lights while he undid the cuffs, pulling his shirt from his pants and sliding the belt from the loops. He undid the buttons, exposing his smooth chest. He pulled the heavy drapes closed.

Marcus folded his clothes.

Completely undressed.

Only when everything was put away did he turn off all the lights and go to the shower. He soaked in hot water until he was soft and supple all over, then soaped up his arms and chest, cleaning every part of his body. Even between his toes. When he was finished, he powdered and clipped his nails and stood in front of the mirror as God intended.

All man.

All flesh.

Clean and ready to do work.

Marcus turned the lights out and stepped out of the bathroom. He went about his nightcap without saying another word.

CHAPTER TWENTY-SIX_

Nix's friends went to a doctor's office when they were sick, where there were magazines in the waiting room and they got a sucker when they were done. Their doctors were in a clinic or next to the hospital, where they had to wait their turn.

Nix didn't have to wait. He went to Technology Park.

The buildings were made of glass. The pond out front was clear with a large fountain. Three flag poles soared near the front doors, flags whipping on top.

When Nix got sick, he didn't feel like other people felt. He didn't get sluggish or throw up. He buzzed. It wasn't anything someone could hear, just an intense humming that sizzled all over. His sister couldn't hear it, but she could tell just by looking at him.

The buzzies are back.

The man in the glass building fixed the buzzies; Nix remembered that day well. He followed his sister up the wide steps. Avery held onto her hand, a pacifier plugged in her mouth. Cali wore a pin-striped skirt and jacket; the white lapel of her silk shirt flipped in the breeze. Her office was in the same complex, different glass building. She took Nix out of school.

He had a special box attached to his hip. It looked like a phone, but it didn't make calls. It emitted harmonizing sonar that equalized the buzzing biomites. It was experimental. Everything they did was experimental when it came to Nix.

Nix was only eight, but he knew what experimental meant. He knew he was different than everyone else. Cali explained that his biomites sometimes didn't get along with the blood cells and there was a fight. When things got bad, he got shaky and the sonar box would hum loudly. Sometimes he felt better, instantly.

Sometimes it took a while.

And, sometimes, there was war.

They stopped at the receptionist desk, this metal, curving wall in the giant foyer. Five people could sit behind it, but there was only one: a guy with short hair and always a phone in his ear. He pushed a button to let them through the door and said hello as they approached. Cali's heels echoed off the hard floor. Above them—three stories up—was the ceiling, where large bird sculptures hung and twisted.

In Search of Knowledge, Harmony and Freedom.

That was carved behind the desk, engraved on a gold plate in cursive. Nix didn't know what that meant. He just knew that whenever he was there, something was going to hurt.

Always.

But, afterwards, it felt better.

He had nowhere else to go.

They went to a small room with five chairs. There were no magazines, no TV. Just chairs and a clock. Nix watched the second hand tick around the face while the sonar box hummed.

The doorknob turned.

Dr. Merrick didn't wear a stethoscope or a white coat like most doctors. He always wore tan pants and a wrinkle-free shirt. He kept his hair cut really short.

"Dr. Cali." He crossed the room in three steps and hugged Nix's sister. "How are things on your side of corporate?"

"Oh, you know. Grants are still in limbo, so our hands are a little tied with the development of the last biomite generation."

"What about this one?" Dr. Merrick squatted. Avery hid behind Cali, making pacifier noises. He tried to tickle her, but she stayed on the move.

"Young man."

Dr. Merrick held out his fist. Nix gently punched it.

"You feeling all right?"

Shrug.

"What's this?" Dr. Merrick shrugged back. "Yes? No?"

Nix didn't feel like smiling. His guts felt like they were on an elevator.

"Let's take a look at you." Dr. Merrick held the door open. Nix followed Cali into his lair, an office in the back where there were no good memories.

"I'll be right back. Stay with Uncle Nix."

Cali peeled Avery's hands off her leg and plopped her in the seat next to Nix. She held out her arms and started crying around the pacifier. It was just as loud as if nothing was plugging her up. Cali tried a few more bribes. Nothing worked until Dr. Merrick pulled a purple lollipop from his pocket.

He does have suckers.

"I was ready today," he said.

Cali peeled off the wrapper.

Avery was transfixed by the color. Cali made her escape. It wasn't far. They were on the other side of the door, their voices muffled. Avery opened her mouth and let the pacifier drop on the floor to make room for the sucker.

Nix pulled the sonar box off his belt. Sometimes it worked better if he pressed it against his stomach. He picked up Avery's pacifier. There was no sink to wash it off. There wasn't much besides a couple of chairs and an office desk with computers and microscopes and things that caused pain.

Nix sat back down, held the dirty pacifier and stared at the only picture on the wall. It was a big green mountain with a long granite cliff. Water fell from a hole in the stone wall, drifting hundreds of feet to a blue sea below. He'd been in the office before, staring at that scene while Dr. Merrick prepared one of his special injections. Sometimes he'd stick it in his leg, sometimes the hip or arm. Once he got one in the back of the head. He always numbed it so he didn't feel the sting, but there was nothing he could do about the pressure.

That would last for hours.

Nix cried every time. Grown men would, too.

He didn't like this place. He wanted to be somewhere fun. Somewhere nice. Somewhere normal people went, do things that normal families did. That was impossible. At eight, he knew normal was gone.

Avery began exploring the office with the white stick poking between her lips. She opened a drawer and found a pad of paper. There was a pen attached to a clipboard on the back of the door. He thought maybe he could untie it and give it to her. Avery loved to draw.

"I know it hurts," he heard the doctor say. "But the results look good."

"I've got another generation that will be ready for testing in a couple weeks," Cali said. "I'd like to inoculate Nix, starting with a spinal tap—"

"Let's be patient. I expect..."

Nix couldn't understand what he said.

He pushed his ear against the door.

"I got to be honest," Cali said, "I'm little worried. He says his body tingles..."

The sonar box—

Heavy.

His insides stepped off the elevator and dropped to the center of the earth. The box—pressed against his stomach—was the only thing holding Nix on the ground, and when it left his hand, when it tumbled from his fingers, he zoomed like a helium balloon cut loose.

His stomach fell out.

The room spun.

And the buzzies went electric.

His bones vibrated like over-modulated components, emitting heat waves that elevated his temperature. He was being electrocuted from the inside.

Black edge—

Floor—

Door opening and a deep breath and a hand on his arm—

A salty warm rush into his throat—

And the room—

He smelled green, like when he cut the grass.

He was on the ground with trees overhead. Vines strangling the trunks. Sunlight filtering through the leaves.

A bird called.

Something jumped in the branches.

"Cali?" Nix sat up.

This was weird. This was... he was just in Dr. Merrick's office and now they were... *camping?*

He stood up. He felt a little numb, but it wasn't the bad kind. It wasn't anything like a buzzy. It was just... dull. Couldn't really feel stuff, could hardly smell it. There was a path that wandered between the trees. It was narrow and weedy. Nix didn't feel scared or alone. Not like he should. He felt good. Felt solid. No buzzies.

He just wanted to know where his sister had gone.

So he took the path. He followed it to the end. He heard something roaring. It sounded like a big truck. He saw an opening and a blue sky. The roar was deafening. He felt it in his chest, vibrating all over him. He slowed and carefully stepped to the edge of a cliff. He looked down hundreds of feet to see...

The waterfall in the picture.

The lagoon was born when Nix was eight.

All he had to do was close his eyes.

CHAPTER TWENTY-SEVEN

"Momma?"

Avery's voice was tiny. So far away.

Cali's eyes hurt. She'd been squeezing them closed for... how long?

She didn't hear Avery return.

Didn't hear the machines beeping.

Only heard the words shooting into her mind. Over and over. Over and—

"Momma?" Avery tapped the back of Cali's hand.

She opened her eyes.

It was so bright.

Her daughter was kneeling on the other side of the bed, leaning on the railing. She could see all of Avery's silver braces that lined her teeth. She was smiling. And pointing down at the bed. Something smacked.

Nix's lips were moving.

Cali leaped to her feet. She stopped from grabbing his cheeks. She didn't know what to do with her hands. They ran up and down her sides and over the bed railing. She leaned over and felt his rotten breath on her cheek. It felt wonderful.

"Nix," she whispered.

His eyelids batted back the light, rapidly fluttering. His blue eyes peered through the slits. It took a few moments to process the big face hovering over him. His lips cracked when he smiled.

"Hey." He squeezed weakly.

Cali squeezed back. "How are you?" she asked.

"Better than I look."

Cali nodded. She knew what he meant. "Good, good."

[*We don't have much time,*] she thought to him.

He heard it. His new breeds picked up her thoughts like a radio wave, transmitting them like spoken words. Still, he was surprised. His eyes bulged slightly. It took a moment to comprehend, to understand what the hell just happened.

She waited patiently. Let him calm down, form his own thoughts.

Cali sat down and gave him space. He smacked his lips, calling for water. Cali handed him the cup and stuck the straw between his lips. He only took a drag off it. His head was too exhausted to stay up and drink more.

He was going to need all his strength.

"Where's Avery?" The words scratched his throat.

Cali wiped her cheeks and pointed to the other side of the bed. Nix turned his head slowly. He lifted his hand for her to take. Avery's hand looked so small in his.

"Does it hurt?" the little girl asked.

"You look so pretty."

Avery bowed her head, smiling and giggling. Her bashfulness evaporated in seconds and she jumped up to show Uncle Nix her new shoes, demonstrating them with some swift dance moves.

"I missed you," Nix said.

"Then don't sleep so much," Avery sang.

He watched her dance some more and tell the story about the flowers she found in the lobby and used them to decorate his bed, that he would've loved them, but her mom made her clean them up.

Nix listened patiently. A good uncle.

[*You're* 49.9%,] she thought.

He turned back to her. He worked his lips, closed his eyes and focused.

[*I know.*]

While Avery began telling another story—this one about a prince that went to save his sister from a red dragon—Cali sent her escape plans.

He closed his eyes, nodding.

CHAPTER TWENTY-EIGHT_

Dr. Erickson had been the chief physician of bionanotechnology at Northwestern Memorial Hospital since the wing had been dedicated to the science of biomite healing.

That was seven years ago.

At the time of its dedication, he was excited about the future of humanity. He'd seen too many things go wrong. As a doctor, good came with bad. But medicine was so much more complicated than it was in the old days. Now there were lawsuits and unrealistic expectations and insurance... those were not the reasons he chose medicine as his profession. He wanted to help people, wanted to give them a second chance. But they needed to help themselves.

Too often, that was not the case.

When bionanotechnology was introduced, he was skeptical. *Machines that imitate human cells? That's science fiction, not reality.*

But all that changed.

All that changed when he witnessed the simplicity that occurred at the microscopic level, that these miniscule artificial cells were programmed like stem cells to transform into anything inside the human body. He'd witnessed miracles.

He was not a religious man, but there was no other word for it.

Miracles.

But humans have a way of corrupting everything meant to be good and proper. In the few short years that Dr. Erickson oversaw the development and implementation of biomites to save faulty organs, to restore sight, and repair damaged bodies, he became embroiled in the politics that went along with it.

He opened his office door and was reminded, bluntly, of such corruption.

"Why are you in here?" Dr. Erickson said.

Marcus Anderson stood in front of a large saltwater fish tank. He bent over and smudged the glass with his finger, pointing at the anemone.

"Amazing how a clownfish survives, Dr. Erickson. It hides in the poisonous tentacles, resistant to the sting itself."

"Evolution is amazing."

Marcus turned. "And God's grace."

Dr. Erickson dropped his clipboard on his cluttered desk and sat down. The office was dimly lit, chiefly from the tank's light. He kept his office that way intentionally. It was a place of respite, a secret room from the hectic matters only a few short steps outside of it. It was remarkable how it could be disrupted by a diminutive man such as the one still fouling the tank's glass.

"Can I help you, Mr. Anderson?"

The small man straightened up as best he could—the bump between his shoulders vaguely noticeable—and came over to the desk. He didn't bother sitting. He fished a Jolly Rancher from a dish and unwrapped it.

"I came to inform you, Dr. Erickson, that I will be overseeing a biomites shutdown this afternoon."

"I hardly see how that involves me."

"It will be conducted on this wing, in a room at the end of the hall."

"That is against hospital policy."

"You'll have to make an exception. The subject is incapable of transport. Unless you can reduce his biomite population, it will be conducted on these premises."

Marcus sucked on the green block of candy, rattling it over his teeth from one cheek to the other.

"We cannot oblige, Mr. Anderson. There is a Hippocratic Oath that we take seriously here at Northwestern Memorial, and I intend to uphold it. I will file an appeal to suspend Nixon Richards' shutdown until he is able to walk out on his own."

"And die somewhere else?"

Dr. Erickson rapped his fingers on the desktop. "I don't approve of shutdowns anywhere, Mr. Anderson."

"And neither do I."

Dr. Erickson's expression was blank.

"Doctor, the fact is, you have no choice in the matter. There is nowhere to request a stay of shutdown, no one to hear your plea. The Halfskin Laws are executed whether you and I approve of them or not. When any person reaches 50% biomites, he or she is shut down. I am sorry for that, I am. But the world has been warned; they make their choices. They have to take responsibility for their actions. If they don't like the consequences, they shouldn't seed themselves."

"What about those that need them to survive? Accident victims, genetic disorders, you name it. Life happens to them and they receive biomites to survive only to be told there's a law that forbids it?"

Marcus leaned over the trash can and spit the candy out. It banged the bottom.

"We have to have order, Doctor."

"You should reconsider your policy."

Marcus stretched his chin and straightened his tie. "Perhaps you should consider your own policies."

"And what policies would those be? That I want health and well-being for the people that come here?"

"You're turning people into machines."

"We're using technology. Prescription glasses, hearing aids, medicines... no difference."

Marcus nodded. "Does your computer have a right to life, Doctor?"

"My computer?"

Marcus nodded at the monitor. "Shouldn't you consider its feelings before you unplug it one of these days for an upgrade?"

"A computer was never human, Mr. Anderson. It has always been a machine."

"The past doesn't define who we are. It is only now. We were not meant to live forever, Doctor. There are limits to our survival. Perhaps death should not be held in contempt. Without it, where would we be?"

Dr. Erickson leaned back, sighing. His hope in the human race continued to wither. Especially when speaking to a man like this. A man with power.

"We'll be conducting a shutdown this afternoon, Doctor. We prefer to keep it quiet. You may attend, if you like."

Marcus filled a paper cup with water, the water jug chugging with air. He crushed the cup and dropped it into the trash.

"Neither of us can stop it," he said. "Whether we want to or not."

Dr. Erickson decided the man's smile indicated he not only didn't want to stop it, he looked forward to it.

He felt no less deflated when Marcus left the office. Just more hopeless.

CHAPTER TWENTY-NINE_

Cali folded the last of Avery's shirts and squeezed it into her bag.

Her daughter was curled up on the chair. They needed to get out of the hospital for a lot of reasons. And they would. In three days, they would be somewhere else where there was fresh air and freedom.

That was the plan.

She packed her belongings. Three days was longer than she wanted to wait. She was prepared to dash now, that morning, but Nix wasn't ready. He could barely walk.

He was asleep. *And not in the lagoon.* She made damn sure he wasn't expending energy on his inner world. They needed every bit to restore his health. The new breeds couldn't conduct a secret siege on his body, taking the place of the older biomites that compromised nearly 49% of his body. She was certain the new breeds could flush the old ones out, but since the hospital readers couldn't see the new breeds, they would think his biomite population was declining.

And that would lead to suspicion. That would not help.

Everything needed to look normal. Nothing going on here. Everything was the same. Any close examination could bring her best-laid plans to a halt. There was no hope if that happened, so it was business as usual.

Nix slept.

Cali monitored him.

Yes, she read him like a computer. Even she was surprised by the recent developments. Not only could she telecommunicate with Nix, but she was using them to wirelessly communicate with every wireless device in the vicinity. She was a wireless router that heard everything around her.

Phone calls.

Emails.

Network servers.

I'm a computer.

It was all data streaming through the atmosphere, vibrating against her new breeds that downloaded and interpreted it all into words and sounds. But it was too much to understand. It was white noise, the chatter of a thousand voices, at first. That's what she'd been hearing for the past few days and had thought it might be a malfunction. The new breeds were breaking down, they were learning. Evolving.

She thought-commanded the new breeds to tune it all out. Perhaps, at some point, she could filter out what she wanted to hear. For now, she focused on her little brother, listening to his new breeds report his health and stats.

Bones mended.

Organs stable.

No fever. Blood vessels healed.

He could walk, but she needed more than that. It was going to take a lot to get out undetected. They needed time for him to heal. Stay too long, he goes halfskin. Leave too soon, there's biomite failure.

Sleep. Heal, my brother. Heal quickly.

In the meantime, Cali discovered that she could access her computer through thought-commands. The new breeds made a connection through her secure portal. If she closed her eyes, she could see the interface as if it was a monitor in her mind. She arranged a hotel reservation at the Red Roof Inn. It was close to the hospital—too close—but Nix would need to recover. She arranged Hertz to deliver a car to the parking garage and drop off the keys to an alias.

After those arrangements were complete, she explored the hospital's network. The new breeds slipped easily past passwords, speaking the language of computers. She spied through a multitude of cameras like a thousand eyes inside her head. She knew who was on duty, where they were, what operations were scheduled and even what the cafeteria was serving.

None of that did much good. Not now.

She decided to stretch out. She jumped into the Internet and found Marcus Anderson's home computer. He'd upgraded since she hacked his personal information a week ago, but she flew past it like a ghost. She opened his email, searched his voicemails, office memos, etc. She decided to download everything to her cloud storage.

He's the real threat.

That man wouldn't stop. She and Nix could leave the hospital and very few people would care. They might even elude Mother. But this man, he would dog them to the end of the world just so he could watch them die.

He needed to be addressed. Permanently.

The door swung open.

Cali jumped back from the bed. She blinked a few times, bringing her vision back online. The images inside her head faded slowly. There were two men stepping inside. Twins, at first.

But now there was one.

She focused on Marcus Anderson.

He was smiling.

CHAPTER THIRTY_

Marcus left the doctor's office, cursing beneath his breath He never uttered such language, never made it a word, but he let the cursed thoughts settle, melting like dirty mints.

Because he hated this place.

He hated the smell of hospitals. The peculiar scent clung to his sinuses, coated the back of his throat, and swabbed his nostrils. It would take days to purge it. Even candy couldn't mask its odor.

He stopped outside Dr. Erickson's office and placed a few calls. He had approval to conduct the shutdown in the hospital. There wasn't an option, but it was nice to have others in the administration on board. The sooner he was out of Chicago, the better.

He hit the door harder than he anticipated, his thoughts elsewhere. Cali was caught by surprise, kneeling next to her brother's bed, hands folded against her forehead.

She's praying.

It warmed his heart to see this godless scientist succumbing to prayer when times were dark and hopeless. All scientists came to the Lord when times became desperate. And if their heart was open, if they were prepared to admit their sinful ways, He might accept them into the gates of heaven. That was how good the Father was. He held no grudges, only love.

She stood.

"No, no. Don't let me interrupt. Please." He gestured to the bedside. "Continue."

"What do you want?"

Marcus noticed the bag. None of her stuff was scattered around the room. "Going somewhere?"

"My brother is healing. He'll be transferred soon. I want to follow him... back to wherever you're taking him."

"I see."

Marcus unbuttoned his coat, reached inside and let his hand rest for a moment. The woman looked so vulnerable, so afraid. She knew something was coming. He wasn't there to pray, though.

"I'm afraid I have bad news."

He walked softly to the bed, pulling his hand out of his jacket to reveal the biomite reader. He placed it gently on Nix's exposed throat. A number appeared a moment later. Marcus knew what it would read. He was not disappointed.

He lifted it in her direction.

49.99%.

"Wrong," she said. "That's wrong."

"You're lucky." He turned the display, reading it again like a man that lost his bifocals. "An upgrade now allows for an accurate reading to the hundredths. Your brother would be shut down already."

"It's wrong." Her fists clenched. "And you know it."

She acted like she knew he was lying, but even if she did, she couldn't prove it. Mother was not one to argue.

"I won't let you turn him off."

"You think my finger is on the button?" He smiled like a victor. "I'm simply an ambassador, young lady. I only confirm when the Halfskin Laws are applied. That's all. I have no part in the rest of this. I don't enjoy it."

"Lie."

"I wasn't talking about this." He pointed at Nix. He enjoyed that. Wouldn't say it out loud. "I mean, I don't enjoy witnessing the erosion of the soul. I don't enjoy watching Man play God. It's sinful, at best."

His left eye twitched.

"Evil, is what it is."

"I believe you're the one playing God, Marcus. You're deciding who lives and dies. You're responsible for the bill that brought all of this into play. You're playing God."

His lips thinned. "You, Cali, with your degrees and engineered biomites, are spreading the disease responsible for this, not me. It is a disease. It is consuming the human body. You tell me, what will you be when your body is 100% biomites, mmm? Where is your soul then?"

"Biomites won't consume 100%."

She was lying. She didn't know that.

"Man's greed is insatiable. The laws I helped put in place are meant to stop humanity from self-destruction, whether they like it or not. All these years, we thought the nuclear bomb would bring about our extinction. Turns out our greatest threat is a microscopic entity that mimics our self-centered greed."

Her hands quivered. She looked at Marcus with intense concentration, like she was trying to will him into death, like lasers would shoot from her eyes to carve him up. He shuffled a step, a bit nervous of what she was capable of doing. Desperation can crack the strongest. And she was cornered.

But then she appeared to wilt.

Shoulders slumped.

Whatever she wanted to do, she gave up.

Marcus waited at the end of the bed. Cali took a seat, pushing her hair back, cradling her face. Yes, she'd resigned to the end. Marcus was positive. He'd broken many spirits. He knew the sight of one that had crumbled, only needing swept up and disposed.

Still, he waited. He waited until the door opened and James

stepped inside. He considered whether he needed security in the room. It was wise to play it safe. When James was next to him, only when his big body was between him and the wasted young woman, did Marcus pass the biomite reader to her.

"Take it."

She held it, confused. Marcus gestured with a bent finger to her throat. She raised her head. Her eyes widened slightly. He was sure that she knew what would happen before she hesitantly pressed it to her flesh.

Read the number.

She held the biomite reader without protest.

"We'll be doing a double shutdown at approximately 15:00 today. I'd like to conduct this event with dignity, Dr. Richards. I would prefer you shut down next to your brother. I'm sure you would prefer it that way, too."

Marcus took the biomite reader. He went to the door and stopped, hardly turning his head.

"Check the news feed. The video of your brother's assault has been released. The real one, Dr. Richards. Any other videos that may pop up will obviously be considered forgeries by talented engineers like yourself."

She didn't bother looking up. She'd been cornered. Knew her little stunt with the security video would only hold leverage for so long, knew he could get his people to make one do what he wanted. Whatever she was planning, she waited too long. And her shoulders slumped just a bit more.

Marcus would sweep up the pieces later on.

Rick Mansfield buried his hands in his coat, hunching his shoulders against the cold. Traffic ripped down the street, turning snow into ashy slush. The sky felt like a steel plate.

He skipped across the road, all six lanes, and dropped his foot in a pothole. Icy water soaked his sock. He hopped over the curb and hustled into the building with blacked-out windows, through a door below a bright sign: DREEMITE.

He stomped his shoes on the rug, his foot already numb. He grimaced. His upper lip cracked. It always cracked in the winter from the dry furnace-air. In Canada, there was a lot of furnace-air.

A few people sat at a small round table, sipping coffee and cappuccinos. Two men—one bald, the other reading a paper—sat at the bar; a woman worked behind it. The foamer whooshed with steam. The bald guy dropped his mug on the bar and started toward the door.

"I got minutes, I got minutes!" Rick raised his hands, surrendering. "I got minutes, Stan, I promise."

Bald Stanley didn't listen, grabbed Rick by his army green coat and hoisted him toward the door.

"Mr. Connors, I got minutes, I swear, I do!"

Mr. Connors didn't look up. "Scan him."

Stanley stopped like a Labrador hearing a whistle. He dropped Rick's coat and stepped back. Rick straightened himself up and spread his hand out, palm down.

"This a goof, Mansfield, I'm throwing you in the street," Stanley said. "Head first."

"No goof, Stan. No goof. See, real deal." Rick flexed his fingers. "It's my hand, not synthetic. Not a fake one, not like last time. Go ahead, scan away. I got minutes."

Stanley eyeballed him. He pulled a tablet from the inside of his jacket. Stanley put Rick's hand on it like he was in court, swearing to tell the truth, the whole truth, and nothing but.

"Two minutes?" Stanley held the tablet up for Mr. Conners to see. "Kid's got two minutes. What the hell's he going to do with two minutes?"

Mr. Connors shrugged.

"Two minutes is two minutes," Rick said. "I'll take what I can get, you know what I mean, Mr. Conners." He raised his voice. "I'll take what I can get, even if I HAVE TO PAY DOUBLE!"

"You're about to go on the street," Stanley said.

"I'm just saying, if you want to make some money, I'll pay double."

"Feds are watching, Mansfield. Skimming minutes will pull our license. Losing our license for you ain't worth it."

Rick shrugged off his coat. "Then two minutes it is."

The barista slid the cappuccino to Mr. Connors. She went to the computer and punched the screen. "Eight is open."

"Pay first," Stanley said.

"Cash," Mr. Connors added.

Rick dug into his pocket and dropped two crumpled twenties on the bar. "Two minutes, forty dollars."

The barista ran a pen over the bills to make sure they were legit. She nodded. Stanley took Rick's arm and guided him through the black curtain hanging over a doorway to the right of the bar. Rick yanked away from him.

The doors were numbered. Odds on the right. Evens on the left. Eight was at the end of the hall. Stanley pushed it open, revealing a solo chair in a closet-sized room.

"This won't take long," he said. "I'll wait."

Rick closed it behind him. A light came on and he locked the door. He dropped his coat and sat down. The chair was thick and comfortable with a firm headrest that cradled his skull. He leaned back, stared at the hanging light, and pressed the back of his head into the cradle until his biomites communicated with the plate embedded in the chair.

Closed his eyes.

Heard the winding, like a rocket preparing for liftoff.

His brain swirled.

Three, two, one...

And the bottom dropped out. He fell into the inner world. The plate made his brain biomites sizzle with excitement, releasing hallucinatory hormones. Rick saw colors. Warmth bled down his shoulders.

Lights.

Sounds.

And... crowds.

He saw the bodies. Saw the people. A nightclub full of them. All jumping to the beat, lasers fired in time to the music. And when he stepped onto the floor, they all knew him. They were all happy to see him. They raised their hands, they hugged him, slapped his back, wanted to take pictures with him.

Rick pushed them out of the way, sorting through them like collector's items. Each woman was hotter than the next. Black, white, Asian, Pilipino... it was so hard to choose.

And he didn't have much time.

He put his arms around two women. One was a blonde, at least six foot, a sparkly dress that revealed half her rack. Her lips were full and her breasts ripe. The other was a limber Chinese girl, perfect skin, big eyes and delicate fingers.

His groin twisted like a wet rag.

He sprinted for the stage. The band welcomed him. The guitarist started a slow, rhythmic solo. Rick wanted everyone to watch. And the crowd roared. The crowd adored him, paid to watch him perform on stage. That's all he wanted, was everyone to recognize him. He deserved that.

He hooked his finger beneath the blonde's strap, tugging it off her shoulder. Her ample breast popped from the top, revealing a large, circular hard nipple—

The light turned off—

Silence.

And Rick Mansfield fell back into his body. He opened his eyes, looking at a naked light bulb. Hands holding winter's chill.

And he hated life.

He hated it.

Hate. Hate. Hate. Hate. Hate.

CHAPTER THIRTY-ONE

Oxygen came in short supply.

Cali took little gulps, twisting her fingers like origami. Staring. Staring at a dead boy.

Her eyes couldn't get any wider. The shock rode her pulse like waves, scratching the walls of her circulatory system as her blood carried toxic emotions to her numb and wooden body. Bones turned to steel.

Skin, sun-dried paper, singed at the edges.

She looked around the room, looked for ghost killers. Looked for their executioner. Felt the ceiling fall, the floor cave. The walls collapse.

Her world blacken.

Dry and desolate.

And dead.

And dead, dead, dead, DEAD, DEAD, DEADDEAD-DEADDEAD—

[*Stop.*]

The tiny blip of light that was Cali—rational Cali, intelligent Cali—was going under, tossed beneath waves of thoughts and panic and rage...

That little bit called a halt to the madness.

And the new breeds released a tsunami of endorphins to deaden pain, to release the tension. To stop the thoughts.

Cali's eyelids dropped like shutters. Her breath leaked from her nostrils. She pulled a draught of fresh oxygen, long and deep, and exhaled once again. When she opened her eyes, she saw her brother. He was alive.

And she could save him.

Okay.

All right.

Deep breath.

Cali slowly let her thoughts engage her awareness. She needed to piece together what happened, what needed to change. She had expected to lose the leverage of the security video. It got her into the room. She knew they'd make their own, but they moved faster than she expected, but it was not a surprise. She began reaching for her phone to search the newsfeed, to see what the government was saying, when something twanged at the back of her neck.

Something felt familiar, easy.

She was using the new breeds to communicate with her computer, to think directly into the Internet... she didn't need her phone. She thought-commanded a search into cyberspace, looking for the last news on Nixon Richards. The results were recent and plentiful.

Biomite-Crazed Teenager Attacks Detention Guard.

She activated the video link and streamed it directly to her retinas. Her eyes glazed over as the video formed, surreally, over Nix's head. It started with him standing in his room, the footage grainy. The door opened and George stepped in with a tray of food. He smiled at Nix and appeared to say something that made them both laugh. The fat, jolly guard placed the tray on the desk and went to the door and, just before he opened it, Nix pounced, driving the man's head into the wall.

Her brother slammed the door.

He climbed on top of the obese, hairy man—eyes wide with adrenaline, teeth bared to the glistening gums—and began to wail.

There was no sound.

But there was blood.

Lots of it.

And the sheer gore of the video would carry it around the world in seconds.

Cali didn't bother reading the interviews. The press was sure to find someone that claimed Nix's sister was crazy, that she was losing it, that she'd lost it after the accident. Her co-workers might slip that she was on a medical leave of absence, that she'd seen a psychologist. The public would label her crazy, case closed.

There were sure to be inconsistencies that were swept under the public rug. The anti-biomite protest groups would ignore the obvious forgery. The conspiracy theorists would be dismissed as kooks. And even if it was proven false, even if Nix's innocence was heralded in the Supreme Court, it wouldn't matter. It wouldn't matter, not one damn bit.

Because they'd already be dead.

They'd be shut down.

And nothing could bring them back. That's how that game was played.

It was mid-morning. Chicago was full tilt. Bumpers on bumpers. Sidewalks hustling.

That was one of the reasons Cali planned for Nix to be transferred to Northwestern Memorial, to be in the city. She wanted people around. Millions of them, all with biomites.

This would all be easy to resolve if Marcus was seeded. The man was pure. She'd scanned him when he was in the room, her new breeds chattering all over his body and finding nothing but organic flesh. And that was a stroke of luck because if he was seeded even with the smallest amount, she would've killed him where he stood.

She would've reprogrammed his biomites to consume him like

microscopic pit bulls or discharge a power supply, boil him from the inside.

Eat his brain like zombie tapeworms.

She would've dropped him, killed him, murdered him... and then there would be no escape, not right then. Even though he deserved it. He deserved to die.

He plans to murder me.

Cali wasn't 49.9% biomite. Her registered biomites—the ones Mother could see—held steady at 39%.

Mother was rigged for moments like this. How easy it would be to get rid of a problem by calling it into Mother, overriding her monitor with a false number and then push a button and—

POOF.

It was murder. And he'd told her with a slight smile. He knew that she knew. He wanted her to know that she'd stepped into a lion's den when she brought the security video to him, forced him to play her game. Wanted her to know that she'd lost.

But the game wasn't over.

First, she needed to get Nix far away from this place. As she watched a taxi wedge its way into traffic, her accelerated thought process put together a plan. There was no time to run an analysis on it.

She tapped into the hospital network and requested a wheelchair be brought to their floor and parked around the corner. Her shirt tugged off her shoulder.

"Momma?" Avery had a handful of her shirt. "Are you all right?"

"Sweetheart."

Cali fell into her chair and wrapped her arms around her. She murmured apologies, over and over. How long had she been there, calling her name? Worried something was wrong?

Bad mom.

Cali held Avery at arm's length. "Honey, I need you to do something by yourself. Can you do that?"

Avery nodded.

"I need you to go to the Red Roof Inn; it's just down the street. I'll give you directions. You'll go to the front desk and there will be a key there, waiting for you. Tell them your name is Avery and your mother left the key for you. Can you do that?"

"I'm scared."

"I know you are. So am I. But this is important. We all have to find the big person inside us. I just want you to be safe in the room and wait for us."

"I'm afraid you won't come back." Avery sniffed.

"Oh, honey, we'll be right there. Uncle Nix just needs to rest a little longer and then we'll be there, okay?"

"Is that bald man going to hurt you?"

"No, no. He's not going to hurt anyone. I promise."

Avery puffed out her bottom lip. She nodded.

Cali showed her directions to the hotel on her phone and hugged her so tightly that Avery couldn't breathe. She walked her to the door. James sat in the hall and looked up from his paper. Cali watched her daughter walk bravely to the other end of the hallway, past the nurse delivering a wheelchair parked around the corner.

Nix was still asleep.

Cali sat next to him.

And began to think.

CHAPTER THIRTY-TWO

Nix dreamed of the lagoon.

It wasn't the same as going there. Dreaming was more like thinking, but it was better than nothing. So Nix dreamed his dream. He flew with his arms out, over the white-tipped waves that washed foam on the north shore. He brushed over the tropical trees, the leaves shimmering in his wake. He imagined his girl there, waiting on the beach for him, where they'd sit by a fire and wait for the moon to illuminate the still waters.

Excitement buzzed the sky.

Warmth bled deep into the jungle.

Nix felt safe.

Peaceful.

If he was lucky, he'd stay that way, maybe never wake up. Just bask in the sweet healing glow of the dream. It had been so long since he'd felt that way. He knew it was the new breeds that soothed his nerves and calmed his mind, but he'd felt that way before. He'd felt safe and wanted when he was younger, when he was composed of so many less biomites.

When he was mostly organic.

It was mostly when he went to bed, all curled up beneath the comforter with his head sunk in a pillow. The adult voices murmured from the front room. When his parents died, Cali and Thomas took over for the voices. Theirs were sharper and higher, but just as safe. Sometimes it was just the two of them talking about their day. Sometimes they had friends over and glasses would clink and bottles pop, but no matter how many cars rushed down the road or how many creepy sounds the house made, Nix was safe.

Nothing would touch him. He'd throw the cover over his head and melt into the safety of their voices.

When Cali was nervous or scared or worried, he could always count on Thomas to bring the safety back. He was strong and smart. He knew how to hunt and how to drive a boat. He could bait a hook in seconds. Nix still had a picture of his first offshore catch, ten years old, holding a yellowfin tuna—Thomas helping him hold the silver-sparkling fish high enough to take the picture.

And then there was the time some guy got weird outside the market. He asked for money. He smelled bad. His eyes red where they should've been white. He grabbed Cali's wrist and Thomas chopped the guy in the neck, dropping him like a tree branch. Said he learned that in the service.

Nix never felt so safe.

And he deserved it.

After everything he'd been through.

And when the phone rang, when Nix was twelve years old, watching TV, and his sister answered and her mouth opened and closed like the yellowfin tuna's did when he reeled it onto the boat's floor... he knew.

He knew.

It happened again.

Another car accident.

The details, irrelevant.

Nix was exposed again. No security blanket. No safe feeling. He'd lost, again. That's what no one in the world realized, what everyone took for granted, what Nix never did...

You can lose everything at any moment.

So he reveled in the dream's security. He rolled in the warm emotions like salty bathwater. If he could make it happen, he would never wake up.

Stay asleep. Forever.

But then Cali's voice echoed in the dream, calling down from the blue dream-sky like God.

He would have to wake up.

Cali needed him. He had to *be* the security blanket. She needed him.

He stayed in the dream and listened to her projecting thoughts into his mind. Plans had changed.

He would have to wake up now.

CHAPTER THIRTY-THREE_

James adjusted his weight.

His left butt cheek was numb. The chair had no padding. If it did, it had been mashed thinner than rice paper by three hundred pounds of security guard. He'd already paced back and forth to get the blood flowing through his lower portions, but it only worked his bowels into a tizzy. He couldn't hit the toilet until he was relieved, and Mr. Anderson was dead set on leaving him there until everything was squared away.

Sometime that afternoon.

James snapped the paper open and began reading the sports section for the third time.

Some said the job of a security guard was 90% boredom, 10% adrenaline. James felt it was closer to 99%. Had he known he was training to read newspapers and open car doors, he might've had second thoughts. But it paid the bills and he wasn't digging ditches, so he shut the hell up and shifted his weight near the middle of his left and right cheek.

He was somewhere between the Chicago White Sox ninth inning collapse and the suspension of a biomite-enhanced recruit when the buzzing started. It wasn't anything noticeable, sort of like a head rush when standing too quickly or temporarily seeing spots. He chalked it up to eating Mexican. Taquitos at 7:00 a.m. can wreak havoc.

The buzz crept around the back of his neck like fingers massaging his jawbone. It crawled over his gums, his teeth, up into his sinuses and around his temples. The backs of his eyeballs itched.

He blinked back the odd sensation and rubbed his eyes with finger and thumb. He was going to have to call in a backup and explain that Mother Nature could be an insistent bitch. Somehow he didn't think dropping a Mexican deuce in a bedpan was going to cut it.

He took a breath, wiping his brow. Maybe the Want Ads would get his mind off it. He was thinking about a dog anyway. His watch reported 11:00 a.m.

Never going to make it.

He plowed through the pet section and ended up studying real estate. He hardly noticed the buzzing. It was still there, just wasn't bothering him. Wasn't in the way. Seemed normal.

The door opened. Just a crack at first.

James looked up from the funny pages. Cali looked back with one eye. She seemed to struggle with the heavy door; then it swung open.

She just stood there, in the doorway. She stared. He stared.

"Going to get something to eat," she said.

James blinked.

The edges of her face were blurry. Kind of glowing, like the soft light photographers use to dress up wedding pictures. James folded the paper under his arm and gouged his eyes again. When he opened them, the girl was past him. She took half-steps, trailing her fingers along the wall as she went. She stopped after each step, paused, took another. She didn't look back, just kept going until she reached the turn. She crossed from the right wall to the left with three quick shuffles, bracing herself against the wall. It took a couple waves to finger the armrest of a wheelchair peeking around the corner, like she didn't have another step left in her.

Cali fell into it. Her head sagged like dead weight.

Bells went off in James's head, the kind of bells that were drilled into security guards. The kind of bells that sound like something between a car horn and a fire alarm. The kind that push a guard to his feet and shove him down the hall, made him ask a few questions and poke a few holes.

Skip. Skip-skip.

Click.

James dug his fingers into his eyes. Shook his head.

She was gone.

She'd already wheeled away, down the hall, going to the cafeteria to get something to eat, because the woman just hadn't been eating. I mean, she hadn't eaten more than an orange slice since she'd gone in that room. Couldn't say anyone could blame her. Her brother was near the end of a ship's plank, about to be switched off like a light. And the news only got worse. She was going, too.

Woman couldn't catch a break.

The alarm bell was drowned out by a new wave of buzzing, this time reaching over the top of his scalp and pulling his upper lip over his eyebrows. His eyes hurt from repeated grinding. The bells were still in the distance, like an ambulance going in the other direction, now around the bend. Danger over there. Not here.

He rattled the paper and decided to start with the front page. He'd read every story, starting at the top. That's how he stayed awake when things began to grind. Pay attention to details, listen to sounds, see everything. Nothing would get past him.

The door opened.

Cali stepped out. "Forgot my bag."

She slung a heavy canvas bag over her shoulder and walked down the hall, all the way to the end without touching the wall or stopping for balance. No wheelchair down there. She turned the corner.

The alarm bell was deafening.

James stood, reached for his phone, took a step—

Zzzzzzzzzzzzzzzzzzzzzzzzzzzzzz.

Next thing, he was sitting. Face in hands. Both cheeks numb.

There was a bell in his head, but he didn't know exactly why. In fact, he couldn't recall what that sound even meant, forgot what he was all about. But then it came back; he remembered. He considered looking in the room but knew there was no reason. Nothing could get past him. They couldn't crawl out the window; they'd have to walk past him to get out.

And he hadn't seen anyone in hours.

James rattled the paper. Started at the top of the front page. He'd read every story, top to bottom. And the taquitos had passed.

He felt better already.

CHAPTER THIRTY-FOUR

Nix lay in bed, staring at the ceiling. Waiting. Waiting for Cali.

She slumped in the chair next to his bed, head back. Eyes closed. If anyone walked in, they'd think she was sleeping. Anyone watching the cameras would believe the same.

[*Okay.*]

Her voice was inside his head.

[*They're watching,*] she thought to him that morning. [*They're watching.*]

She relayed everything he was supposed to do into his head. It was weird, talking that way. At first, it was like talking with his ears plugged, echoing with the volume up. It took some adjustment, some getting used to, before he was able to exert some control. She explained the new breeds were like wireless computers aggressively taking over his body and brain.

[*We need them to outnumber the old-generation biomites.*]

[*Why?*]

She didn't answer that. He imagined the new breeds were super soldiers, Pacmen gobbling up cell after cell, biomite after biomite. He didn't ask the obvious question, didn't ask... *Am I becoming a computer?*

[*Okay,*] she whispered into his mind again, eyes closed.

Nix pushed onto his elbows. His ribs ached. He took a second before pulling the covers off and sliding his feet over the edge. The floor was hard and cold. His skin, tired. He covered his eyes. A spotlight was blazing through the window; the sun was a beam of pain stabbing his brain.

His fingers crawled over the bed and snatched up the clothes Cali laid out. The top was an orange sherbet blouse, the white pants rolled at the bottom. It took longer than usual to put Cali's clothes on. A few weeks ago, they would've been snug.

When he was dressed, he moved his weight onto his bare feet. His bones were fragile. Joints popped, ligaments creaked. He turned back to the bed, stuffed the extra pillows beneath the covers and pulled the sheet up high like someone was sleeping in the comfort of darkness. He made it to the end of the bed and stopped, taking a breath.

His skin sizzled with the heat of active biomites. *New breeds.*

The door was five steps away. He focused on the handle. Five steps, that was his goal. Get to the door handle first. Get to the door. He took deep breaths, let go of the bed and started after it. Earlier, his sister helped him to the bathroom. He pulled out his catheter with the help of new breeds numbing the pain in his urethra as the balloon-end popped out. He walked back on his own, but he was wobbling.

Like now.

He held his hand out. The last two steps turned into three. He caught the handle and hit the door with his shoulder. The impact made his insides quake. Rattled his lungs. He needed a moment, took one and then another—

[*Go.*]

Cali's voice was a whip, lashing his hand into action. He pulled the door open—

A big man looked up from his paper, sitting outside the door. Not happy.

Nix watched him, waiting for him to do something. But he only stared. Confusion swirled in the glassy orbs beneath his thick brows.

[*Go.*]

Nix yanked the door with unexpected strength. Weakness shook his brittle bones. His muscles were taut. Renewed vigor surged through his nervous system. He was burning adrenaline and needed to go before it hit empty.

"Going to get something to eat," he muttered, like his sister told him to say.

The big man seemed to be working out what the simple phrase meant, like he'd just heard a thick accent and the pieces of what he was seeing and hearing weren't fitting. Nix didn't wait for Cali to jar him with another thought. He started down the middle of the hall before shuffling to the wall for support. He stepped quickly past doorways.

The wheelchair was there, right around the corner. Waiting.

He focused on it and didn't look back. His goal was to get to it.

Nix panted.

He stopped across from his goal. Summoning the courage, he took three quick steps across the hallway's gulf to the other side. The tank had reached empty. There were no steps left in him. He fingered the wheelchair closer and collapsed into the cushioned seat.

Made it.

There he was, in the hall. In the wheelchair.

The big man reading his paper.

Nix backed up.

Out of sight.

Where he waited.

CHAPTER THIRTY-FIVE_

CALI WASN'T A JUGGLER. BUT SHE MANAGED TO KEEP SEVERAL
balls in the air.

So far.

She sat down and appeared to take a nap. She looked exhausted.
She was exhausted and she did need to sleep, but when she curled up
on the chair and closed her eyes, she didn't slumber. Her mind
expanded, feeling the various networks and biomites within a certain
perimeter. Her reach wasn't unlimited—she couldn't connect with
people on the streets—but she was expanding. The new breeds were
learning, were dividing and evolving far quicker than she guessed.
She was becoming a technological telekinetic, wirelessly talking to
anything that chattered computer-speak.

First, she penetrated the security camera fastened in the corner of
the room. Once she tapped the video loop, she followed it back to the
security servers and downloaded several minutes of Nix lying in bed
while Cali stood at the window. She stitched that into a loop and put
it on a seamless repeat cycle. It would fool any passing eyes for a few
hours, and that was more than enough.

Next, she sensed the security guard outside the door. James
was bored, reading a paper. She passively observed his behavior.

There were moments when she could actually see what he was seeing, as if through foggy glass. His biomite content primarily enhanced his reflexes and senses, in particular his sight and hearing. He was naturally suspicious and calmly disciplined. Despite the boredom and aches of long periods of waiting, he remained vigilant.

She didn't want to do this. If it failed, it was all over. But there was no other way. Now or never.

Now or never.

[*Go.*]

Cali occasionally checked on the security loop while firmly maintaining a connection with James's biomites. Her next diversion was Nix. She stayed connected to monitor his health and strength. Even if everything went right, this might be too much. She could end up pushing him too far, drive him into overload. There would be no need for Marcus to come shut him down.

She might do the job for him.

When he was dressed, Cali began to manipulate James's biomites. Slowly, she took control of his sensory input. When Nix reached the door, when he pulled it open, she made him see what she wanted him to see.

It was a struggle, a delicate balance. If she pushed too hard, he'd go unconscious and draw attention. He had to believe what he was seeing. He had to put his suspicions aside and see her going to the cafeteria like she'd done several times over the past week. Those memories supported the false input.

Nix started down the hall.

James's suspicion eased. He accepted what just happened. But that wasn't the hard part. He needed to forget she just left, needed to believe that she'd walked past him to get her bag. Cali opened her eyes and grabbed the bag off the floor. The security loop was still showing Nix sleeping, her staring out the window.

When she opened the door, James nearly slid out of her mental grasp. His biomites shuddered like molecules put to flame, threatening to slip from her grasp like ornery children who didn't want to do as they were told.

She squeezed him.

It was a tiny jolt, one that temporarily knocked him into a blackout. It would feel like a head rush, and while he was senseless, she planted a reasonable explanation in his unconscious, that he was bored and tired and achy. And there was no way Cali and Nix could escape, not when their biomites were being monitored. If they left the hospital, an alarm would go off and they could track them. And if they got too far away, they could shut them down.

There was hardly a need for a guard.

Nix was in the wheelchair. Three nurses were down the hall. Cali connected with their biomites and simply commanded that they weren't their patients, no one that they should be concerned with. Cali turned the wheelchair around and pushed it to the end of the hall and waited for the elevator.

Nix sat with his arms in his lap. His complexion was good, his head upright. She liked what she was seeing. His strength was better than she anticipated. The elevator arrived. Cali sensed it was empty before the doors slid open, accompanied by the sound of a bell.

She pushed him inside and hit the button. They both stared down an empty hallway while the doors slid closed. She resisted hugging him. Instead, they stared at each other in the warped reflection of the silver doors. They made it this far, but it was only the start. And hardly that.

[*Ready?*] she thought.

Nix nodded.

They instinctively took deep breaths, preparing for a deep dive into the unknown. Cali closed her eyes. She was firmly connected with Nix's new breeds. She held her next thought-command on the edge of her mind, like the crosshairs aligned with a target, finger on the trigger.

[*Off.*]

Cali's legs buckled. She caught herself on the wheelchair. Her skin tingled as her new breeds compensated for the sudden deactivation of ALL the old-generation biomites. She'd shut down a third of her functioning body. The new breeds struggled to keep her from passing out, to keep her organs functioning and her brain from freezing.

Nix was limp.

But he was breathing. His pulse a distant rhythm.

He was alive. Barely.

They needed time to recover, for the new breeds to complete the transition. Now that the old-generation biomites were off.

Now that they were invisible.

Cali's gut dropped as the elevator lurched upward.

CHAPTER THIRTY-SIX_

BAD FOOD.

Swamps soaked James's armpits. A toxic fog lingered behind his eyes; fuzzy edges haloed the newspaper. He needed to call in backup. He wouldn't be any good puking on the floor. Not that there was anyone he needed to be chasing down, but he was going to be in the bathroom within the next ten minutes.

He reached for his phone—

The doctor trotted around the corner, his lab coat fluttering behind him, a nurse on his heels. James stood up. They passed him, not paying any attention to him, hit the door and rushed inside. James wandered in behind.

The doctor yanked the covers back, exposing pillows. "Where is he?"

James filled the doorway, hand on the heavy door. He didn't have enough sense to even shake his head.

"This was in the bathroom." The nurse handed the catheter to the doctor.

He put his hands on his hips, looking around the room like Nix might be hiding in a corner. He even bent slightly, peering under the bed.

James hadn't moved.

"Call your boss," the doctor said, pushing past him.

James was going to puke, for sure.

Rodney Chandler was a superhero geek.

His dad boasted the world's greatest collection of comic books, all cataloged and sealed in mold-proof sleeves and stored in the basement. He would let Rodney look at the covers, but not take them out. God, no.

But when the old man was away, Rodney slipped into the musty downstairs and flipped through the paperbacks organized alphabetically and by edition. Superman, Green Lantern, Thor, Hulk, X-Men... he never knew where to start, the colors so vivid.

He'd read them by flashlight, afraid to turn on the light in case someone passed the house. The old smell of the pages tingled his sinuses. And the thrill of getting one over on his old man twisted his guts. Made him smile.

He watched all the movies, collected the posters. Bought his own vintage comic books and hid them from his old man's grubby mitts. When he was old enough to get seeded with brain biomites, he experienced submersion films: virtual trips into the world of superheroes. He became the Man of Steel, flew around the world, stopped speeding bullets and saved the distressed. After a while, he played the villain. Sometimes he even won.

But even that got stale.

Eventually, the submersion film ended and he woke up, plain old Rodney. Nothing special, nothing good.

Just another street rat.

But there were people that could help, people that had money and access to biomites that others didn't. And didn't cost Rodney a dime. All they asked in return were favors. That was it.

It'll be painful, they said. It'll hurt like a bitch until the biomites acclimate, change your body. You understand?

Rodney half-listened. He was in, no matter what. He was tired of being Rodney. He'd give anything to matter.

But they weren't joking. Rodney sweated out a recovery that lasted months in some dirty basement room. He hardly remembered it, just the pain and the screaming.

After that, the power.

They gave him a phone, told him they'd call, and that he better answer when they did. Months went by before his first call. In fact, he'd forgotten about it. He was way into the new powers. I mean, he was a superhero, for Christ's sake. He considered moonlighting his powers for the good of the city, but the people told him absolutely not, under no circumstances was he allowed to exercise them.

Just wait.

He listened, sort of. He went back to his apartment and practiced. They couldn't expect him to be any good if he didn't. He set up scenarios and pretended to be the good guy. Always the good guy. By the time he'd gotten his first call, he'd saved a thousand imaginary victims.

But now he was standing on West Twenty-Third Street outside a tall building. New York was especially cold that winter, but Rodney didn't feel it. He pulled the hood over his eyes not because he was cold. He leaned against the building and watched the traffic with head bowed. Maybe someone would tell him to move on, but he wasn't begging.

He was waiting.

He flexed his fingers inside the front pocket of his jacket, keeping them limber. There was a metal ball beneath his tongue, filling his mouth with a metallic tang. He switched it from cheek to cheek, watching traffic.

Watching traffic.

When the black limo rolled around the corner, he almost swallowed it. His throat seized, hidden fingers clenched. Fear froze him against the wall. He shifted his weight and dipped his head as the limo stopped at the curb. Car doors opened.

Rodney slid the phone out and swiped his thumb over the glass. A picture illuminated the screen, a photo of a man with gray hair. The photo the people sent him. They needed a favor. And he was their man.

He kept the phone out, watching the fatneck security guard stand next to the back door while another fatneck opened it. He felt them watching him. He was far enough away to be harmless, unless he had a gun. And if that happened, they'd move. So they watched him while the silver-haired man stepped out of the limo. He was speaking on a phone, eyebrows knitted in anger, lips pulled back over white veneers.

Rodney rolled the weighty ball onto his tongue and curled the edges around it like a fleshy barrel. His chest expanded slowly. Expanded fully. No one would notice.

No one would expect it.

He'd practiced it so many times, so many ways. Always getting the bad guy, always the ones that deserved it. Somehow, Rodney knew this guy was bad.

He unleashed a powerful burst of wind, firing the metal ball through his biomite-reinforced tongue. There was a sound of a cork as it passed his lips.

The wet sound of it popping the silver-hair's right eye, sinking into gray matter.

His head snapped.

The fatnecks looked around.

People stepped off the sidewalk; some began to gather. Others called 911. Rodney pushed off the wall and hustled away from the scene. He felt like he was falling, a thrill spun in his groin like he'd pulled a vintage comic from its plastic and inhaled the musty flavor.

And when a beefy hand landed on his shoulder and spun him around... when the security guard clenched his neck, cut off his air, began to drag him back... blades slid out between his knuckles and plunged into the fatneck's belly. He tasted salty blood, licked the man's intestines with the blades like razor-sharp tongues.

Felt the cold chill as he pulled them out.

Felt the wind on his cheeks as he ran away. Ran faster than a man should run, the biomites fueling his muscles with adrenaline, the biomite-blades retracting into his arms, stinging in their slots.

He was a superhero.

CHAPTER THIRTY-SEVEN_

MARCUS DRUMMED HIS FINGERS ON THE COUNTER. THE HOTEL clerk tapped on the keys, checking in a woman with frizzy hair and a kid attached to her leg, a thumb in his mouth. The rugrat stared at Marcus, a snot bubble swelling with each breath.

Marcus turned his back.

His driver rolled his luggage to the car and put it in the trunk. He'd wait for Marcus to call, swing by and pick him up when all this was done.

Marcus looked at his watch. 1:00. He didn't want to be in Chicago a minute longer. When it hit 3:00, those two halfskins were getting shut down and he wasn't going to linger. He'd wasted enough time on this charade. This was done, 3:00, on the dot.

Mother was an honest system. She was a machine only interested in data. She recorded every event, watched where people went, alerted the authorities when they went redline, and shut them down when they went halfskin. She had no feelings, had no investment about who lived and died. It was a simple system, an honest one.

But Marcus reserved the right to keep it that way. Sometimes, honesty can make the wrong choice. Dr. Cali was clearly damaged from her biomite seeding. His people had interviewed her co-workers and neighbors; they'd done a full analysis. Her basement was a fully operational biomite lab that had been cleansed of data. She was up to something and smart enough to cover her tracks.

And while her biomite content mysteriously stayed below the redline, he was sure that she had rigged it. Somehow, she was fooling the meters, changing what they were reading. Marcus had been around enough halfskins to know when they were over the line. He could smell it. They had a way about them. They were slightly hollow, distant and mechanical.

Machine-like.

That was her. Cali was halfskin, he knew it. If she thought she could walk around fooling him, she was wrong. She met the one person that could remedy her deceit. So, yeah, Marcus set the record straight. It wasn't his meter that cheated the reading, he simply changed what was being reported through Mother.

She would shut her down.

"I want smoking," demanded the woman with the snotty kid growing off her leg. "I said that already."

Marcus sighed, drumming the counter with his fingernails. The woman glared at him, giving him a chance to say something. His phone buzzed. He put it to his ear, not taking his eyes off her.

"Yeah."

The kid made sucking sounds around his thumb. Marcus wanted to wipe his nose with the mother's dress.

He barely heard what was said.

Not because he was distracted. Because it was impossible.

"What do you mean *disappeared*?"

CHAPTER THIRTY-EIGHT_

EIGHT NURSES.

Three med techs.

One janitor cleaning up vomit down the hall.

Cali sat in the corner of room 512. Eyes closed. Mind plugged into the fifth floor's network, reading who was clocked in. She didn't know what they were doing, except for the janitor that was just called up after Mr. Craven regurgitated his chicken salad on his way to the bathroom.

She sorted through the database and read the patient list. She knew this room had recently been vacated when Ms. Sheila Hartley had been discharged after hernia surgery. Cali immediately filled the room with an alias Mr. Calvin Brown, a man that suffered from diverticulitis. His mother would be in the room with him, sitting in the chair with her eyes closed.

Mr. Brown was currently sleeping.

Cali had triggered a shutdown of their old-generation biomites, the very technology that allowed Mother to follow them, to monitor them, to pass along their location, health and activity to anyone with authority to receive it. Namely, Mr. Marcus Anderson. And now that all the old-generation biomites were deactivated, they were invisible.

Mother couldn't see them.

Nix wasn't ready for the shutdown. There were still too few new breeds to support his body without the assistance of the old-generation ones. But there wasn't a choice. If they stayed on the second floor, if Marcus shut them down with all the bodyguards around them and Cali and Nix survived, suspicion would drop like a hammer.

The new breeds would be discovered.

She had to get them away, to hide. To survive. Invisible, they could make their escape. But she couldn't just wheel Nix out. She could barely stand and she was in much better shape than her brother, and even that sudden loss about did her in. They needed to rest, give the new breeds time to flush their systems and take the place of the old-generation biomites, to keep their organs functioning, their muscles contracting, nervous systems firing.

Cali went to the sink, filled the pitcher with water and drank. She'd been to the bathroom multiple times, excreting the dead biomites that were filtered through the liver and kidneys. She filled a cup, bent the scrunchy elbow of a straw, and lifted Nix's head. He wasn't asleep, but conscious just enough to feel the plastic tip on his lips, to pull the water. She was constantly reminding him to drink, to drink more. She couldn't move him to the bathroom; he had to do his business right there. In the bed.

She'd worry about that later.

Cali sat back down. Felt like she'd run a marathon. She wanted to sleep, needed it badly. Right now, she needed to watch, needed to wait for their opportunity. When Nix was ready to move, they'd have to move. Hiding inside the hospital wouldn't last, even if she could manipulate the computer database. Eventually someone would come looking: they'd see past her illusions.

She closed her eyes.

She listened to the chatter of intercom calls and secure phones. She caught fragments of medical talk and concerned families in waiting rooms. She stayed open, listening. Watching.

Waiting.

CHAPTER THIRTY-NINE_

Marcus marched out of the elevator.

His shoes hammered the floor. Coat unbuttoned. White shirt puffed over his belt and tie slightly undone. He went down the middle of the hall, eyes ahead. Others moved to the side. He turned the corner, hand out, punching open the door.

Several people were inside.

Most were dressed darkly, unassuming clothing that cloaked security guards from standing out in a crowd. Their chatter was cut still.

The balding man stopped. He looked around, hands on hips. He met all their eyes.

"Someone," he said, drawing out the word, "tell me what the *hell* happened."

The last word hissed with steam.

James was the only one in the room sitting. He worked his tongue to moisten his lips. He stood up. He explained that he might have been poisoned, or maybe it was just bad food, but whatever it was... he couldn't quite remember. Cali left the room to get something to eat, and then they were gone.

"What do you mean, *gone?*"

He shrugged.

"Use your training, son. Did the woman have her brother stuffed down her pants? Did she fold him up and tuck him into her bag? HOW THE HELL COULD HE BE GONE?"

Again, shrug. No one had answers.

One of the security agents, a tall skinny man with thinning hair, recounted what they knew. Marcus paced the room, listening while he peeked in the bathroom, looked at the bed, picked up a water pitcher. They'd interviewed everyone on the floor; no one had seen either of them leaving. The security camera was running a loop of them still in the room.

"How could they do that?" he asked.

"We're looking into that," the skinny man said.

She had no access to her laptop. Her phone, perhaps, had hacking capability, but that would require a significant amount of time to set up and execute. Certainly, they'd know what she was doing if that was it.

Impossible. Just... impossible. There was no way she could shut herself down, shut her brother's biomites down, and disappear. Their bodies had to be somewhere. It was not possible to survive without biomites. She wasn't halfskin, not like his reader reported. No, she was probably redline and that would be enough to cripple her. But the kid... he'd be dead.

The bodies have to be SOMEWHERE.

And she couldn't make them invisible. Mother was synchronized with the unique strands of artificial DNA strands that composed every single biomite in production, artificial DNA that allowed them to function. Even if that was somehow sidestepped, even if she was able to recombine the biomite DNA, there was the mitochondria power supply. Mother could follow that.

The woman was a brilliant scientist, but she couldn't accomplish something like that. None of the biomite corporations were allowed to experiment with off-grid synthesis of biomite production without the consent of the government without risking loss of license. The Army Corp of Engineers had been working on developing invisi-biomites and hadn't even come close.

Have I underestimated her?

No. Impossible.

Had to be another explanation.

"Sir?"

Marcus jerked around.

"They were last located in the elevator," Skinny said. "The elevator went up and stopped on every floor. No one recognized them, but there's no evidence they went down. They might still be in the building. The exits are all covered and we're going floor to floor."

"Good," Marcus said. "Check all the rooms, all the closets. I want everything turned over. I want IDs checked, I want every syringe, every cottonball, every last Band-Aid examined for these two people, do you understand?"

They nodded.

"Do not notify the Chicago police, not yet. If they're still in the building, I want to handle this."

They didn't ask questions. They knew a media shitstorm was on the horizon. Once the media got wind of a problem, it got harder to solve. And if they heard that two people went off the grid and hadn't been found—whether they were alive or not—it was going to create a landslide of legal issues.

This was a potential Hydra.

Marcus's thighs were cold. Uncertainty swirled.

James's eyes were still a bit hazy.

"Get him checked out," Marcus said. "I want to know what happened to him so it doesn't happen again. And get the doctor, now. Where is he?"

"On the way."

"I want all the records of this Nixon Richards now. I want to see all the blood analysis, all the tests they ran since he arrived. Make those available ASAP. If his sister somehow tampered…" He stopped, not wanting to utter it out loud, even though they were all thinking it. "I'll be in the doctor's office."

They moved out.

James was the last to go.

CHAPTER FORTY_

Chug-chug.

Chug-chug.

Machines. Chugging and pumping. Working in synchronicity, a majestic symphony of artificial sounds.

The sound of work.

A furnace glowed red hot, somewhere. A furnace burning with friction, with energy. He felt it, out there, warming the universe.

Vibrations jittered on the skin of an invisible membrane, a body that contained the identity known as Nix. It quivered and jiggled and sang. Somewhere, ants crawled along that barrier, their legs touching and marching and going *chug-chug.*

Chug-chug.

Colors mixed with sound and energy. Primary colors shot like stars, crossing paths, running parallel, overlapping to make secondary colors. Sometimes they swirled and curved. He'd recognize a face, eyes and a nose, that would quickly melt away in the growing heat as the furnace pumped exhaust into the world. Sweat tracked the skin somewhere out there, tickling small hairs and tiny nerves.

He began to sink. Down he was going, down somewhere on a

smooth ride, like an elevator taking him to the basement, dipping him in an essence that was warm and cleansing.

And slowly he went. Slowly he went.

Nix sank closer to where the furnace was burning.

He sensed there weren't floors where the ride was going, it was just sinking and sinking and more sinking. To the center of the furnace where the *chug-chug* banged away.

Deeper, it went.

Hotter, it became.

Nix knew where the ride would lead if it did not stop. He knew it would take him to the center of existence, into the heart of the fire. To oblivion.

If it did not stop. Did not stop.

And the *chug-chug* rang like a gong.

It hammered.

It sang. It called. It created.

And it burned.

Nix felt the fabric of his life—his existence—was curling and graying like the edges of a parchment meeting the freshly struck tip of a match. He was thinning, fraying, and fading.

He could take no more.

If he went deeper.

He would be no longer—

But the ride began to slow—

Slow—

Stop.

Near a furnace, a surface red hot, filling everything with light. It surged like a belly, like breath filled it, a heart beating inside.

Beating to the *chug-chug*.

Nix felt the elevator that held him so close to oblivion; it clung by a delicate thread that could be easily snipped by the edge of a butterfly wing. He waited, dangling precipitously close to touching the surface, a touch that would melt everything.

He felt his skin peel.

Bones char.

He melted into a fleshy puddle of goo that would leak through the cracks of the elevator floor and drip on the furnace and sizzle and evaporate and become nothing, become nothing, become—

And then it lifted.

Ever so slowly, he pulled away, lifted up. Carefully. Lovingly.

He inched away from death. Away from the furnace.

No longer a puddle.

And up he went where it was cooler. Where there were streaking colors and sounds again. He remembered things. Remembered who he was, entertained thoughts of what he looked like and where he'd been. He wished he could hide in the lagoon, like he could call it up and go there, soak in the ocean's buoyant grip and lay his head back, bathe in the soft droplets floating from the waterfall.

And upward he went—

Through the thoughts, through the colors and smells and images until—

Wake up, Nix.

He felt a membrane wrap around him, sealing him inside. Defining him. It felt like plastic wrap.

He recognized, finally, his body.

He opened his eyes in a dark room.

CHAPTER FORTY-ONE

A FACE LOOKED BACK FROM THE MIRROR. SUNKEN EYES, CAVED cheeks. A cold sore—red and angry—shined on her upper lip. She ran the tip of her tongue over it and felt the sting.

Felt good.

Cali's hands quivered on her eyes, her nerves quaking with doubt.

Biomites were artificial clones of biological cells. They required oxygen and nutrients. Food, something she hadn't had in thirty-six hours. Or more. She had no appetite and figured she could go another thirty-six hours, if needed.

She was still drinking water. Her urine had cleared and lost the biomite smell—something like putty. She suspected the majority of the old-generation biomites had been flushed out.

The blinds were drawn. Darkness was outside. After midnight, somewhere in the range of 2:00 a.m.

The hospital was quiet, except for the sounds of some of the suffering down the hall and the hushed tones of late-shift nurses. She programmed their computers to show their room was empty due to equipment failure. Nurses wouldn't need to open the door until maintenance arrived in the morning.

She listened to the radio and phone chatter, eavesdropping on conversations, but heard nothing except gossip and sorrow. No security guards reporting their positions.

No Marcus Anderson.

She dared not hope for the best. She wasn't desperate enough to believe they'd gone to the streets of Chicago in search of them, leaving the doors wide open. Her head was stuffy, brain a bit sluggish as it readjusted to the flushing, but she wasn't delusional.

They were out there.

I'm not delusional.

Nix looked good, his vitals improved. She'd thought she lost him shortly before midnight. His pulse faded. There was nothing she could do but wait. And he came back from the edge. The new breeds wouldn't let him die; they kept him alive. His forehead was hot to touch, but that was good. They were fighting.

She wasn't going to lose him.

But she needed him moving normally. If they could leave the hospital at full strength, walk out like a healthy pair, she could handle interference much more effectively, alter what people were seeing and believing. They could do it when visiting hours had closed, when the day shift had gone home and surgeries were done and nurses were just trying to keep people asleep.

They'd do it then.

She sat down and rested her head, fully aware she might fall asleep. All was quiet and maybe she could get a few hours, setting an internal alarm to wake up. Her eyes were instantly weighted, like the thought gave her body permission to check out for a spell.

If she'd had that thought seconds earlier, if she'd decided not to visit the restroom, the ending would've been different.

Her eyelids were on their last drop, preparing to lock down, when a disturbance snapped them open. A nurse protested with hushed tones, but harshly enough to carry through all the doors along that wing. She was answered by a man with no ability to whisper.

Cali jumped to her feet.

She was at the door, eyes wide, mind scanning. There was nothing in the airwaves, but the nurse was obviously agitated. Cali felt her anger. It was late; there was no way the man was going to look in every room, not on her watch. If he had any questions, he could ask and she might be able to tell him, but there was no way he was going to—

The man was done talking.

The nurse was unable to stop him.

Cali's heart slammed her ribs. She touched the door, head against the cool surface, hoping to get an idea of where he was going. The nurse's voice was trailing. She might be going off to search for help. Or she was following the man.

She quieted her racing mind, reaching out to sense biomite activity in relation to where she was. She picked up on the nurse's. And the man's.

Cali hovered on the fringes of his biomites, careful not to influence them in any way, wary they may be expecting manipulation after they examined what she did to James. She simply watched what direction he was going.

The C-wing.

He would come this way, though. He'd stop in the room. Cali might be able to influence what he was seeing, but it was a risk. Any hint of manipulation could set off an alarm and bring a mob of gun-toting maniacs. And if this turned into a chase, Cali and Nix were not going to win. Not from the fifth floor.

They had to leave. *Now.*

"Wake up, Nix." Cali bent over the bed, gently shaking his arm.

Nothing, at first. She shook again and, this time, his eyes opened with effort. There was no focus, plenty of confusion. His breath was humid, rancid. Lips coated with gummy residue, skin flaking off his cheeks.

Cali pulled back the sheets and looked away. She swallowed back the acrid bile that erupted past her tongue. He'd been eliminating urine where he lay. She could clean him up when they were ready. That wasn't now.

Nix was already falling back asleep. She sat him up, whispering what they were going to do. She couldn't hear the nurse anymore. At the pace the man was going, he would reach the end of the wing in five minutes and come back in their direction.

She got new pants on Nix. They were her pants, but he couldn't go without clothes. Not naked.

And not soiled.

"One foot," she whispered, leaning him forward. "Put your weight on it, then the other."

Nix followed her directions like a compliant zombie, lifting one foot then the other. He supported his weight, standing and swaying with her help. She led him to the wheelchair.

That was good.

He was moving, responsive.

And not dead.

Cali ran to the door and cracked it open. The hall was empty.

A nurse would later report seeing a woman and a boy on the elevator around 2:00 a.m., just before the doors closed. She didn't think much about it at the time. She couldn't explain why.

CHAPTER FORTY-TWO

Marcus unbuckled his watch and rubbed his wrist. He shut the laptop and made sure it was locked before getting up. Another stretch, this one for the lower back. The nurse paid him no attention. She was busy at her station, behind the counter.

He dropped the laptop in a leather saddlebag and slung it over his shoulder. There were plenty of people coming through the nurses' station, plenty that never looked at him. No one seemed that happy in the middle of the night on the biomite wing.

The floor was quiet except for an occasional moan from the B wing, some old man that suffered burns over half his body when his tractor turned over. Biomites were rebuilding the skin and dulling the nervous system, but still he moaned. Marcus would gamble the old man moaned on a good day.

He waited for the elevator, watching the lit arrow as if that would get the car there faster. He wondered if Cali and Nix used that elevator to leave the hospital. Wondered if they were still in the building. Wondered how the hell they even left the room. He hadn't told the Secretary about the event. He glanced at his phone.

Fourteen unanswered calls.

Come daylight, he'd have to answer one. Just through the night, that's all he wanted. The first twelve hours were the most important. He'd reluctantly released photos to the Chicago police without a full explanation. Names and faces, that's all. People of federal interest. Their help would be much appreciated. There was a chance the two were on the streets, hiding in an alley or passed out in a car. If they tried to use a credit card or the phone, Marcus's people would fall on them like vultures. Marcus needed to be patient. They couldn't be far.

Couldn't be healthy.

But how the hell did they disappear?

That's why he needed to find them more than anything. They fell off Mother's radar, somehow erased Nix's test results, masked the security camera... this was the real problem. They had done the impossible and Marcus needed to find out how. It was no fluke. And if it had happened, if it spread to other people, to other biomites... this was something the doctor failed to understand. Of course, how do you make sense to a biomite sympathist like him?

That's why Marcus was working from the nurses' station. He had commandeered the chief doctor's desk. The man walked in and stood in front of his decadent fish tank.

"Out."

Marcus didn't look up from his work. "I'll only need your space through the night, Doctor."

"Not in here, you won't."

"I don't think you understand." Marcus punched a few keys. "Two halfskins escaped your floor. They have also escaped detection, something you haven't been able to explain. Their capture is imperative."

"We don't call them halfskins."

"They're 50%. What else are they?"

"They're human, Mr. Anderson. Biomite-enhanced humans that, otherwise, wouldn't be alive."

"Whether you call them halfskin or not does not change what they are. It does not change the fact that they are in violation of a federal law that no human being can be composed of more than 50% biomite replacement, Doctor. That is the law and I am enforcing it."

"Not from my office, you won't."

Marcus finally looked up and sat back. They stared like gunfighters.

"You think you're saving them?" Marcus asked. "You're only delaying their death."

"Medicine has been doing that for centuries."

"Medicine? Is that what you call this? You replace their bodies with microscopic machines, a little at a time, and you call that medicine?"

"Modern-day medicine, Mr. Anderson."

"Medicine involves antibiotics and repairing the flesh, not replacing it. What you're doing is killing the soul, selling pleasure for a price they can never pay."

"Pleasure?" The doctor slid his hands into the front pockets of the lab coat. "Walk this floor, Mr. Anderson, and listen. Do you hear pleasure? There's a boy that needs a new heart valve, a woman that needs a kidney, and a man with a brain tumor. They'll all survive because of biomites. It's what we do in a hospital, we heal them. Biomites have made that possible like never before."

The doctor pulled the door open.

"Now, I'll ask you to leave once more. Don't make me call security."

Marcus considered the demand. Certainly he could force the doctor to reconsider. This wing benefitted substantially from federal funding. But he couldn't play that card, not yet. He needed to operate quietly. For now.

He snapped the laptop closed and pushed away from the desk. He stopped on his way out. "You know where they are, don't you."

The doctor shook his head.

"When this is over, if I find out you helped them escape, your career will be over."

The doctor was unperturbed.

The elevator arrived.

Marcus stepped into an empty car and went down to the cafeteria for some coffee. He'd sit there and monitor his agents from a booth. He checked his phone again. There was about three hours of daylight left to do it.

CHAPTER FORTY-THREE

Their reflection in the elevator door was distorted. Still, that couldn't hide the vacancy in her eyes, the dark pockets they stared out from. Nix looked like an invalid, head cocked to the side, mouth open. His cheeks were pale and shiny, like a frost victim. She leaned over, inspecting the tiny cracks along his cheeks. The skin was flaking off, like a snake shedding skin. She rubbed her own cheeks. Skin fluttered like dandruff. She peeled a sheet from her arm.

They passed the third floor. She felt five people as they went by. They were blips on her radar, their biomites signaling like stagnant ships on a sea of ether.

Second floor, three more. Two nurses, one orderly.

The world was unfolding around her like another dimension, her body interconnecting with everything with an electronic pulse. The language was unspoken, belted out in waves and particles, falling on her like photons on a light-sensitive plate, patterns that were immediately translated.

Connecting. I'm no longer separate from the world.

The elevator slowed. Stopped.

Cali held the button down on the panel, keeping the doors closed. She reached out with her mind. There was no one within range. She didn't expect anyone to be in this part of the hospital where janitorial and maintenance clocked in and out. Not this time of night. There was an exit to her right, down the hall and through the loading dock. Her finger slipped off the button.

The doors opened. She looked in both directions.

Nix's head bobbled as the wheels bounced out of the elevator. Cali pushed at a half-trot. She kept her mind open, her feet moving. The loading dock was at the end, to the left. There was a doorway that led through a locker room that—

SOMEONE.

The wheels squeaked. Cali's feet tripped up; she almost let go. She stopped in the middle of the hall, fingers trembling. Someone was up ahead. Someone at the loading dock. She stayed there, in the hall, afraid to move.

But she had to move.

She had to keep going.

They were out in the open. Hiding wasn't an option, not anymore.

The chair eased forward, the rubber wheels silent again. Cali was on her toes, breath bouncing in her throat. She closed her eyes, reaching out to feel the body that was between them and the exit. She read the person's biomites like seeing words through a telescope. She knew who he was before peeking around the corner, seeing the man with short hair standing in a doorway, holding the door open to blow smoke.

Federal security.

They had the exit covered.

Had them all covered.

She leaned against the wall, head bouncing lightly. Her brother, still silent in the chair. She needed to think, just for a minute. They couldn't outrun him. The second they were recognized, they would be caught. They needed a head start. A big one. If she tried to blind him like James... no, they'd be ready for that. She assumed they'd know what she did to get out of the hospital room. They'd know when their biomites were being manipulated.

She took a minute.

She thought. *They'd be expecting her.*

And then closed her eyes. There was no other choice.

CHAPTER FORTY-FOUR_

Sam Craven was still considered a rookie.

He'd been working for the feds two and a half years, but they still called him rookie. He'd been on numerous assignments and saw nothing but boredom. He'd fired his gun plenty of times at the range and bagged deer during the season, but when on duty, nothing ever happened.

And he didn't expect anything to happen this time.

The suspects were harmless, although that could be deceiving. A couple of halfskins on the run. How that happened, they weren't told. Just a brother and sister due to be shut down and somehow fell off the grid. Intelligence suggested they were on their way out of town, but there was no evidence they ever left the hospital, so Sam was holding down one of the exits.

Hours went by and he stayed at attention. But the room was stuffy and he was jonesing for a smoke. He leaned the door open and fired up a Winston, pulling the first drag deep. The smoke hit the nighttime air, thick and white. The paper crackled with satisfaction.

He wasn't distracted. He had an eye on the outside and inside. No one would get within twenty feet without being seen. And if he saw them, his biomites would automatically trigger a facial recognition alarm and the rest of the team would converge. *Lights out, halfskins.*

But they weren't here, not in the building. No way.

If those two could brain-scramble James, if they could loop that camera, then they wouldn't stick around the hospital, now would they? Holding down the loading dock was a waste of time, really. They should be on the street, interviewing people, analyzing biomite activity... all the shit he'd been trained to do. Not acting like a doorstop.

The third drag, his head buzzed—

The cigarette cherry popped on the concrete in a shower of embers.

Sam let the smoke leak from his nostrils.

Looking in. Out. And back.

Something was buzzing. They were prepped for this. This was what James experienced before the escape. There was an analysis of his brain waves recorded by his biomites, a manipulation of his perception that made him blank out, almost skip time.

Sam put his finger to his ear.

He didn't want to call, not yet. Give it a second. Just a second and then he'd report it. He wasn't 100% sure it wasn't a cigarette buzz, and if it was, he was sure to catch—

Snip.

A black flash covered his eyes.

Just a moment, like a movie skipped a few frames.

He wasn't sure, did he blink, or was he thinking, or was he... he was just so confused...

"*What is it, Craven?*" a voice called into his ear.

Sam's lips moved. Nothing came out.

"*Craven?*"

He needed to say something. He must've called out and reported the disturbance; he wasn't sure. He couldn't explain it was an accident; something was happening. He couldn't talk, couldn't talk, couldn't think straight, he just needed to open up and shout for help—

THERE! THERE!

In the lot! Across the lot! A woman pushing a wheelchair.

They got by him.

They got by him and he couldn't...

"SUSPECTS IN SIGHT!" he shouted. "AT THE LOADING DOCK, WOMAN PUSHING A WHEELCHAIR."

Whatever gripped him had let go.

"IN PURSUIT!"

It had him paralyzed, had him trapped, but she was out of range, lost control of him before they could get out of sight. And now he saw them. Now he knew where they were. And it was only a matter of time. Once there was visual contact and the chopper was overhead, it was over.

Sam was off the loading dock, carefully following. He didn't want to get too close just yet.

His hand dropped to his gun.

Maybe this time.

CHAPTER FORTY-FIVE_

Her mind was a delicate hand.

It observed the man in the doorway, blowing smoke, wishing for something better. Something more exciting. His name was Sam Craven. He was twenty-six years old. Never married. Had dated a few times but preferred to keep his options open. He went home for Christmas every year, argued politics and kissed everyone on the cheek when he left.

He was a good man.

A reliable one.

Alert.

Cali sensed his paranoia, knew he was looking for her and Nix as well as any strange sensations. He was primed to pounce. And she preyed on that. He was looking across the parking lot. She could see what he saw—as if she rented his eyesight. There was open asphalt and faded yellow lines. Several cars were spread out beneath the sodium lights. Nothing moved.

Nothing at all.

Cali imagined what she wanted to see in that open space. She pictured it in her own mind as clear as if she had conjured it up on a screen. She played it out, all the way to the end, made sure the details were rich and convincing. Once through was all she had time for. Once through to make it work.

All at once, she projected it into Sam Craven's mind. He felt the manipulation first, buzzing at the back of his head like wires had been yanked from a secret door just below his hairline and short-circuited. Alarms fired. He began to look around, began to call for backup, but not before the image crossed his mind like footprints in freshly laid snow.

He saw her pushing a wheelchair. Saw her hustling to get out of sight, surprised when she turned around to see him pursuing. Saw her race the wheelchair to the sidewalk and around privet hedges to the street beyond.

His voice trailed off, shouting for his companions to hurry. He had them. He had them dead to rights. He was in pursuit.

The doorway clear.

Cali slipped out of the loading dock and turned to the right. Her mind open, searching for others, she pushed her brother around the corner, under a rampart and around another corner until they reached an empty street.

She didn't stop running, despite the weakness in her legs and dimness in her vision. She rushed down the sidewalk, across the street, in the opposite direction of the federal agents.

She hurried toward freedom.

CHAPTER FORTY-SIX

Marcus was one of the last to reach the loading dock.

His hard-soled shoes weren't meant for running on linoleum and he bit it on the first corner out of the cafeteria, catching his knee on the corner of a vending machine. He managed a skip-run the rest of the way, slowing around the corners. He couldn't feel his leg. His breath labored, heart slamming in his ears.

Craven had called on the radio. Marcus spilled his coffee while he stuffed his laptop into his briefcase. At first, he thought he'd apprehended them. *I GOT THEM! I GOT THEM!*

The radio crackled with updates as Marcus worked his way to Craven's position. He couldn't be sure, it sounded like they were still in pursuit. He couldn't imagine how they were still chasing after a woman pushing a wheelchair, but there were many scenarios. This was new ground they were embarking upon. They needed to catch these two.

Had to.

Agent Starling was standing on the loading dock. Marcus stopped in the doorway, leaning over to catch his breath. His pant leg was stuck to a dark spot that was growing over his knee.

Starling raised his finger. "That way, sir."

Marcus nodded. He went down the ramp, hopping mostly on his good leg. His other leg stiffened. He struggled across the parking lot, his chest tightening. The lights turned his skin the color of porridge. He was walking when he turned the corner at the hedges. Across the street, only fifty yards down, three of his men were gathered outside a six-story parking garage. Marcus walked easily, catching his breath when he arrived. The briefcase repeatedly hammered his hip. He set it on the sidewalk.

"Update," he demanded.

A short man built like a roadblock told him that the suspects had slipped past the automated gate; they were last seen fleeing to the second level. All the exits were covered. Three men were currently searching the levels. They were on the third floor. So far, no sign.

"It shouldn't be long, sir."

"Where's Craven?"

"On the other side of the building."

"Get him over here."

Marcus sat on the edge of a concrete planter. His knee wouldn't bend. He left it out straight. Craven hustled over a few minutes later and stood in front of him. Marcus sat up, but didn't try to stand.

"What happened?"

Craven went through the details. He was on post at the loading dock when his biomites acted funny, like James had described when the woman and boy escaped. He managed to stay conscious when he noticed them halfway across the parking lot. At that point, he gave chase while calling for backup. Craven saw them enter the parking garage but lost them in the dark as they headed for the second deck.

"And there's no way they could've escaped?"

"No, sir. I took up position next to the elevator and stairwell with the ramp in view. There is no way out of this parking garage, unless they jumped."

Marcus shook his head. Thinking, thinking.

Craven wanted to go back to his post. He wanted to catch them. Marcus jerked his head, telling him to leave. Craven acknowledged him and stopped to speak with the other agents.

The distance from the privet hedge to the parking garage was only fifty yards. The parking lot was about fifty yards. A guy like Craven—someone fit, lean, and young—could cover that distance in fifteen seconds. Maybe less.

And a woman pushing a wheelchair...

"Why didn't you catch them?" Marcus coughed.

Craven turned his head.

Marcus pointed back to the hedge, taking a breath. "Why didn't you catch them?"

"They were almost across the parking lot when I started after them."

"You said they were halfway across, not almost across. Which is it?"

"A little farther than halfway."

Marcus stood up. His knee was frozen. "I can't imagine she could reach the parking garage before you, but I'll give her the benefit. But how did you not catch her before the second deck?"

Craven thought. "She turned the corner, disappeared in the darkness."

"Disappeared?" Marcus looked through the entrance. "Did it occur to you that the corner is a hundred feet up the ramp?"

Craven remained still.

"So you were on her and then she reached the end of the ramp in, what... three seconds?"

Marcus limped in front of him.

"Pushing a wheelchair."

Craven's lips worked without words, running the memory over and over. He was sure it was there, it had happened. He saw it.

"You said you felt the buzzing," Marcus continued. "When did it stop?"

"Right about here."

Marcus nodded. He started back toward the hospital.

"She's in there, I saw it!" Craven shouted. "My eyes weren't buzzing; I saw that person inside the parking garage. They're in there!"

Marcus waved without looking. He slung his briefcase over his shoulder and abandoned the parking garage. They could stay there, finish the sweep. They wouldn't find anything. And Craven would continue to swear what he saw. The fact was, if he doubted it, he'd fall apart. If he faced the reality—that he saw something that wasn't there—he'd never trust his senses again. He'd be done as an agent. When they turned up nothing, he would convince himself and others that the woman and her brother had somehow slipped out an uncovered entrance.

Somehow.

Marcus limped over to the loading dock. His knee was working a little more fluidly now that he was moving. The briefcase, however, felt like a bag of concrete.

"When did you arrive?" he asked the agent posted in the doorway.

"Sir?"

"When did you get here to guard this exit?"

He thought. "About a minute before you arrived."

Marcus looked around. The parking lot was surrounded by brick walls and shrubbery to his right. There was a sidewalk to his left that went around the building. He handed the briefcase to the agent, telling him to hold it. Told him there was sensitive data in there. It was the most unadvisable thing to do, hand something like that over, but he cared a lot less than he did only fifteen minutes earlier.

He made it around the corner, making his knee bend as he went. He followed the path beneath a portico and past the entrance to another building to the street beyond. He stopped there, looking left and right.

It was almost 4:00 a.m.

Crickets were the only thing that disturbed the distant interstate.

He reached inside his coat and took out the phone. It was time to make a call. Time to tell his superiors what had happened.

Tell them it was over.

THE KEYCARD SLIPPED FROM CALI'S FINGERS. THE CORNER rebounded off the standard hotel carpeting and bounced to the other side of the hallway. She put her hands on her face. Her fingers cold. Cheeks burning.

Legs quaking.

We made it. We made it this far.

She steadied herself on the wheelchair's handles. Nix's head rested at an odd angle. The clerk at the front desk was more interested in a magazine than the sleeping kid in a wheelchair, and checked them into their room.

We're on our way to meet family, Cali told her. *Just running a little late.*

The clerk pursed her lips, tapping at the keys. *Jenny Meggett?*

Yes, that's me.

Tappity-tap-tap-tap. The girl coded a keycard and handed it over. She didn't ask for a credit card; there was already one on file. Cali hesitated at the desk, then pushed towards the elevator. She wanted to ask if a little girl had checked into her room, but thought better if she didn't. She wanted to know, but thought better if she went and looked herself.

So now she was on the second floor, staring at raised numbers on the door. The keycard on the floor. Nix sleeping.

She held on and bent over, prying the keycard off the dense carpet with a fingernail. The plastic was slick, the edge biting into her palm. She aimed it at the slot and stabbed the lock with a quick motion. A green light ignited. Gears turned.

She stared until the light went out.

Again, she keyed the door. This time she pushed the handle down before the light expired.

It was dark.

The smell of clean drifted from the room.

Cali backed inside, pulling the wheelchair with her. The light switch was around the corner. She locked the door and stood there. The heavy curtains were drawn. The beds made.

TV off.

"Avery?" she whispered.

Cali's hands shook with renewed force, her fingers rattling over her lips as she covered her mouth to keep any more sounds from squeaking out. She was a horrible mother. She'd sent her little girl out on her own to wait for them and they almost never made it. What would've happened to her if they were shut down? Where would she have gone? She had no one if Cali disappeared.

No one.

Cali looked on the other side of each queen-sized bed, the corners crisply made and tucked beneath. She pulled the curtain aside and looked down into the city. The street was empty and wet. Drizzle streamed down the glass like tears.

"Momma?"

The bathroom door opened. And her little girl, her treasure, stood there with a toothbrush, wearing her nightshirt, the one that said Little Princess. Cali fell on her knees with such force that, despite the carpet, pain shot up her legs. She held her arms out and her little princess jumped. Avery smelled like Colgate.

"I'm so sorry," Cali whispered. "I'm such a bad mother. Such a bad, bad mother."

"No, you're not. You're the best."

"I'm sorry," she repeated, over and over.

"It's okay, Momma. It's okay. I just waited for you."

"I know, I know... I just..."

And she squeezed her girl harder than a girl should be squeezed. And it felt good. A momma holding her cub to her bosom, never letting go.

Never letting go.

"Is that Uncle Nix?"

"Yes," Cali said. She held her hand and knelt next to her brother.

His breathing was shallow. Drool hung from his lower lip. His complexion was still yellow but blotchy with patches of dry skin flaking off like scales. Like a new body pushing away the old.

A new breed.

"He smells funny," Avery said. She leaned closer, wrinkling her nose. "What happened?"

"He's been sick." Cali pushed her brother's hair off his forehead. Clammy and wet.

"He's better?"

Cali nodded. "Yeah, he's better."

She smiled.

"He's a lot better."

Avery, despite the odor, wrapped her arms around Nix and pressed her head against his. Toothpaste dried on her lips like primer. The little princess smiled with her eyes closed, glad to see her uncle home and safe.

Home and safe.

CHAPTER FORTY-EIGHT_

THERE WAS NO SENSE OF TIME.

Like anesthesia. Like a portion of consciousness snipped from his life. If he had to recall his last moment of awareness, and it took great effort to do so, Nix remembered the silver doors of an elevator closing. Remembered his reflection looking back and his sister standing behind him. She said something—

Fire and furnace.

The images of hallucinatory dreams marched through his memories like pink elephants.

And now there was darkness. Blackness so perfect, unmarred by variations of smudging or the hint of shapes and depth. Just black.

Just night.

He wasn't sure that time was passing, although it seemed to be, since he was aware—on some level—of this absence of light. Of this night that went on forever, where there was no sensation. There just was.

Just is.

Until there was a pinpoint of light.

He wasn't even sure when it appeared. As he became aware of it, he was thinking that perhaps it was there the whole time. That perhaps he just didn't see it.

And then there was another. And another.

Like a black sheet draped across the sun and something poking through it. Some holes bigger than others, some brighter, but none bigger than the head of a needle. All there, filling his vision, filling the darkness like a can of sparkly paint flipped from a brush to spatter the night.

Stars. Those are stars.

Nix was grossly aware that he had a realization. That there was thought in this world. Before, the dark and the pinpoints of light were just knowledge, something that he just knew. But he felt a movement —something shifting—when he recognized the lights for what they were. That they were stars.

That he was lying on his back, looking into a pristine night sky.

And, like the lights had eased into his awareness, so did the sound of water beyond his feet, ebbing and flowing and shooshing and crashing. The heartbeat of the ocean was somewhere beyond his vision, but he could hear it. He could smell the salt, the sea life within it. Feel the sand beneath him.

And he lay there, motionless. Watching the stars glitter. Listening to the ocean call. He stayed that way for longer than he would remember, for a period of time that he could not measure, remaining in the present moment.

Just seeing.

Just hearing.

Smelling. Feeling.

Until smoke was in the air. Wood burned and crackled somewhere to his right. Nix turned his head, the sand grinding against his ear. He saw the fire glowing, flames licking the darkness somewhere between the hard-packed sand and the line of trees. Sparks danced like insects.

Perhaps he knew where he was and didn't recognize it. Of course he wouldn't. Because never before had he ever experienced the inner world with such clarity. Never could he smell its richness, breathe its wonder. Feel its beauty. Perhaps, he thought, he was somewhere in the outer world. That, holding that last memory of the elevator and sister closely, Cali had taken him far away from the hospital. Perhaps they were in paradise, after all. Just like she promised.

They escaped.

Because, if this was the lagoon, if this was his inner paradise, his dreamland, surely he would see—

She would be—

And a form stepped from behind the fire, the light flickering on her dark skin. Her bare feet pushing through the sand, hips swaying. Arms swinging at her sides. Her features faded as she stepped closer, the firelight now at her back, hiding the smile that touched her lips.

Nix went up to his elbows. He sat with arms crossed on drawn knees. He looked at the star-choked sky and cresting waves. Felt his longtime companion near him. Fully aware that the new-breed biomites had fleshed dreamland, made it as vivid as skin and bone.

Or maybe this is real.

Raine's hands were warm.

Her embrace soft.

CHAPTER FORTY-NINE_

Marcus rapped the counter with his fingernails, tapping a rapid succession of bullets with no particular rhythm, just something to cut through the barbiturate fog. His leg, stabilized in a blue wrap, still pulsed.

The doctor was late.

It was cold in the room with jars of tongue depressors and old magazines. Marcus tapped and stared straight at a poster—the only adornment in the room—framed in a thin black border beneath a layer of clear plastic: a picture of an old man and his wife walking through Hyde Park. He was two feet in the air, clicking his heels like a goddamn fairy on Broadway.

BIOGEN. Stem cell biomite technology to have you on your feet and out the door. Ask your doctor if it's right for you.

Tap. Tap. Tap.

Tap. Tap. Tap.

Tap. Tap. Tap.

A week had come and gone. Still in Chicago.

The pain, excruciating. When the adrenaline was exhausted, he'd smashed against the reality of a shattered knee. He attempted to fly home but was told to stay in Chicago. The investigation was ongoing and they needed him there to mop up. And in the meantime, get that knee fixed.

They knew he wouldn't take the biomites. They knew his stance. And he knew they kept him there to let him stew in the raw scream of nerve endings that blared like never-ending fire alarms. Sometimes pain brought a man's beliefs down, shattered the foundation on which he built his life. Pain, when there was enough, broke down all ideals.

But not Marcus Anderson.

He was certain, now more than ever, that biomite technology would be the end of humanity. Where once he held onto the thread of hope—bare and frayed at the ends—that people would see the folly of their tireless attempts to create happiness with technology, it was now all but dissolved.

They need me now more than ever.

The public was unaware of Cali and Nix. Thank God, the media, either. So far, all they knew was that a mistake had been made. As far as authorities were aware, the brother and sister were wanted for questioning. But they hadn't broken any laws. And, for the love of God, they certainly weren't halfskins that Mother couldn't see.

And that should be impossible.

The only way to escape Mother was to develop a new brand of biomites. Geniuses had yet to crack that case, but if Cali did... if, in fact, she developed something that knocked them off the grid and this wasn't a fluke... well, then, Marcus was fucked.

We all are.

Everyone would figure out how to avert the all-watching eye of the government; they'd be out on their own, doing what they wanted, infecting humanity with a new brand of biomites that were, perhaps, stronger, faster and telepathic.

Marcus was sure that he'd live long enough to see the ugly end. He'd see humanity consumed by microscopic machines. And he would sit back with the other purists in the world and laugh.

Laugh as biomites ate them like flesh-eating bacteria.

Laugh and say it, say it loud.

I told you so.

The door opened. A doctor entered and extended his hand. Asked Marcus how he was feeling.

Marcus grunted. And tapped.

The doctor dropped a folder on the counter and leafed through several documents. He pursed his lips and whistled. His lips wet. The sound happy and piercing.

The doctor tapped the counter. It came to life like a computer tablet. Marcus removed his hand from the lighted surface. The doctor went back to whistling, moving objects around. He double-tapped a folder and the wall in front of Marcus transformed. The framed poster turned out to be a projection.

Lights danced.

An X-ray flipped into view.

"That's your knee." The doctor used his fingertip to draw a red circle on the wall. "Your patella is shattered and you tore the patellar tendon."

Marcus didn't need the X-ray and all the red arrows pointing to the black lines that spiderwebbed his kneecap. The knee was destroyed.

"There's a procedure that utilizes cadaver tissue to rebuild—"

"No." The thought of a dead man's skin inside his body was revolting.

"When the swelling is down, we'll replace the entire knee."

The doctor explained, with more red lines, how they were going to enter Marcus's knee, where they were making cuts, and what materials they would use to substitute for bone and ligament. He would have an artificial knee that worked almost as good as the one he was born with. He could expect trouble as he got older, but it beat the hell out of the alternative.

"There is another option." The doctor swiped the desktop. The red lines vanished.

Marcus's jaws flexed.

"You're an ideal candidate for biomite regeneration. There have been some recent advancements in biomite knee reconstruction. The seeding is relatively painless and the results are complete within a month. We could start today, don't even have to wait for the swelling to go down."

Marcus took in a long breath. The doctor pretended to organize his folder.

"No," Marcus managed to say, and that was it.

The doctor nodded. He turned the desktop off, pushed the folder to the side, and sat on a stool. Marcus let out a small sound when he unclipped the brace around his knee.

The pain lanced the fog like a spotlight.

CHAPTER FIFTY_

The room smelled like a stale armpit.

A week of recovery, of sweating out waste, of dead skin peeling off them like burn victims, was about all Cali could take. It clung like cigarette smoke. She felt better stepping out of the shower and wrapping up in a robe. She leaned over the sink, piling a generous helping of toothpaste—compliments of Red Roof Inn—onto the bristles and scrubbed her whole mouth. The armpit was even on her tongue.

Her spit was foamy red—blood and toothpaste.

She pulled her lips back, spilling lines of blood over her teeth. Her finger squeaked over her gums, massaging the blood away. They had receded.

Cali stepped back, looking at her reflection. She wasn't pasty anymore. She opened the robe and exposed her body to the mirror, revealing saggy breasts that drooped over a series of speed bumps that were her ribs. Her pelvis jutted from her hips like brackets. No matter what she thought-commanded, the biomites weren't putting weight back on her.

She'd been eating, even though she wasn't really hungry. She assumed it was just a caloric deficiency that was causing the gaunt affliction, but nothing had changed. Her distress haunted her, reminding her something was wrong each time she looked in the mirror.

Another self-analysis, just to be sure.

"All right, in you go." Cali clapped her hands. "Into the shower, young lady."

Avery jumped on one bed; Nix lay on the other, hands folded over his stomach. "Momma," she said, the impact of the jump bouncing in her voice, "we're doing this game where I jump over to the other bed and... and..."

She jumped a couple times and caught her breath.

"And Uncle Nix tries to... to... grab my feet before I can get back and... and... we're keeping score."

"What if you hit your head?"

"No, no... he hasn't caught me yet. I'm too fast, Momma."

"She's too fast?" Cali looked at her brother, his eyes closed.

"Too fast for me."

Avery squealed with delight, bouncing almost to the ceiling. Cali pulled the towel off her head and wrangled her daughter onto the floor, kicking and laughing. She smacked her bottom as the young lady padded into the bathroom. Cali turned on the shower for her.

She dug through her bag, looking for the least gross thing to wear. Nothing had been washed in over a month. She hand-washed the T-shirts and underwear in the sink, but they still seemed rank.

The armpit contaminated everything.

She threw on a baggy sweatshirt and shorts, nixed the underwear. She closed the bathroom door and retrieved a black kit, sitting on the bed.

"Let me have your hand."

"Do I have to?" Nix answered.

"Come on."

"Use one of my toes. I can't feel my fingertips."

"I've got a baseline with her fingers, now hand it over before I pull a sample off your lip."

He made half an effort. Cali grabbed his pinky and pressed it on a small box. A needle took a droplet. Nix pretended it hurt, sucking air through his teeth.

"Baby," she said.

Cali set it down on the round table next to the window, the curtains drawn. All levels were exactly where she expected them to be. His nervous system was up to 60% function. Respiratory was 88%. Circulatory, 95%. Brain function was near 100%.

Punching all cylinders.

"How are you feeling?" she asked.

"How are you?"

She waited for an answer.

"Maybe you should put that thing on your finger," he said.

"I will. Don't worry. You're the only one who skirted death, so tell me how you're feeling. Any unusual aches, pains, sensations? Anything abnormal?"

It had been a week. His recovery was unbelievable, really. She'd just hoped he'd survive, that she could push him out of the hotel looking halfway normal.

Still, it could all go wrong.

"Well?"

Nix shook his head. She stared, just in case he needed a little pressure to find the right answer. He folded his hands and closed his eyes. She pressed her finger on the black box and watched the readout. Her levels were better than his, just something about the brain function was a little off. It was operating at full capacity; the only difference was the anomaly in the algorithm, something that was always there as long as she could remember. She could never figure out what was missing. It was similar to Nix's readout when he was dreaming up the lagoon.

Going there, as he put it.

But she didn't have a dreamland and that made her wonder if there was something the new breeds were doing that she wasn't following. She would have preferred that they be better—stronger— but they couldn't stay in the room any longer.

They'd been out once. It was the second day after Nix woke up. She took him on an extended walk to the ice machine. They walked the entire floor and stopped at the end. She didn't like being in the open for so long, but the exercise was refreshing. And the view of Chicago was different from that end of the hallway. They sat for an hour. No one bothered them.

When they returned, maid service had been through. Thankfully, nothing was out of the ordinary, nothing that would raise an alarm. She thought about switching rooms, but that seemed too obvious.

"How's it look?" Nix asked.

"What?"

"Your analysis."

"It looks fine. Now, I don't want you to push it. Tomorrow morning, we'll be walking through the lobby to get to the parking garage. I'll go first and find the car and have it ready. Avery will go with you. If you feel weak, you can lean on her. You need to conserve your energy. That means no extracurricular activity."

She snapped the black kit closed.

"No dreamland."

Avery was still singing in the shower.

Cali went to the mirror and brushed her hair. It was thinner than before. Nix lay motionless. She tried to ignore him but plopped her hand on Nix's.

"Look, I know you miss her. I know you miss... *Raine.*"

The name came out sharp. She didn't try to sugarcoat it.

"But, I'm sorry, she's in your mind, Nix. She's something you constructed with thoughts, something you made up when you were little."

She squeezed his hand.

"You're saying she's not real?"

Cali shook her head.

Nix nodded. He closed his eyes again. Then, a few moments later, he tapped his skull.

"I think this is a new reality, sis. I've no more control of her than I have over my heart beating or hair growing. She's a part of me that lives and breathes. I think the biomites give me access to the new world."

"Did you dream up that world?"

"In the beginning, yeah. But now, it's just more... real."

"But every detail you have created, right? You've pictured every color, every image since you were ten. You built that world with your mind."

He didn't answer.

"You told me it started in the doctor's office with the poster and the waterfall, that you kept adding to it by visualizing something new. First, you made the ocean, then the forest and the fish... and then her."

Cali touched his forehead like she was checking a fever.

"It's all right, Nix. It's just not real. You invented it. The only difference is that it's inside your mind. Not out here, not in the flesh."

He stared at her, like he was really listening. Maybe this time he would understand. This time he would believe and stop wasting time in dreamland.

"If I'm the only one that sees her," he said, "does that mean she's an illusion?"

"Yes." Cali nodded. "Sorry. Get some rest. We'll go over things again in the morning. For tonight, get some real sleep. Promise?"

He nodded, once.

Cali opened the bathroom. The song jumped out, loud and clear.

"Enough showering. No one else in the building will have hot water."

"Yes, Momma."

Cali turned the shower off and dropped on the bed while Avery dried off. She flipped on the television and scouted the news stations. Still no word on their escape. She had the queer sensation that something was missing.

Couldn't quite put her finger on it.

Maybe if she'd noticed the missing wheelchair, things would've been different.

CHAPTER FIFTY-ONE_

Every bump sent spikes through Marcus's knee. Even in the OxyContin-induced fog, he felt the pain.

We don't get many of these anymore, the nurse teased. *I can't remember the last time a doctor cut open a knee to operate, honestly.*

Honestly, he didn't give a shit.

He was supposed to stay another month to rehab. And while he was there, continue overseeing the case of the missing brother and sister.

Plans changed.

Just before surgery, his superiors informed him that Jack Parsons would be arriving to go over Marcus's notes. Marcus could go home and recover peacefully. The day after surgery, lying in bed, mouth open, pain-sweat beading on his head like it was freshly waxed, he received the news that Internal Affairs wanted to talk to him.

They scheduled a chat for when he returned to D.C.

While he was stuck in Chicago, his office had likely been raided, his interns sequestered. His records scrubbed and combed through and picked apart. Dr. Erickson, chief of biomites, probably blew the whistle and reported their conversations. The bastard probably recorded them.

Marcus knew what would come next; he'd been part and parcel of witch trials of this sort. They would paint him as a religious sycophant bent on destroying biomite technology, that he secretly manipulated the system and caused the premature death of hundreds.

Eventually, they would say, *thousands. Millions.*

They would paint that picture, they would show it to him as a warning. *Go down quietly, Marcus. If you don't, this is what you'll see.*

Perhaps he was wrong. Maybe this was all a misunderstanding. He was good at his job. If he wasn't, he would've been replaced long ago. Maybe he was just too biased to be trusted. His hatred for biomites colored his perception, tainted his thinking and actions. Truth be told, he was perfect for the job and the Secretary all the way to the president knew it. If someone was planning on casting Marcus as the goat, they would make a mistake.

He was a scrapper.

They knew what he'd been doing. He managed his job with the tools they gave him. When he had to distort reality for the good of the country, he stepped up, did what needed doing.

He shook his head.

His thoughts were getting away. Even if he felt old and broken, he was the founder of the Halfskin Laws. If he fell, a lot would follow.

He was rolled out of the hospital to wait for a car to pick him up and take him to the airport. Fly him home. His phone buzzed. He looked at the number, silencing it. His wife had nothing that he wanted to hear. He would be there by nightfall to hear it all in person. If there was one bright side to Chicago, it was the silence of his hotel room. There were no extra voices around unless he wanted them.

Marcus watched for his driver in the downtown melee. No sign of the black Mercedes.

But there was something interesting.

Down the street, about a block away, was a man in hospital

scrubs. An orderly was pushing an empty wheelchair. Marcus watched him instead of the traffic. The man bounced his head to the rhythm of buds buried deep in his ears. Normally, Marcus would've silently cursed about music in the workplace, even though the man was just pushing a wheelchair.

He didn't notice the car pull up to the roundabout. The driver had the door open and Marcus was pushed forward.

"Hold on." He put his hand up, eyes on the approaching orderly.

"Hey. You." Marcus snapped his fingers. When the orderly didn't notice, he grabbed the nurse. "Get him."

The nurse, hesitating, reached out and gently touched the orderly, who pulled one of the cords from his ear.

"Where'd you find that?" Marcus shouted over a passing truck.

"This?" The orderly pointed at the empty wheelchair. "Got reported found. I'm picking it up and bringing it back."

"Where?" He twisted in the wheelchair, sparks lighting up his knee. He grunted. "Where was it?"

"Red Roof said they found it in a room." He pointed at the back of the wheelchair, where it was written, *Northwestern Memorial Hospital.* "Happens all the time, man. You know how much these things worth?"

The orderly waited for more questions. When there weren't, he plugged his ear and continued on.

A certain thrill rolled through Marcus's insides. A delicious feeling, it was. Something he was all too familiar with. A feeling he got when he was right. Or when he found treasure.

This was both.

CHAPTER FIFTY-TWO

THE TASTE OF COFFEE STILL LINGERED.

Cali wished for a mint or something that would make her feel new and fresh. Something that would wash away this feeling of waste. She was certain it would be different when she escaped the room, the hotel. When they were out in the open and away from danger. That was when she would feel normal again.

Fresh and new.

The door clicked quietly behind her. She smoothed out the wrinkles in her shirt, with no lasting effect. Body odor clung to the fabric like a stain. The carpet felt spongy. She sensed the occupants of each room she passed. Most of them sleeping. A few reading *USA Today*. One couple was having sex.

She smelled it.

The lights buzzed in their sockets, throwing an iridescent glow down the hall. She passed the elevator alcove, pushed open the door to the stairs and descended, sure that someone had vomited somewhere in the long trail of treads within the last couple nights. Cali stopped at the bottom step and took a deep breath.

Nix and Avery would stay up in the room for fifteen minutes, then come down and meet her in the parking garage. She'd have the door open, car running. She was sure he had the strength to walk normally through the lobby. She only wished she were there to help. Just in case.

The door's cushioned hinge resisted her initial shove. If she was superstitious, she might see that as a sign. *Don't go any further, stay in the room.* But she'd been up there long enough. Cali leaned her shoulder into the red door and entered the main lobby.

The ceiling was high, the room spacious. She stopped to collect her thoughts. She considered thought-commanding her heart rate to slow down, but adrenaline served her well. She was stressed, needed additional oxygen. She just needed a moment. A breath.

A continental breakfast room was past the desk. There were donuts and bagels, cold cereal and orange juice. Even a waffle maker. Three people were sitting at small tables, reading newspapers and chewing. The lobby was nearly as empty. A middle-aged couple and their daughter sat on a couch. Cali felt their thoughts and figured they were waiting on the grandparents. They were checked out, ready to go home.

There was one clerk at the desk and a heavyset woman talking to her.

Cali needed to pick up the key, that's all. The rental people parked the car in the garage and dropped the key off at the desk. She'd specifically instructed them to bring it to the room, but the front desk called when he left it there. Probably didn't want to spend the extra time. No big deal, but Cali hoped her only challenge would be to walk through the lobby unnoticed.

Now she had to talk with someone.

She queued up behind the extra-large customer. Her swollen fingers gripped the counter while she ground her words through a triple chin. Her dress had faded floral patterns and a stain on the sleeve. Built for comfort.

"I did not make those charges; take them off," the woman said.

The clerk was a tired woman in her early thirties. Her shift had ended, but her replacement was running late. Way late. Nothing out of the ordinary, the prick had done that sort of thing on a weekly basis. He'd lose his job pretty soon, but not soon enough. And now she had to deal with this self-centered mountain of flesh and three pornos racked on her account.

Cali's stomach curled. Sweat trickled down her ribs, soaking into her shirt. She couldn't smell herself anymore, overwhelmed by the scent of baby powder that gummed the fat lady's skin folds. Cali smelled cellulite.

Fat woman placed her half-empty soda on the counter. She looked past Cali, her breath labored, as if exhausted from breathing. Cali wanted to ask if she could just ask for the key, it would only take a second. But the fat woman—sliding her oversized glasses up her pudgy nose—wouldn't take that kindly. And she was taking all the attention away from Cali, so she'd wait.

She'd wait.

"Ma'am," the clerk said, "I've taken the extra charges off your account. You'll see a refund on your credit card, but it won't show up for a couple of days."

"It better not say what was purchased. I am embarrassed to even have to ask about this. Can you imagine having movies like that?"

"I'm sorry, ma'am." The clerk couldn't look at the customer. She'd heard that bullshit too many times. The hotel's policy was to refund their money, no questions asked. But the lying irritated her. Dishonesty always did.

"It's all taken care of, ma'am. Is there anything else I can help you with?"

The clerk looked at Cali, wanting to move on.

"Yes, I'd like the name and number of your manager. I'd like to be compensated for my pain and suffering."

"Pain and suffering?"

"Are you listening, missy? I'm embarrassed by this and I want a free room. Give me your manager's name and number so I can call him."

"Her." The clerk tried to bite her tongue. "My boss is a woman."

"Well, soooorry. *HER*. Give me *her* number." Fat lady swallowed some flat soda. "I'd like to call her. And I want your name, too. Want her to know how rude you've been, she'd probably want to know that. I doubt I'll ever come back to this place again."

Cali felt the tension winding around the clerk's throat, her fingers poised over the keyboard, contemplating what she wanted to say. The customer, she'd seen them before, was baiting her. Say the wrong thing and get compensation and someone fired.

Sick.

Cali kept her attention on her surroundings. One of the men left the breakfast nook, carrying a Styrofoam cup of coffee. The family on the couch was watching the show at the counter. Cali moved off to the side and considered leaving, going back up the stairs. She could come back later, maybe even the next morning. The thought of spending another day in the room sank inside her like a trapped animal.

No one paid her any attention. She didn't see any thoughts relating to the shabbily dressed woman—the one that looked like an anorexia patient—standing in contrast to the obnoxious fat lady. Cali could wait another minute, just one more. Her hands were shaking—

Small fingers slipped between hers.

"Avery?" Cali looked down. Her daughter squeezed her hand.

"It's all right, Momma."

"I told you to wait with Uncle Nix." Cali spoke quietly, her lips barely moving.

"I'm worried about you. I just wanted to make sure you were all right."

Cali listened to the clerk make a call. Listened to fat lips suck a bottle.

The people on the couch watched.

The clerk steamed.

Avery's hand was warm and soft. Cali squeezed it, but felt something twist inside. *This is wrong. This is all wrong. She shouldn't be out here, not in front of all these people. Nix needed her.*

"Honey," she said, hissing, "I want you to go."

The fat lady's head turned like a heap of flesh on a spike. Her nostrils flared. She looked directly at Cali, her eyes magnified through the lenses. Avery stepped behind Cali, still holding her hand. She held her gaze for several moments, neither of them talking. Fat lady wanted to say something; she was fired up, ready to take on all comers. She thought Cali was talking to her, maybe; thought maybe Cali told her to get going. She wanted her to go, but that wasn't what she meant.

The phone hit the cradle. "Ma'am."

Fat lady turned.

Cali pulled Avery around and knelt in front of her. Held her daughter's cheeks with both hands while staying aware—remaining very aware of the couple on the couch and the two people in the breakfast nook, sensing their biomites like radar, no one else around—and whispered, "Go back to the room, darling. I'll see you in a bit, I promise."

Fat lady was agitated. She glanced back, but the clerk held out a phone, the manager or someone with authority on the other end. Avery nodded, tears brimming.

"Why are you crying?" Cali asked.

"I'm scared."

"Of what."

Avery bit her lip. She did that when she was nervous. When she was little, she sometimes wet herself; now she just bit her lip. Her eyes flicked toward the hotel's front doors, but Cali couldn't sense any active biomites, no one back there.

"I don't want to leave," Avery whispered.

"It's just for a few minutes, honey. I promise. Just for a few."

Avery danced in place. She was going to go if she didn't settle. Cali took her hands. She heard something behind her, something that didn't register.

Avery stopped jumping.

Her lip popped out from between her teeth.

"I love you, Momma."

Cali felt a cold shank of fear drive through her organs. Something was about to shift. About to change.

She sensed a phone call behind her. Someone called the authorities.

She recognized the voice.

Marcus Anderson was at the doors, propped on crutches in all his biomite-less glory.

"What are you doing?" he said.

CHAPTER FIFTY-THREE_

Buzzing.

A different buzz. A good one. This one potent, tight. This one powerful.

Nix sat on the corner of the bed and checked the time. A few more minutes and he'd follow. Just give her enough time to get to the garage, to get the car and be ready. He wasn't concerned whether he could reach it or not. He was only thinking of his sister getting there. He wanted her out of this situation, far away and safe. Then he could relax. He could let go.

In the meantime, he buzzed with anticipation. Buzzed with excitement.

He distracted himself by running his hand over his scalp, the fuzz gripping his palm like Velcro. He missed having hair.

Nix was tempted to close his eyes, make a brief visit to the lagoon, tell Raine he was all right, that he was coming back soon. But he had promised. He had enough energy to stay there all day and be just fine, he was sure of it. His legs were wound springs. But he'd promised he wouldn't. After that morning, he could go all he wanted. He needed to get through the morning.

He thought about what she'd said. She never liked his dreamland.

When he was little, she restricted how long he could go. She was probably right because, if she let him, he'd close his eyes and stay there for days.

Maybe never come back.

Yeah, she was probably right.

But she was wrong about the reality. Raine wasn't just some thought that seemed real. He was sure of it. She wasn't a construct of his mind. He had a theory that the biomites manipulated reality, that they were able to take her from the vapor of another reality and spin her into existence where only he could see her. Where only he could go. The biomites were some sort of portal into a new dimension, something that made dreams reality. That maybe the human body was just a garden to grow the mind. Once it was mature, it existed somewhere else.

Dreamland.

He wasn't deluded; he knew the difference between one reality versus the next. Knew when he was in the lagoon, when he was in the flesh.

He checked his appearance in the mirror. His stomach tumbled like broken glass. There were still blotches on his cheeks, but the peeling had stopped. His eyebrows looked close to normal, but the eyelashes were lacking. At least he wasn't lugging the ring around his neck. A hairless teenager would certainly be easy to pick out in a hotel lobby.

"All right." He checked his breath in his cupped hand, not sure why. "It's time. Let's go."

THE BUZZING ENERGY turned to ice water, filling Nix's legs.

He wasn't as strong as he thought. Or maybe it was nerves. Whichever, he stood at the bottom of the stairwell, his hand on the red door. *Breathe, breathe. And think.*

He wished he could see outside and know what was coming. He

closed his eyes, the buzz crawling over his scalp and tingling like millipede legs. He sensed spots of activity around him, like a field of snowy static where lumps of density could be felt. This was what Cali was talking about, using the new breeds like scanners. Nix had focused on George, manipulating his biomites, but this was like an electronic net that plugged into multiple people. He was a virus that could watch and feel all the players in the field.

Most of the spots were quiet and pulsing. One of them, though, was bright and spiky. His hand slid across the door like he was feeling for direction. This one spot was big and dense.

Agitated.

Disturbed.

Cali should be in the garage. That couldn't be her.

She wouldn't still be there.

But then he heard her. This wasn't in his head; he heard his sister's voice beyond the door. It was shrill, calling a name.

Nix pushed the door open.

A large woman was at the counter, the clerk on the other side. Cali was gone, but the disturbance was coming from somewhere around those people. That was what he felt. Maybe he imagined what he heard. Maybe his panic manifested as his worst nightmare: *Cali searching for Avery in public.*

She wasn't out there. She wasn't in the lobby. But the people weren't moving, they were looking at something. Nix moved toward them. As he came around, he saw her. She was on her knees.

This time, he heard her.

She was calling. Panic strapped her voice, making it tight and piercing. She was calling out for Avery. Over and over, she slung her daughter's name out.

In public.

She was looking for Avery in public, in front of others.

Her eyes wide, filled with blankness. She didn't see him coming. Couldn't see anything. Her lips trembled, spilling a name over and over. Over and over.

Nix ran to her.

He reached down and picked her up. He wrapped his arms around his sister, like she'd done so many times with him. She shivered with fear, her skin on fire. He closed his eyes, trying to connect with his sister, send a thought, soothe her panic.

"Don't move," a man said.

Nix ignored it.

He sent an image to his sister's mind, trying to reestablish an illusion that would keep her from falling completely apart. Tried to make her believe that Avery was standing next to them.

CHAPTER FIFTY-FOUR

IMPOSSIBLE.

Marcus tried not to smile.

A man of his stature, with his power, should not smile like a child. The odds were long that he'd find them at the hotel, but he had a feeling. He believed that God graced him with senses beyond the ordinary. He always had a gut feeling that told him when good things were about to happen. Something turned in his stomach, like a shot of sugar straight to his veins. He sat in the back of the car, watching the city street pass by.

With a smile.

The black Mercedes rolled to a stop. The driver ran around the front of the car and opened the back door. He reached inside, set up a pair of crutches and helped Marcus out. The whole incident took five minutes.

Marcus waved the man off, telling him to wait in the car. He'd be right out.

He didn't know what he was looking for. He needed to call it in, let those on the case handle it. It was a long shot, probably nothing. *It happens all the time,* the nurse told him on the way to the car. *Hotels get a reward for returning hospital property.*

Nonetheless, it wouldn't take much to just look, ask a few questions. He didn't know what was driving him. He hated loose ends. If he was honest, he hated losing. They beat him. Made him look like a fool. He wasn't sure, just yet, how much they'd taken from him. It could be everything.

That was why he looked.

One step inside the lobby—

THERE.

An intoxicating fire, his heart pumped full of fuel, his veins surged with pure joy, the Blood of Christ...

She was there.

She was in the lobby.

She was on her knees, begging forgiveness. Her sins weighed heavily, pressing her to supplicate right there in front of the witnesses, to cleanse her soul. She felt her redeemer coming; she knew Marcus was there, at the door.

She was ready for him.

Cali Richards had reaped the harvest. She had been to hell. She had withered to a faint shadow of a woman, the complexion of a prisoner. The color of death. The drab misery of guilt surrounded her like a toxic cloud.

Marcus moved slowly. He didn't want to scare her, not until he made his call. He speed-dialed one of his guys, speaking softly, calmly, never taking his eyes off her. Cali turned her head. First, she looked up, as if listening. Then she looked directly at Marcus.

"What are you doing?" he said.

Her eyes widened.

White, all around.

"It's over." Marcus held out his hand, stop sign. "It's over; don't run."

She didn't move.

He wasn't sure if she was breathing. He didn't feel the air shimmer, didn't feel the pulse strike the others but saw them simultaneously flinch. A fat lady turned around. A clerk dropped a pen.

People on the couch stood up. An old man and young kid entered and stood stone-still. The old man held a bagel.

Marcus adjusted the crutches, backing up a step. He wanted the driver to come inside. He couldn't leave, couldn't turn or call. But he needed someone in there, someone on his side.

"Avery?" Cali's head shook. She scuffled around the big woman, grabbing her grubby dress to move her, like she was hiding something.

Marcus cocked his head. He knew the name. He knew her file, her history. Her family.

Her tragedy.

"AVERY!" she cried, on her hands and knees. She was calling out her daughter's name.

Her appearance reflected her mind. Undone.

She was calling for her daughter. The woman's eyes were wide, crying out the name over and over.

Marcus raised his hand again. Forcefully, he called the woman's name. He got her attention and delivered the message, one that would slap her back to reality.

"Your daughter!" he shouted, cutting through the thickness.

She stopped.

"Your daughter is dead."

Frozen, again.

CHAPTER FIFTY-FIVE_

HE'S A DEMON.

Her daughter was there, holding her hand—the warmth still lingering—and now she was gone. She was nowhere. And she couldn't feel her. Avery was an independent girl, but Cali could always feel her. That's what struck her in the gut, scraped her brain and stretched her nerves. Turned her into a blank slate.

She's gone.

Cali felt it. Her daughter was gone.

She sat there, slumped on her knees, throwing her mind out to find her. Her awareness crawled through the lobby, out into the halls. It seeped into the rooms. She sensed waking minds and sluggish bodies. She felt their thoughts and knew their intentions. And none of them—NONE OF THEM WERE HER.

She shouted.

She wanted her back. A hole had opened inside her, where she used to be. The love she gave, the warmth and tenderness borne from her womb. She wanted her back.

I'm a bad mother.

"Avery!"

Bad mother!

Cali shoved the fat woman aside, crawling around her.

"AVERY!"

Marcus Anderson was saying something.

She felt him stiffen. Smelled his doubt. His fear tanged the back of her tongue like acid. She couldn't feel him, couldn't read him and his biomite-free body. He was invisible to her new breeds, but she sensed his body. And it was weak.

And she hated him.

Perhaps if he didn't hold up his hand, if he didn't say the next thing on his mind, things would've been different. Something dreadful would've happened. Cali wouldn't just be a bad mother... she would've hurt him, permanently.

"Your daughter..." he said... the words slurring in slow motion, his lips delivering the truth like a surgeon's blade... he said... "is dead."

Dead.

Dead.

DEAD.

Everything is dead.

The world is cold and empty and dead.

The world is useless.

Bad mother.

Cali didn't see anything. Felt nothing. She saw shapes but didn't recognize them.

Heard sounds but didn't know them.

Her world was dead.

It was all dead.

She felt something shift, something move. Something wrapped around her, lifted her. Her feet were wooden paddles, rocks scraping the earth. Legs were logs, arms were twigs. Cali didn't recognize her body or the one embracing her. She felt nothing.

She knew nothingness but the blizzard of static that frayed reality.

Until.

A soothing presence moved through her, eased the dullness, lightened her heart. Filled her mind.

Until she could see.

See the boy next to her.

"What's happening?" she asked her brother.

CHAPTER FIFTY-SIX

THEY COULD RUN.

Marcus didn't have a weapon. There would be nothing he could do.

But it wouldn't matter; it would just be a matter of time now. The federal agents had downloaded the latest effects of the last episode, knew what to look for if they were influenced by Cali, knew when to call for help, hopefully blocking any attempts. At worst, they could hunt them down, wear them out, if they ran.

But they weren't running.

The woman was a sobbing mess. Reality came down hard. The table on which she rested her life just had the legs kicked out and parts and pieces that made sense to her had been scattered. She reaped what she sowed. She used the biomites to delude herself, to make believe her daughter existed, had never died.

Now look at her.

Look at her, coming undone. Her mind frayed, the seams dissolving. Perhaps she would shut herself off, now that she saw the lies. The self-inflicted lies.

Marcus stood vindicated in the hotel lobby. There, in front of him, was the proof on which he based his argument. Give humans too much power over life and they abuse it. We are children of God. We can't make those decisions for him. We can't decide when to die, how we should look, how we should think... we can't BRING BACK THE DEAD!

It doesn't work that way.

We're human. We have limitations.

We're imperfect.

Repent.

For some, perhaps, it was too late. Perhaps not.

Marcus said, "Son—"

"Shut up!" the kid snapped. "SHUT UP!"

The room fell silent. Except for Cali's sobs coming in quiet waves. Nix whispered things to her, things a mother would say to a child, things to comfort her. She probably didn't hear them, but she felt them. She was no longer hysterical.

"What do you know about us? About her? What she's been through. You can pull the file and read about her, interview others, listen to what they say... but you got no clue what she's been through. No idea what it's like."

Cali blubbered something. Her face, buried on his shoulder, her words underwater. The kid didn't understand, he just patted her head, went *shhhhhh,* like that would make her sane.

He knew the score. She was a goner. Marcus had seen people go over the edge. That was it, right there.

They weren't going anywhere.

"Police are coming," Marcus said. "We'll get you help, kid. We'll get your sister help."

Long pause. Cali quieted down.

Nix drew a sidelong glance in his direction. "Help? Is that what you call it?"

"It's what's right."

"What gives you the right to decide?"

Something twisted. "Look at her. She's an abomination. Her systems are failing. She's crashing."

"You don't know what hell is, Mr. Anderson. You don't think you'd reach for a cure if hell came to your life, but you would. When you're ground down to the bone, you'd reach."

"She thinks her daughter is alive, kid. That's not helping."

"She did the best she could. She could only take so much, she broke down."

"Life is like that."

"Then don't deny her the chance to fix it."

"She didn't fix it. We all die. That's how it works. None of us have the right to live forever."

"Some die before others."

"Always been that way. God only knows."

Marcus shifted his weight. Pain throbbed through the medicated dullness. Sweat was breaking on his forehead. The room, closing in. He needed to get off his feet but wasn't about to move, not until someone else was there.

A siren called in the distance. Not long. It would be over soon.

It was so quiet inside the lobby. The witnesses hadn't moved. They appeared catatonic. The family on the couch sat and stared. The fat lady stood behind Nix and Cali like a faded floral mountain of flesh, breathing through her mouth. Eyelids drooping.

Something beeped. It came from behind the counter. The clerk held the phone near her shoulder, staring like the others, the sound of repeated beeping telling her to hang up. Marcus looked around like he might see what happened to them, like the marionette strings lay on the floor.

"What did you do to them?" he said.

"Afraid?" Nix answered. "You're outnumbered."

"You sold your soul, kid. Don't take them with you. They haven't done anything."

"What's it matter? You'll be flipping the switch on them tomorrow or the next day, maybe next year. It's just a matter of time before you visit them."

"Is that what you think, kid? You're some kind of victim?"

"I did nothing wrong. Maybe it's the rules that are wrong. We're not hurting anyone by existing."

"You're hurting *everyone*." Marcus wobbled forward, pain radiating up his thigh, dampened by anger. "You people are the first step to the end. Change is slow, kid. Biomites are going to eat up humanity if we don't do something. We're going to give our flesh—our God-given bodies—to satisfy our desires. No, you're not hurting anyone, not now. You're not hurting anyone's feelings or breaking any bones, you're just the first step in the extinction of the human race."

"You don't know that."

"It's common sense, kid. It's logic. You've given in to your weakness, letting sin live your life."

"You don't know what we're supposed to become, Mr. Anderson. Maybe we're supposed to become this; we were given a brain to develop technology, to hone our bodies, to improve our lives, to develop our minds. Maybe we're something more than this... this skin... and maybe biomites are the bridge to another world. Maybe it's supposed to be that way."

"You're talking about heaven."

"No. You don't know why we're here or what happens when we die, no one knows that. NO ONE DOES!"

"To become that?" Marcus nodded at Cali. "Is that it?"

"She's not perfect. Neither are you."

"You were made in the image of God. Only the devil tinkers with that."

"I'm human."

"*Half.*"

"That's right." The siren was louder. "I'm half a human. But I don't deserve to die."

"Not everything deserves to live."

"Who decides?"

"God does, kid."

Cali looked around. Vacant eyes, she seemed to be seeing something else. Maybe looking for her nonexistent daughter, maybe hearing her voice. Her mouth moved silently.

"It'll be painless, kid."

She gently pushed out of Nix's embrace, still looking around like she was blind. Marcus stumbled backwards on the crutches, grimacing against the pain. His chest was tight and cold. He took several quick breaths. The siren rounded the corner. It was outside the building. He just needed to maintain until someone came inside and corralled these two. Then he could relax. Then it would be over.

Nix watched his sister. She didn't go far. She faltered. A tiny sound leaked from inside, but she held steady. She didn't run. She didn't know where she was. This world or some other that she invented, somewhere in her mind where a little girl lived.

"It's over," Marcus whispered.

Blue lights flashed through the glass doors, strobing around the walls. No one blinked.

"I know." Nix took his sister's arm. "I know."

The door opened. Someone—heavy-footed—came in behind Marcus, daring not to take his eyes off them, afraid they were just an apparition, not wanting to see them vanish.

Everyone flinched simultaneously.

Like a dance move, everyone listening to music in their heads.

Marcus turned his head. The Chicago police officer had stopped behind him. He was listening to something, maybe to the inaudible voice coming through the mic attached to his shoulder. But he looked unnatural.

Frozen.

Nix guided Cali away from them. No one noticed.

"Stop them," Marcus said, but no one heard. The officer was mired in the same biomite trap as the rest of the idiots. He needed one of the federal agents, not a goddamn cop! These two had to be stopped. They had to be shot.

Marcus grabbed his phone; he had to get the agents here, NOW! They would need to track them, follow by car and air until they could subdue them. Tranquilizers or electric shock could be used to overload their systems—

That's when the fat lady woke up.

Seconds later, Marcus's arm was pinned behind his back. No one heard him shouting.

CHAPTER FIFTY-SEVEN_

Kate Farmer had trouble breathing. More so than usual.

This sort of thing always happened when she was working a deal. Doctor said her blood vessels contracted when she was under stress and seeded her with a dose of muscle-relaxing biomites that were supposed to manufacture low levels of dopamine when she was working a deal, so she wouldn't be uncomfortable.

She wanted those fat-eater biomites, but they were too goddamn expensive. Besides, they weren't going to make her feel good, just skinnier. She'd been fat all her life. A hormone imbalance, doctors told her. She could get that corrected, probably didn't cost all that much, really. She always swore that was her next seed, but then there were the iris biomites that made her eyes emerald green. Those were pretty cool. And then the hair removal biomites, the ones that made all the hair on her arms, legs, and pits fall out. That was sweet.

Next, she'd correct the imbalance. Swear.

She'd do that to keep skinny bitches like the one behind the counter from thinking the thoughts she was thinking. Kate couldn't read thoughts—if there were biomites for that, she'd put that at the top of her list—but, honestly, she didn't really need to read them. She knew what people were thinking just by the look on their faces. They judged her. All skinny people judged fat ones. They didn't know what it was like to have a hormone imbalance. I mean, Kate could gain two pounds from a vanilla wafer. What does this skinny bitch know about that?

Nothing.

Right now, Kate was all worked up. She'd watched those dirty movies, just didn't feel like paying for them; they were like fifteen dollars. *Each.* She wasn't going to pay that. Besides, she didn't like the look on that girl's face.

Didn't seem like it was worth the aggravation. Kate wiped the sweat from her upper lip and gripped the counter. She just wanted to feel good, that wasn't too much to ask. Then that skinny bitch held out the phone, calling Kate's bluff; well, that really pissed her off. And then some mental case began talking on the phone and that really wedged a bolt up her ass. She was about to turn around, tell the bony meth-head to keep it down when she noticed the lady wasn't on no phone. Unless she had some communication biomite seed. She'd heard about those, biomites that took the place of a phone.

She sort of forgot about the woman behind her. She was more sick than skinny, one of those people that looked diseased, like AIDS or tapeworm. She looked worse than Kate felt, and that was low. She just wanted to feel good. Not too much to ask. She was an American citizen. She had rights.

So when the warm buzzy feeling melted through her—starting at the top of her skull and pouring inside—she relaxed. Kate's eyelids drooped in ecstasy. Whatever she was tasting, she liked. The doctor said that once her biomites synchronized with her organs and reached a certain threshold (30%, maybe) she'd feel good about everything. And this was exactly what Kate wanted.

Good about everything.

She watched skinny girl behind the counter, tapping on the keyboard, hoping she'd straighten things out. If not, no big deal.

That's what she was thinking. Kate rubbed her gums with her finger, her mouth suddenly dry.

Someone was talking.

She heard it, but distantly. It was hard to hear over the sound of static, like the ocean was rolling through the lobby. Kate imagined she was standing on a boat, listening to a waterfall. She'd been to Niagara Falls, that's what it reminded her of. They were on the boat wearing slickers, touring the bottom. Wet. The sound, deafening as they neared.

Louder.

And whiter.

Voices blurred in the static.

The skinny woman behind the counter disappeared in droplets of haze. Kate didn't notice it so much. She had melted into a puddle of buttery joy. Dry mouth. Tingly teeth.

Lost in it.

Loving it.

And then, like the boat emerging from Niagara's mist, she came out.

The warm buzziness faded, leaving behind a burning pit, a dry socket of emptiness. The skinny woman and the counter were gone. Kate was facing the doors and looking at some shriveled bald man on crutches. She didn't see the boy and the woman, only the gimpy bald man. And, somehow, she knew he was responsible for her problems. He'd deprived her of the yummies.

Didn't know why she thought that, just did. Just believed it.

Just knew that he was bad.

And that he was up to bad stuff. Like harassing that couple over there. She knew that bad baldy was pissed off at the world and harassed those good people, probably slapped the man and fondled the woman. Kate was sure of it, she remembered seeing it. And she, for one, wasn't going to stand for it.

Kate didn't back down.

Not when she felt like this.

When that cop walked in, she told him flat out what happened. That baldy was up to no good. He needed arrested.

And he got arrested.

CHAPTER FIFTY-EIGHT

Jim Freisen was only a couple blocks from the Red Roof Inn.

He was halfway through a shift, bored out of his skull. The call was to assist federal agents in the apprehension of a couple of half-skins. He wasn't so sure why they didn't just shut them down, but whatever, he answered the call. He hit the lights and moved traffic out of the way. He loved that feeling. Hit the lights and people move.

A black Mercedes was out front, driver leaning against the hood. He jumped when Jim pulled up, front bumpers nearly touching. He killed the siren, but left the lights twirling. Jim called in his position. He was the first to arrive. This could be good. This could be nothing.

Surprise, surprise.

He looked through the front doors—appeared to be a standoff in the lobby. No weapons, no screaming or shouting or any sign of violence. Just people staring. He didn't bother resting his hand on his weapon, pushing open the door.

Sand pellets.

Like he was showered with a sandstorm, only they were invisible, like things driving beneath his skin, seeding his thoughts. Scenes flashed once, twice, clicking like channels changing. No one moved, nothing changed. It all looked the same, he just felt a little different about the people inside. He didn't know any of them.

There was just a sense of danger.

Someone was up to no good.

And then a heavyset woman was there. She stepped out of the fog and raised her arm, extra skin swinging. "HE DID IT!" she screamed. "I SAW IT! THAT BASTARD ATTACKED THOSE POOR PEOPLE! I SAW IT!"

Her arm swung to Jim's left.

There were people standing in front of a couch. A man and a woman and a young girl. They were nodding but not much else. Nodding and nodding. And then pointing where the heavyset woman had pointed. Right in front of him.

Right in front of Jim—he palmed his face, all rubbery and fat and stuffy—was a smallish man holding himself up on crutches, his right leg in a brace. He turned to look at Jim, an expression of disbelief. That's always how they looked, though. It was always *It wasn't me, I swear*. No one ever did anything.

But Jim knew, right from the start. He could feel guilt, see it on a face from a mile away. And this bastard was guilty. Gimpy or not, he'd done something and it would get sorted out.

"What are you doing?" the bald man said. He shifted away from Jim's clasping hand. "Officer, you've got it wrong. Think, son. Think how you feel right now. Someone has altered your perception through the biomites—"

Jim twisted his wrist.

"No! NO!" Baldy hopped on his good leg. Pain mixed with anger, slurring his words. "Wait! Don't move, officer. Stay here, wait for the federal agents, they'll be here in moments, they'll tell you what's happening—"

Jim didn't need to wait. He'd been a police officer for seven years. He knew how to keep Chicago safe. It started with getting self-righteous pricks off the street. These good people didn't deserve this, that's what he was thinking. And it sickened him to the point of rage when the heavyset woman told him what he'd done.

The perp struggled at first, but even with two good legs he wasn't a match for Jim. He could wrangle this guy with one hand, if needed. A little pressure on the wrist and the right twist and baldy spun right around, facing the door.

"You won't get far!" His face turned red. His scalp was inflamed. "I WILL NOT REST, YOU HEAR ME? I WILL FIND YOU! I WILL FIND YOU!"

A little extra pressure and the man was on the move. Jim didn't know who the hell he was talking to. He shouted at the corner of the lobby. It was empty over there. Clearly, he'd lost his mind, seeing things. Probably a biomite misfire. Jim had seen many of those over the last couple years; now it was biomite tweakers causing all the trouble. This guy didn't look like the type, but nothing ever surprised him.

Jim got him into the backseat of the squad car as a few more cars arrived. He wasn't going to wait to explain. He had an impulsive feeling: he needed to get this guy as far away from the hotel as fast as possible. Call it a gut feeling.

It wasn't until he was a block away that the buzz faded.

CHAPTER FIFTY-NINE_

"Keys."

Nix held out his hand, staring at the clerk. She was still in a muddled state, swimming in the frayed field of static that Nix was sending. He wasn't sure he knew what he was doing, just commanding every biomite within his range to jitter like excited atoms, disturbing their frequency, throwing them into a state of confusion.

Of static.

Including his sister.

Cali was slipping through her delusion. This day would come, Nix just always hoped they could ease into it. He expected to sit down with her and pull back the curtain a little at a time. It would be easier for her mind to accept it on its own time, but Marcus Anderson had burned the illusion to the ground, opening a trapdoor.

Cali was falling.

If he didn't catch her, she might not come back.

So now she was swimming in the same fog as everyone else. A field of nowhere.

"Car keys. There's a rental car waiting for us to pick up."

No use. He couldn't risk selectively lifting her from the morass without clarity returning to the others. The police officer had accepted the implanted thoughts as his own. He was ready to march the enemy out of sight.

Nix slid over the counter and looked around, pushing papers and folders. There, a key attached to a simple fob, by the computer. He snatched it up and grabbed Cali as she began sliding against the counter.

"Come on, easy steps," he whispered, guiding her toward the side exit that led to the parking garage. "Easy steps."

First, get her to the car. Get her out of here.

But it needed to be quickly. Nix already felt icy weakness in his knees. His neck was stiffening under the strain of controlling all the biomites around him. The back of his eyes itched. With his arm around his sister, he ushered her as fast as he could, her feet tripping on the rug. They went past the people standing outside the breakfast room and into the hall.

Marcus Anderson shouted his dire warning.

Nix knew that they may never live in peace. But, then again, when had life ever been peaceful?

CHAPTER SIXTY

Cali and Thomas's first date was at the State Fair.

She answered the door and started laughing. They were wearing matching clothes. He wore a red shirt and white shorts. She wore the opposite. They looked in love.

Total accident.

They ended the night on the ride that spun around and pressed their bodies to the inside wall. Thomas held her hand. Cali screamed and laughed. And the world went round and round, round and round. The people on the opposite wall smudged into pastel streaks and water filled her eyes and her head went round and round.

Round and round.

And Cali went round.

She was going round.

The floor dropped out of the ride; people screamed. They were stuck to the sides. Not Cali.

She was falling.

Falling.

And there was no bottom to the ride. No end. Just a gut-dropping fall that lasted forever.

Maybe she sensed Nix holding her, guiding her along the paisley-patterned carpet and narrow hallways, through a side exit into a gray parking garage. She heard the car honk when he repeatedly pushed the fob, but she didn't recognize it as a horn or a car or anything.

Didn't feel the vinyl against her cheek.

Didn't know she curled against the backseat, fingers clawing, grasping. Trying to stop the fall, trying to cling to anything that would find solid ground.

There was no sense of leaving the dank garage or the sunlight lighting half her face or the turns or the traffic. She sensed motion but not the car's stop and go.

Just falling.

Falling.

Until she hit something. Perhaps it was bottom. But she didn't bounce. She went through it like a semisolid wall, one that lacked a real foundation, lacked studs, simply shattered on impact and allowed her through to the other side.

Cali fell into the memories that she'd capped so long ago.

<hr>

Cali knew she wasn't special.

People suffered all over the world. They'd suffered tragedies far worse than hers. But none of that eased her pain. She'd lost all the things that mattered. If her brother did not need her, she had no reason to remain in this world. There would be a painless way to escape, somewhere in the bottom of a prescription.

But Nix needed her.

She needed to be there for him. At least until he was an adult. It wouldn't be fair to take everything from him, too. He didn't deserve that. He was so much younger than her, a surprise, her parents admitted. After Cali, they had no plans for another child. They were Catholic but didn't want the big family. They didn't do much about birth control, so fifteen years after Cali—*whap*—Nix was conceived.

Surprise!

Not that they regretted it. Her father always said it was like swimming in a cold pool: sometimes you just needed pushed in and the water would turn out just fine.

They were better parents to Nix than they were to Cali. She wasn't bitter, just noticed they were more patient, less angry. More loving. She was glad to see that because Nix, he was a good kid.

God's first jab took them away. Cali was old enough to handle that. She was a young adult. She'd found Thomas; she'd moved out and was ready to start her own family. She had a good job and a happy home. The news of their accident was a blow. And with no extended family, Nix was welcomed into their home.

Thomas was a good substitute father. A good man. From day one, he was exactly what Nix needed. He was going to be a good father. So when Avery was born, she was perfect. And their family was perfect and all the scars were erased. They weathered the storm and were stronger. Closer. Cherished each other like no other family.

No one deserved the second blow.

Cali wouldn't wish that on the devil.

The call came, the news delivered. She drove to the hospital, numb. She drove without seeing and hearing.

There was a funeral.

There were guests and flowers and condolences and tears.

And then there was silence. There was a gap inside her, a hole that could never be filled. A vacuum that swallowed her life. It hurt. It howled.

It ate her.

And Cali would not survive it. She could not live while dangling over a pit of fear, that any moment life could be raped and clawed from one's clutches. That God could be so cruel. She couldn't accept the smallness that her life had become.

There were pills. There was booze. There were mood-altering biomites that suppressed thoughts and pain. But beneath it all was the realization that all was lost. There was nothing worth living for. If not for Nix...

Cali knew about suppression therapy, that biomites could remove the memory of painful events. Research had proven that victims of tragedy resumed a normal life when trigger-memories were erased. As if they never happened. People, events, accidents… didn't matter. It could all be gone.

Just like that.

But something was wrong with that. Cali couldn't fathom erasing Avery from her life, as if she never existed. If she forgot about her daughter, if those precious moments were taken—her pink skin at birth, her first smile, first birthday—that would be like killing her all over again. And she couldn't stand another loss.

Not again.

If she were not a biomite engineer, never would it have been possible. She carefully researched the idea and found no evidence of it ever being done. Perhaps it wasn't possible. Cali wouldn't accept that. She built a lab in the basement, using all the money left from her late parents and her dear late husband. She even took money from Nix's trust fund—all of it—with the intention of paying him back. She just needed this first, and then everything would be all right.

Everything would be all right. Just the way it was supposed to be. She deserved that. God couldn't take whatever he wanted. She would be proof. The Richards family might not be impervious, they might not be strong…

But they were smart.

And Cali coded a strain of biomites with memories of her daughter. It wasn't all that difficult, really. She simply planned to erase the memory of her daughter's death and then ran the memory erasure in reverse for her revival. Avery would live just like Cali imagined she would. She would be a perfect little girl.

Cali would see her. She would feel her.

And she would have her daughter back.

On the day she prepared to seed herself, she considered not telling Nix. She was afraid he would be a voice of reason, convince her it was a bad idea. Somewhere, she knew this. But she'd run out of options. *Desperation is a convincing drink.*

Nix didn't say anything. He listened and nodded.

Perhaps he knew there was no use; she'd made up her mind. Perhaps, like an alcoholic's spouse wife, he just wanted to see the pain go away. He'd seen her wither, listened to her weep. He watched his sister's life shrivel to a dried husk.

And he wanted her to live, too.

Maybe, deep down, he knew this was a bad idea. But he was drinking from the same well, tainted with desperation.

He would support her delusion.

He watched her descend into the basement and close the door behind her. He waited for her upstairs while Cali, cheeks wet, pressed the cold tip of the seeder against the base of her skull while she thumbed through photos of her daughter.

Touched the trigger.

And darkness was no more.

CHAPTER SIXTY-ONE_

Nix had no idea what the car looked like or where it was. Luck, for once, was on his side. The taillights lit up ten stalls away: a white Ford Focus. He wasn't sure he could reach it if it were any farther.

He couldn't focus on Cali anymore, couldn't keep her biomites in whiteout, not without completely exhausting himself. Rubber scuffed over the concrete; Cali's shoes pointed behind her.

Nix stumbled into the back door. He rested a moment, out of sight from passing cars. He checked her breathing. It was shallow and slow. Completely unconscious.

Good.

Maybe her new breeds put her to sleep.

A horn echoed in the enclosure, shocking him back into action. He opened the door and pushed her into the back. No one would see her. She could sleep.

She could forget.

Nix sat in the driver's seat for a minute. Back in the lobby, everyone would return to normal. Confusion would reign, memories obscured and illogical. Eventually, someone would show up and figure out what happened. Someone would come looking for them.

Marcus Anderson would.

Nix started the car. He could barely feel the pedals.

He drove carefully out of the parking garage, took a right at the exit and waited for the GPS to show him the nearest interstate. A police car flew past. His knuckles turned white, palms slick on the wheel. He snuck a peek in the rearview, watched the cruiser's taillights ignite and felt a cold twist in his belly before it turned the corner.

The GPS's voice was female. At the next stoplight, she said, turn right.

SOMEWHERE ON I-64 SOUTH, Nix pulled into a rest stop and parked far from the other cars.

He was starving.

And tired. The adrenaline had worn off. He had to pinch his legs to stay awake at the wheel. He needed coffee but had no money. The car had half a tank of gas and it would get them through Indiana, but after that...

He got out and stretched his legs. Cali hadn't moved much. Occasionally, her nails would scratch against the seat like she was trying to claw her way into the trunk. That much told him she was alive. He wanted to open the door, listen to her breathe, feel her pulse. It would look like he was hauling a dead body.

The driver's seat was still warm. He reached over the seat and pushed two fingers against her neck. *Still warm. Still beating.*

Still alive.

He got back on the interstate. They had another three or four hours' worth of gas.

LEXINGTON, Tennessee.

Cali sat up.

Nix's eyes flicked from the road to the mirror, waiting. And waiting. Her face, still haunted by weight loss. Cali's expression was foggy, at best. She didn't seem to look at anything in particular. Just sat there. Nix just drove.

"We're going to need gas," he said.

He didn't know what else to say. That was the most important thing on the list at the moment. Stranded on the side of the road was a losing strategy. But Cali didn't respond. Her expression didn't change. She stared into space. Maybe she didn't hear him. Nix drove another couple miles.

"We need food," she said.

Nix didn't rush his response, sensing she was processing things slowly. "We need money," he finally said.

Her head turned side to side, as if listening. "Next exit," she said.

He thought about asking what next, how they were going to pay for anything. They couldn't use a credit card. Nix, for one, didn't even have a wallet. He wasn't sure if Cali had anything in her bag. Camping in a farmer's field and eating corn wasn't going to last long.

The next exit was ten miles. There was no conversation. Cali looked no less foggy. Nix was dizzy from looking from the road to the mirror. The car rolled into a Sunoco with a Subway and stopped at one of the tanks. He threw it in park.

Cali's hand rested on the door handle. "I'll be right back."

Nix watched her methodically walk inside, like a sedated mental patient. He kept track of her through the glass wall as she walked down the aisles. He lost her somewhere on the other side. Minutes went by. He thumbed the steering wheel, debating going in.

He took a deep breath, envisioning her lying on the floor and the clerk calling 911 and the police arriving—

Never should've let her go in alone.

He grabbed the door handle. The parking lot smelled like sour beer. One foot on the pavement—

Cali pushed the door open.

It wasn't a straight line she walked, but she made it to the car. She tossed a plastic bag of food inside the car and fell in the backseat. Her head tilted back, eyes falling shut. "Fill it up."

"With gas?"

"There's thirty dollars on the pump."

He didn't bother asking how or where the food came from. No one was coming out shouting about a robbery. Nix just filled the tank. When he turned around, Cali was asleep. There was an apple in her hand, a single bite notched out of it. Nix checked her breathing, just to be sure. Then he drove off, shoving candy bars and bananas in his mouth, washing it down with water.

Cali slept until they reached the mountains.

CHAPTER SIXTY-TWO

Marcus was one of the first to board.

The airline assistant wheeled him down the gateway to the plane. The stewardess smiled and tried to help. He just wanted her to get the hell out of the way. He managed to find his first-class seat, sweating through the pain, without bending his leg. There was just enough leg room to lay it out straight.

He sat back, searching for refuge in the painkilling haze. Found none. The ache consumed his entire body, pushing into his thoughts like a sliver. He couldn't sleep, couldn't get comfortable. Just in it. No escape.

"Can I get you a pillow?" the stewardess asked.

He nodded.

The police officer that arrested him came to his senses about a block from the hotel. At first, he just slowed down. Marcus had been wedged into the backseat with his hands cuffed. He couldn't lean one direction or the other without twisting his knee.

"Turn around!" Marcus shouted through the agony.

The car slowed. It finally stopped in the middle of the street. No lights, no siren. Just stopped right in the middle of traffic. His mind was trying to find solid footing. Maybe he remembered nothing or just couldn't put the pieces together; whatever it was, he was stuck.

"Officer," Marcus said, "there are two fugitive halfskins that made you believe I accosted people back at the hotel and filled you with a sense of urgency to get me out."

Marcus had to adjust his leg.

"I am a federal agent. I need you to turn the car around and return to the hotel. Everything will be explained."

The officer looked in the backseat and observed the leg and the clothing. Marcus locked eyes with him.

"Reach into my jacket, look at my wallet."

Five minutes later, they were back at the hotel. Federal agents and police officers were already at the scene. Someone found a hotel wheelchair for Marcus. Despite getting off his feet, the pain was intolerable. He remained long enough to hear from the witnesses.

They remembered nothing.

No one saw the woman and boy, or had any recollection of them entering or exiting. No evidence they even stayed there. All of them described the same experience as the police officer that hauled Marcus down the street.

White static.

The plane began to taxi.

Marcus's phone buzzed. His wife was calling. He punched the ignore button. He'd talked to her earlier that morning. The plane was fully boarded. A small woman sat next to him. She plugged her ears with headphones and opened her laptop, didn't even say hi. His kind of travel companion. As the plane taxied out of the terminal, Marcus's phone buzzed again.

He put it to his ear.

"How's the knee?" the Secretary asked.

"Wonderful. I'll be landing in a couple hours."

"Good. I'm sure Janine will be glad you're home. I read your report."

There was a long pause, like he was still thumbing through it.

Marcus had submitted a detailed report of the hotel incident that morning. If there were plans to cut him out of the loop, that report would highlight his importance.

"A little over the top, Marcus. A bit hysterical."

"Sir, you'll need to turn off your phone," the stewardess said. The woman next to Marcus closed her laptop and laid her head back, eyes closed.

"Nothing about this is hysterical," Marcus said. He cupped his mouth over the phone and spoke low. "We're talking full-scale vulnerability if this gets out. Do you know how long it will take information of this type to go viral? There are garage hobbyists that can code designer biomites if they get the right protocol. They can seed themselves. They're all looking for a way to get off Mother's radar."

"This sounds more like an anomaly. It's happened before, someone gets lucky, finds a new frequency, and Mother cues in on it. They'll be back online within weeks, Marcus. I don't want you releasing anything to the press, nothing that will shake the public's confidence. This will take care of itself."

"No."

"I hope you're not refusing a direct order."

"I'm saying no, this will not blow over. Trust me on this, this is big. We cannot sit back and let this solve itself. I want my staff doubled and put on full priority. I'll need to monitor all Internet chatter, track if she's leaking out her discovery. And, if we find them, we'll be able to access their biomites, find out what she did—"

"Sir? You need to shut your phone off."

Marcus held up a finger. The stewardess lost her happy face.

"I'm not sleeping until this is over."

He hung up and turned it off. Held the phone up so the stewardess could go on her way before others started looking and staring. Marcus stared at the wall in front of him the entire flight. The pain kept him awake. But that was good.

He didn't want to sleep.

CHAPTER SIXTY-THREE_

Cali ate the last chunk of cantaloupe, chewing slowly. Let the juice fill her mouth before swallowing. She sat back and looked off the veranda at the view of the mountains, remembering something someone once said.

Sour makes sweet.

She'd had plenty of sour, to the point she didn't taste the sweet. But now, one chunk at a time, she savored the release of sticky goodness. She'd been sitting at the table since the kitchen opened, one of the first to arrive. The morning was cool. She held a coffee cup with both hands just below her chin, the steam on her cheeks. The sun came up as a hot coal beyond the valley, throwing shadows over the verdant turf as it fought through the low-lying clouds.

It had been her idea to stop in North Carolina.

We're far enough, she'd said, from the backseat. *Find the Asheville exit.*

Nix hadn't argued. Exhaustion had depleted him. But when she told him to find the Grove Park Inn, he threw a fit. *Too public,* he said. *Need to find a dive, somewhere crack dealers sleep.*

Trust me.

She remained in the backseat while they drove another hour in silence. It was dark by the time they found the inn. Nix wasn't surprised there was a room waiting for them and didn't ask how she'd done it. Maybe he was too tired.

He fell on the bed, asleep. Cali stayed up. She pulled open the curtains and sank into a cushioned chair, watching the stars pop out of the sky. To anyone watching, she looked like someone enjoying the view, but it was quite the opposite. Inside, she was surfing the Internet, playing the information on her mind's eye. It was effortless, like a second language. She'd never need a computer again. Currently she was using the hotel's wireless Internet connection, but soon she'd set up a Verizon account under a false name and configure the new breeds to behave like a cell phone. She'd have access at all times.

She was thinking like a computer, speaking a binary language. She'd placed the reservation at Grove Park Inn long before they reached it. She went back to Hertz Rental Car and deleted all records of the car they were driving. Not only had it not been leased to a customer at the Red Roof Inn, it never existed. No one would ever look for a white Ford Focus.

And the ATM at the gas station? She simply withdrew from the last customer's account.

It was stealing, she was aware. And guilty. But she wouldn't continue. Just until they were settled and could create new identities. New lives. Make their own money. It shouldn't be hard.

They spent two days in the room, mostly sleeping. It took a while to get back to normal.

Or as close to normal as Cali could get.

It was the third morning that she went to the veranda and ordered cantaloupe. Nix woke up about 10:00. Cali sensed it. She followed his movements to the bathroom as he looked for her. She sent a thought.

[Come for breakfast. You'll love the view.]

He wasn't thrilled she was hanging out in public, but the tone of the thought gave him hope. She had teetered on the edge of an emotional abyss for days. There was still sadness in her voice, desperation in her thoughts. She could work through her realization.

Surviving was the first step.

Nix sat down across from her, a plate of eggs and bacon waiting. He was hungry but stopped and looked to gauge her condition. When she nodded, he filled his mouth. He was halfway through the food before saying anything.

"Why are we out here?" he asked.

"No one knows us. And no one is looking for us. The incident never really became a story. The feds are keeping this one quiet."

"Someone's looking." Another bite of eggs. "*He's* looking."

Cali blew across her coffee. Marcus Anderson would always be looking. She would be proactive on that front. She needed something to convince him they weren't worth the effort. They weren't hurting anyone.

They just wanted to be left alone.

"He'll stop," she said.

"How do you know?"

"I know."

She didn't mean to say it like that, it was just... she didn't have a whole lot of space for emotions; she was quick to snap. There was still a lot to sort out.

She sipped. He ate.

Truth was, she didn't know a lot of things. There were no easy avenues. There was much grief to process; she couldn't just turn off the thoughts and hope it would go away. She needed to feel the depth of her loss and grieve for the loss of a beautiful daughter and wonderful husband. The loss of so much. And the guilt for, once again, surviving when so many didn't.

So much work to do.

But, for now, there was waking up. There was her brother pushing the plate away and downing a glass of orange juice. His eyebrows had returned along with an inch or so of hair on his head.

There was even the hint of whiskers. Just an eighteen-year-old boy. A hungry one. A healthy one.

That's all she wanted.

"Thank you," she said.

He slid the empty glass onto the table and wiped his mouth. "For what?"

She nearly smiled. "I asked a lot from you when I built the illusion of... *Avery.*"

Her name was a lot harder to say than she expected. She pinched herself for showing emotion like that in public. Like that in front of Nix. *Not now. Not yet.*

"You still supported me, even though you knew it was wrong."

Nix folded his hands on his lap. He looked out across the mountains. There were no tears, no glassy eyes, but his voice was weak. "I miss her, too."

She almost lost it and hid her quivering bottom lip in the coffee cup. She sniffed, holding it together. Didn't want to make a scene, not that anyone would recognize them. If she opened that gate, it would be difficult to close.

Cali didn't have to pretend Avery was there; she didn't have to remember that she had died while she spoke to the illusion.

Nix did.

"It hurts, brother," she whispered.

"I know, but I like you better this way."

They studied the view. Drank more coffee. Nix ate another breakfast. When they were ready to go, Cali put the bill on the room that would be erased before they left. But they would stay a bit longer.

CHAPTER SIXTY-FOUR_

The office doors were wide open.

It wasn't that Marcus didn't close them, he just didn't lock them. The kids hit them like pile drivers, launching the doorknobs into the bookshelves as the hinges groaned. Three of the boys, William, Andrew, and Clifford, chugged into the office single file, like a juvenile train on a mission to see their daddy.

"Ho!" Marcus threw up his hands like stop signs. "Slow down there, boys!"

They lined up at the corner of the grand desk, snickering. Marcus pulled at the edge of the laptop, turning the screen away from them. Not that they knew what any of it meant. It was just habit.

"Now, one at a time," he said. "What do you want?"

They didn't want anything, really. Half-dressed on a Saturday, the boys wondered what their daddy was doing. And to see if they could use his wheelchair. That was the deal. When he was sprawled out on the bed, they could take turns running each other up and down the hallway if—and only if—the housekeeper was there to supervise. Marcus was supposed to be walking on his reconstructed knee, not pampering it with the wheelchair.

The physical therapist could kiss his ass.

William started off with, "Sir, uh..."

Marcus's leg was still braced and stuck straight out, supported by the wheelchair's bracket. William nervously pinched at his dad's big toe. It tickled, but the young man's cold fingers felt good.

"Sir," he started again, "can we use the wheelchair, please?"

"Does it look like I'm using it?"

They nodded, straight-faced. They were old enough to interpret their dad's expression correctly. It was not time to play.

"Have you done your chores?"

"Yes, sir," the three of them said.

"Good. Brushed your teeth?"

"Yes, sir."

"Well, do it again. Teeth can't be too clean."

They didn't really need to brush their teeth, he just ran out of things to say. Their faces slumped. Even William's.

"Tell you what, I'll let you take the chair for a ride after lunch."

He patted Clifford on top of the head, stiffly.

They cheered. Ariel, the housekeeper, corralled them before they stormed out. They weren't going to brush their teeth. No big deal. Ariel closed the doors behind her, without having to be asked. Too bad she didn't lock them.

He turned the sound up on the TV, waiting to hear a story on Cali and Nix. So far, there was none. They'd done a good job keeping it away from the press. He needed to give his staff a bonus; they'd made his life easier, giving him time to make sure this never happened again.

Once he had some documents prepared and had his team ready, he could make a convincing argument for new halfskin thresholds. Clearly, they were waiting too long to detain and observe. He would propose detainment start at 30%, perhaps a weekend check-in arrangement. Extreme, yes. Some would argue it was the beginning of a new-age holocaust, but cancer has to be cut out to be cured.

Marcus knew how to bargain. Start high. His proposals would strike fear in the biomite industry and force them to slow down, force them to conform to the government's regulations. There had to be a precedent that anyone tinkering with biomite transparency would be dealt with swiftly and firmly. There would be no compromise.

Marcus would not rest until Cali and Nix were apprehended, until he had their biomites analyzed. Until those outlaws were shut down.

That's a promise.

Part of his proposal would include an increase in his operating budget to expand his staff. More agents trained for this sort of confrontation. Also, research to develop biomite resistance to outside influence. Ideally, they needed more purists like Marcus, but he was a realist. They wouldn't have many candidates to choose from if that was the requirement. Besides, if he was honest, the enhancement of biomite-seeded agents was nice. His men were stronger, faster and smarter. Hypocritical, sure. He chose to fight fire with fire, as long as he wasn't the one getting burned.

And when Cali and Nix were located and detained—not if, but *when*—he would know the exact coding that knocked them off of Mother's map. They would have that, and that, he knew, would sway his superiors more than anything. Invisibility was something that should be reserved for the government.

He'd already arranged for global scanning of facial recognition and personal asset activity. So far, Cali and Nix had completely abandoned their house, bank accounts, automobile... *everything*. He didn't expect them to come back. But Cali's hallucinatory re-creation of her daughter proved a lapse in judgment. He hoped, on the outside chance, they'd make that one swipe of a credit card, that one withdrawal that would give them a lead.

The doorknob turned. Marcus was about to shout at the kids. He'd make them go outside and play if they came asking again, but his wife stepped inside. He preferred that she knock before marching inside, but it was her house, too. Janine dropped a stack of papers on the desk.

"I need you to sign these."

"What is it?"

"Refinancing on the house. Remember? We talked about this a few months ago."

He flipped the top page. "I'll read them later."

"Just sign, Marcus. I've already been through them."

He never signed anything without reading, even those contracts that came with software where you just click the box and hit OK. He read those, too. Even if his wife said she read the papers and said it was all right, he read them.

"How's the knee?" she asked.

"Better."

"Have you done your exercises?"

"This morning."

She waited, hands on hips. No makeup, just frumpy sweatpants and a loose T-shirt that jiggled without a bra. She looked heavier. Each inhalation pressed her nipples against the fabric. Marcus looked back at the papers.

The laptop sounded off with an email. He itched to look.

"I've got a conference call in ten minutes with a congressman that's interested in hearing what I'd like to propose. I promise, right after that, I'll go through these and sign them."

Janine deflated, dropping her chin on her chest. Her gut pushed out. She was preparing to launch a verbal attack. He'd seen that posture before, she was just lining up the words like bullets. She gazed out the bay window.

Here it comes.

"What're you doing?" was all she said.

He waited for the rest. Instead, she looked at him. Her brow was not stiff, lips not thin. There was nothing there, no expression at all. Like she'd given up, maybe.

A cold quiver stabbed him.

"What do you want?" He threw his hands up. "You want me to stop working, is that what you want? This isn't a forty-hour-a-week job, Janine. I don't punch a clock; I can't just take off when I feel like it. You don't even know what the hell happened, but I can promise you I can't leave it on the desk for tomorrow so I can watch William hit a home run or Alexander ride his bicycle with no hands. The world depends on me, Janine. *On me.*"

He thumbed his chest, a reminder of whose career ranked higher.

"Everything depends on me right now, Janine. You have no idea. So have Ariel watch the kids. That's why we pay her."

Janine didn't move. Still expressionless, she listened. Even looked like she was holding her breath. A series of nods were the first sign that she'd even heard him. She turned around, hands still planted on her hips, and paced away. Marcus, silently, thanked his good fortune. He glanced at the email icon in the corner. He reached for the mouse.

Janine didn't leave the office. She faced the bookshelves near the exercise bicycle, looking up. Thinking. This was unusual for her. Too passive. Was she giving up?

He opened the email. It was short. He read it twice, not understanding.

I can find anything. Leave us alone.

He didn't recognize the username, CNN, no one in his address book that he could remember. He didn't subscribe to that liberal news outlet and it was certainly no one he corresponded with. He had a very good spam filter, but occasionally one would slip through. This one had an attachment, something he certainly wouldn't open. The pointer hovered over the trash icon. He looked at the username again.

CNN.

C and N.

The attachment was an .AVI file.

He downloaded it through virus protection. It came up clean.

Janine was still there, still thinking. Still quiet. Still looking up.

Marcus opened the video file.

At first, he was confused. He looked at Janine, then over her head at the books on the top shelf, then back to the video.

Finally connecting the dots.

Marcus turned the sort of gray that a dead man wears beneath the mortician's makeup.

Fear stabbed him once again, freezing everything inside.

He closed the laptop.

It was a long time before he spoke again.

CHAPTER SIXTY-FIVE

THE HORSESHOE CRAB LAY STILL, HALF BENEATH THE RECEDING wave. The tide was going out, leaving behind ocean detritus to bake in the South Carolina sun. The spiny ridge glistened along the domed shell as saltwater ran off.

A flower—yellow petals with a burgundy center—fell and stuck to the shell. The next wave knocked it off.

Cali clenched the flowers in both hands. Her toes sank in the sand as the water washed it from under her feet. When she was little, long before Nix was born, they lived on an island not too far from there. She remembered seeing—every morning when she looked for sand dollars with her mother—the beached horseshoe crabs, dead and dying. They'd flip them over and, sometimes, see a dead carcass stinking beneath.

A living fossil, her father would say about the horseshoe crab. *One of the only things still alive that has fossils dating back 500 million years.*

Cali wondered how they were living when they seemed to die so easily.

She wondered if a horseshoe crab cared when it died.

Some kids screamed in the waves. Judging by their sunburns,

they were on vacation. She did the math and figured they were Avery's age. If she was still alive. She would do the math like that whenever she saw kids. She'd do it for some time to come.

The curtain had been lifted. No more giggles. No more hugs.

Avery is gone.

She'd been gone a long time.

Cali remembered laying daisies where she was buried. She'd picked them out of a neighbor's yard. Didn't ask, just wandered through and grabbed a bundle. No one stopped her from such eccentricities, not when they knew what happened. They looked much like the flowers she was now dropping into the water, watching the waves drag them out.

Watching them go to the ocean.

Watching them disappear. Forever.

Nix's shadow covered the horseshoe crab. He remained silent until the last flower fell. It stuck on the sand. The next wave pushed it between Cali's toes. It bobbed in place, waving at them until the wave receded. The foam took it under. The color paled beneath the green wash.

"I've got some food." Nix held out an apple.

Cali took it. She picked at the sticker and shined the red skin with her thumb.

"You okay?" he asked.

She nodded. "Yeah."

She took a bite and smiled. She said, once she swallowed, "You say hello to Raine for me?"

"Not yet."

Guilt kept him from meeting her eyes when she brought up the dreamland. After all, he still had his delusion. Long ago, he had told her all about the lagoon—the crystal water and black sands, the funneling waterfall and clear sky. And his beautiful girl. His best friend.

She knew what he was thinking. She could have that, too. Cali could create her own lagoon inside her head. The new breeds could make it as realistic as the sand beneath her feet, the water on her toes. The flowers in the water. She could have anyone there.

And I would never leave.

She'd had enough of illusions. She'd fooled herself for all these years; it was time to live right here and now. Perhaps there was nothing wrong with Nix's lagoon. He insisted there was something more to it, that it wasn't just a lucid dream.

Delusions, though, can be pretty convincing.

"You sure you're all right?" Nix asked.

Nod.

"You want to come in, grab some dinner?"

The sun touched the horizon. "Think I'll go for a walk first."

"You sure you should be out like this?" He looked around like Marcus Anderson might be on vacation down the beach. "I mean, shouldn't we lay a little... lower?"

Cali reached down and plucked a flower out of the water that rode a wave in. She tucked it behind Nix's ear. She touched his cheek, the stubble rough on her hand. She remembered when he was little, when his face was smooth. When he needed her. Her brother was like her child before there was Avery.

"No one will ever come looking for us, brother."

She almost smiled. Smiling, though, was a long ways away.

Nix didn't ask about Marcus Anderson again. Whatever she did, he believed her. With Cali, nothing was impossible.

She walked along Folly Beach by herself. A beach known as the Edge of America.

A place where she was scared to death.

Where she would be for quite some time.

CHAPTER SIXTY-SIX_

Nix lay back.

All it took was closing his eyes, like going to sleep. Only he didn't drift into unconsciousness, he stayed awake for the ride.

Like falling down a long dark hole.

At some point, it didn't feel like falling. He couldn't exactly decide when motion stopped. It just became normal. And then he didn't feel the pillow or the couch. He never once felt like he left his body, only transitioned from the physical world to dreamland.

Like stepping through a door.

He heard a macaw. Palm fronds rustling. The roar of the waterfall, somewhere out there.

Water lapped his toes. Nix felt the weight of his eyelids but kept them closed. Instead, he savored the green scent of the jungle and the salty breeze. *The lagoon is alive.*

The new breeds brought it to life, opened his senses. Or clarified his connection. Whatever it was, there was no discernible difference between his two worlds. He imagined brightly colored fish—gold, yellow, and orange—with long tails and spiny fins.

He opened his eyes. There, near his feet, was exactly what he'd pictured. He waded deeper, sank his hand in the water and let them nibble on his fingers. He floated on his back, tasted the seawater on his lips, and felt the fish tickling his back as he paddled along the shallow water.

It was possible that his sister was right: the lagoon was a construct of his mind. He had gone way beyond a halfskin. A part of him was still organic, but he'd stopped checking just how much.

There was no going back.

He flopped his hair out of his eyes. A spent fire was on the beach. Charred logs sat among a gray bed of ash. Nix dripped on the ring of stones.

Raine?

She was usually waiting for him. He closed his eyes and imagined her there, bare feet digging in the sand. Skin bronze.

But nowhere.

Weird.

Nix walked the beach, tempted to shout her name. Words were as good as thoughts at the lagoon. He thought he saw her paddling in from the ocean, but it was just the sun reflecting off the waves.

A subtle feeling of panic clenched inside. He'd never considered the lagoon without Raine. Never had to. If she wasn't there, what was the point? But that was impossible.

Why isn't she here?

He continued along the sand until he reached the ocean inlet, where white-crested waves ate away at the sand bars that protected the lagoon. The horizon was flat and endless.

He thought he heard her shouting, convinced it was a wave slapping the sand. Maybe a bird. He shaded his eyes and looked toward the soaring blue cliff, wet with mist.

"Hey!"

It was distant, just an audible bump in the water's roar.

Nix squinted.

Something was at the base of the cliff, just above the trees where the earth sloped down to meet the jungle. It was boxy. The top was angular and shiny. A metal roof, perhaps. Yes. Yes, it was. *A house. A blue and green house with a copper roof built into the side of the cliff.*

And, there, just below it was someone waving.

Raine waved him to come to her, to join her in the home he never once saw, certainly never imagined. And yet, there it was.

And there she is.

Nix dove into the water, stroking his way across the lagoon in the company of the brightly colored fish.

Perhaps, he thought as he climbed the opposite shore, making his way up a narrow path, *falling trees do make sound in the lagoon when I'm not around.*

Janine Anderson loved her children. Loved her career.

But never her husband.

He was a safe bet, that's what he was. Janine was not a gambler. She knew, the day she met him at a conference for medical technology, that he was a sure thing: connected to politicians and dedicated to his work.

He was deep into his forties and, if she gambled, would bet he never would've married had she not asked him out to dinner. Even then, their marriage was more like a business arrangement. She wanted children and he wanted someone to take care of him, legally as well as maternally.

Not a match made in heaven.

So it was no wonder she'd had enough. She knew what she was getting into when she struck the agreement, knew any attraction between them—usually fueled by a bottle of wine—wouldn't last the length of their agreement. She couldn't blame him, really. Maybe that was her fault. She figured she was the one falling on the ugly grenade, not him.

Maybe she overestimated herself.

One thing was certain, she was not innocent. She'd sought relief from their emotionless arrangement, as dry as a sandbag. She accepted the fact there was dirt on her, that if he got wind of Janine's sexual preference (Helen was a very, *very* good friend) and occasional dalliance, she'd lose everything in a divorce. Marcus wouldn't want the children, but he'd take them because he was cold-blooded. He liked to win.

So did she.

That's why their arrangement seemed like such a good idea, in the beginning. They shared the blood of reptiles.

And that's why she installed the cameras.

He was a Washington insider. His office was his inner sanctum, off-limits to everyone in the family for the purposes of national security. She had never suspected anything of a perverted nature, nothing she could pin on him during a divorce. He played politics as dirty as any of the elected, but in marriage he was as clean as a virgin. No cussing, drinking, or smoking.

There was never a reason to suspect Marcus even had a pulse around women. But Janine always remembered Justine.

She was young and slender. Her blouse was unbuttoned one too many, revealing the crack of voluptuous breasts. Janine was distracted and a bit irritated by such a rash display, and the fact that she couldn't stop looking. But the warmth that lit Marcus's cheeks was revealing. He had a pulse, after all.

His gaze lingered on her full lips and caught sight of her display when she looked away. At first, Janine chalked it up to masculine lust triggered by a pair of balls, filling him with an urge against his will. Not that he acted on it, but it was there.

Who would guess?

Just in case it was more than that, she scanned his emails for flirtatious correspondence. But nothing. Taped phone calls. Still nothing. Even hired a private investigator that turned up... *nothing*.

Maybe she guessed wrong. Maybe he was a man that controlled

his appetite. After all, it wasn't disloyal to think about sex. But she couldn't stand around with nothing for long. She wanted out. She wanted a life, her life and all that was in it.

Minus Marcus.

So a camera was installed in the office.

She did it herself. It was the size of a marble that fit into the binding of a book that sat on the top shelf, the pages hollowed out to hold its components. A motion sensor turned it on, wirelessly streaming to her laptop. She tested it multiple times while he was in Chicago. His first night back, he locked himself inside to Skype a meeting. She went into the bedroom and watched him argue at the monitor for an hour.

After that, she only watched the recorded bits at the end of the day, and that she did in fast-forward. Each one more boring than the next. It was the fifth day that things got interesting.

The fifth day he was sitting back in the wheelchair, apparently sleeping, when he looked up. Looked around. He wheeled to the door and checked that the deadbolt was in place. A lock that couldn't be undone with a key. A lock that ensured privacy.

Janine sat up.

Watched him wheel back to his desk.

He closed the curtains, checking all the gaps were secure. That he was alone.

That no one could see.

He spun around—

Nothing.

The streaming cut out. Clipped like an edit. Like something—or someone—had tampered with the video. At first she went cold with fear. He knew. He'd found out somehow and destroyed some evidence. But what didn't make sense was that all the rest of the records were still there. It just stopped at that point.

How convenient.

She would have to check the feed and always make sure it was still there. That it was still working.

But not until he was gone. Perhaps install a backup while she was at it. If he was up to something—and he was—she would catch it. Eventually, she would catch it.

What she didn't know was that her equipment worked just fine. That the video was indeed clipped from the stream and downloaded to the memory of another computer, one that consisted of new-breed biomites seeded into the brain of a woman hundreds of miles away. A woman that had been snooping through their computers, their finances, and pictures and documents until she found what she was looking for.

Quite a home run, it was.

Unfortunately, she did not see her husband reach into the upper right drawer, where a secret compartment was installed deep under the desktop, and retrieve a cube. She didn't see him hold it gently, tenderly, stroking the edges and corners: a cube he'd acquired in Amsterdam, by accident, really. She would remember the trip if he told her.

It was a conference on biomite perversity, how the porn industry was using biomite technology to enhance orgasms and sexual prowess. It was the basis of some of his best arguments, how biomites contributed to the depravity of the human race. He'd be lying if he said there was never a stir in his groin when he saw some of the images, lying if he said he was shocked at how they were using technology.

He truly and honestly had no idea they could do that.

It was just so... real.

It was during that trip he'd acquired the cube that would be with him for years to come. An item he kept hidden, even though its use was of no consequence to the naked eye, to the unknowing observer. A cube that went everywhere with him. Because he was lonely, if he was honest. His life was dry and empty. He needed something to cope, something to manage the emotional isolation he found inside his house. In his life.

He placed it on the edge of his desk and wheeled away from it. It wasn't cheating. It wasn't real. It wasn't flesh.

He laid his head back, watching through slits as the cube unfolded.

Watched the biomite cube expand like magical origami. Watched metallic color turn fleshy, digits turn to fingers and toes. Watched an unfolding lump smooth its rough edges into sumptuous curves and crossed legs.

Janine would never see the biomite perversion cube walk across the room in high heels, watch her husband lay his head back and close his eyes. She would never know this addiction.

Unless he broke his promise to the culprit that clipped that video. If he did, he had more to worry about than his wife.

WHAT TO READ NEXT?_

Clay
Book Two
bertauski.com/halfskin

Jamie wants to be a halfskin.

Her life has become dull and pointless. If she had more biomites—synthetic stem cells that promise hope—she could take control of her life. But Jamie's body is already 49.9% biomites. The rest is clay—her God-given organic cells. Any more biomites and she becomes a half-skin. And halfskins are shutdown.

But there is a way.

Black market biomites, called nixes, can't be detected by the government's halfskin hunter, Mother. Jamie would have to sacrifice her clay to get the nixes, but they would make her halfskin without anyone knowing. Including Mother. But first she has to find them.

Nix Richards can help. He's the first halfskin to escape Mother and

Jamie has something he wants. He'll need her to help him find a fabricator. He'll betray anyone to get it, even those closest to him.

This psychological thriller will keep Nix and Jamie second-guessing every move while they elude Mother and Marcus Anderson, the man that wants to rid the world of biomites. But in the end, they'll all discover just how deep the betrayal goes.

Clay
Book Two
bertauski.com/halfskin

REVIEW HALFSKIN!_

If you enjoyed this ride, please drop a review on your favorite vendor. It doesn't have to be long and complicated. Throw some stars on it and write *Loved it!* or *It was really, really okay!* or *Meh.*

Reviews make the difference.

bertauski.com/halfskin

BERTAUSKI STARTER LIBRARY_

Get the
BERTAUSKI STARTER LIBRARY
FREE!

bertauski.com

My grandpa never graduated high school. He retired from a steel mill in the mid-70s. He was uneducated, but a voracious reader. As a kid, I'd go through his bookshelves of musty paperback novels, pulling Piers Anthony and Isaac Asimov off the shelf and promising to bring them back. I was fascinated by robots that could think and act like people. What happened when they died?

Writing is sort of a thought experiment to explore human nature and possibilities. What makes us human? What is true nature?

I'm also a big fan of plot twists.

bertauski.com